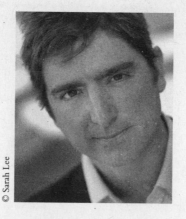

© Sarah Lee

Marcel Theroux is the author of three novels, *A Stranger in the Earth; The Confessions of Mycroft Holmes: A Paper Chase,* which won a Somerset Maugham Award; and *A Blow to the Heart.* He lives in London.

Also by Marcel Theroux

FAR NORTH

FAR NORTH

MARCEL THEROUX

PICADOR

FARRAR, STRAUS AND GIROUX   NEW YORK

www.picadorusa.com

Picador® is a U.S. registered trademark and is used by Farrar, Straus
and Giroux under license from Pan Books Limited.

For information on Picador Reading
Group Guides, please contact Picador.
E-mail: readinggroupguides@picadorusa.com

Designed by Jonathan D. Lippincott

The Library of Congress has cataloged the Farrar, Straus and Giroux edition as follows:

Theroux, Marcel, 1968–
    Far North / Marcel Theroux.—1st American ed.
        p. cm.
    ISBN 978-0-374-15353-3
    I. Title.

PS3570.H395F37 2009
813'.54—dc22

2008049224

Picador ISBN 978-0-312-42972-0

First published in the United States by
Farrar, Straus and Giroux

First Picador Edition: July 2010

10 9 8 7 6 5 4 3 2 1

ONE

1

Every day I buckle on my guns and go out to patrol this dingy city.

I've been doing it so long that I'm shaped to it, like a hand that's been carrying buckets in the cold.

The winters are the worst, struggling up out of a haunted sleep, fumbling for my boots in the dark. Summer is better. The place feels almost drunk on the endless light and time skids by for a week or two. We don't get much spring or fall to speak of. Up here, for ten months a year, the weather has teeth in it.

It's always quiet now. The city is emptier than heaven. But before this, there were times so bad I was almost thankful for a clean killing between consenting adults.

Yes, somewhere along the ladder of years I lost the bright-eyed best of me.

Way back, in the days of my youth, there were fat and happy times. The year ran like an orderly clock. We'd plant out from the hothouses as soon as the earth was soft enough to dig. By June we'd be sitting on the stoop podding broad beans until our shoulders ached. Then there were potatoes to dry, cabbages to bring in, meats to cure, mushrooms and berries to gather in the fall. And when the cold closed in on us, I'd go hunting and ice fishing with my pa. We cooked omul and moose meat over driftwood fires at the lake. We rode up the winter roads to buy fur clothes and caribou from the Tungus.

We had a school. We had a library where Miss Grenadine stamped books and read to us in winter by the wood-burning stove.

I can remember walking home after class across the frying pan in the last mild days before the freeze and the lighted windows sparkling like amber, and ransacking the trees for buttery horse chestnuts, and Charlo's laughter tinkling up through the fog, as my broken branch went *thwack! thwack!* and the chestnuts pattered around us on the grass.

The old meetinghouse where we worshipped still stands on the far side of the town. We used to sit there in silence, listening to the spit and crackle of the logs.

The last time I went in there was five years ago. I hadn't been inside for years and when I was a child I'd hated every stubborn minute I'd been made to sit there.

It still smelled like it used to: well-seasoned timber, whitewash, pine needles. But the settles had all been broken up to be burned and the windows were smashed. And in the corner of the room, I felt something go squish under the toe of my boot. It turned out to be someone's fingers. There was no trace of the rest of him.

·

I live in the house I grew up in, with the well in the courtyard and my father's workshop much as it was in my childhood, still taking up the low building next to the side gate.

In the best room of the house, which was kept special for Sundays, and visitors, and Christmas, stands my mother's pianola, and on it a metronome, and their wedding photograph, and a big gilded wooden *M* that my father made when I was born.

As my parents' first child, I bore the brunt of their new religious enthusiasm, hence the name, Makepeace. Charlo was born two years later, and Anna the year after that.

Makepeace. Can you imagine the teasing I put up with at school? And my parents' displeasure when I used my fists to defend myself?

But that's how I learned to love fighting.

I still run the pianola now and again, there's a box of rolls that still work, but the tuning's mostly gone. I haven't got a good enough ear to fix it, or a bad enough one not to care that I can't.

It's almost worth more to me as firewood. Some winters I've looked at it longingly as I sat under a pile of blankets, teeth chattering in my head, snow piled up to the eaves, and thought to myself, Damn it, take a hatchet to it, Makepeace, and be warm again! But it's a point of pride with me that I never have. Where will I get another pianola from? And just because I can't tune the thing and don't know anybody who can, that doesn't mean that person doesn't exist, or won't be born one day. Our generation's not big on reading or tuning pianolas. But our parents and their parents had plenty to be proud of. Just look at that thing if you don't believe me: the burl on the maple veneer, and the workmanship on her brass pedals. The man who made that cared about what he was doing. He made that pianola with love. It's not for me to burn it.

The books all belonged to my folks. Charlo and my ma were the big readers. Except for that bottom shelf. I brought those back here myself.

Usually when I come across books I take them to an old armory on Delancey. It's empty now, but there's so much steel in the outer door, you'd need a keg of gunpowder to get to them without the key. As I said, I don't read them myself, but it's important to put them aside for someone who will. Maybe it's written in one of them how to tune a pianola.

I found them like this: I was going down Mercer Street one morning. It was deep winter. Snow everywhere, but no wind, and the breath from the mare's nostrils rising up like steam from a kettle. On a windless day, the snow damps the sound, and the silence everywhere is eerie. Just that crunch of hooves, and those little sighs of breath from the animal.

All of a sudden, there's a crash, and a big armful of books flops into the snow from what must have been the last unbroken window on the entire street until that moment. The horse reared up at the sound. When I had her calm again, I looked up at the window, and what do you know, there's a little figure hang-dropping into the books.

He's bundled up in a bulky blue one-piece and fur hat. Now he's gathering up the books and fixing to leave.

I shouted out to him, "Hey. What are you doing? Leave those books, damn it. Can't you find something goddamn else to burn?"—along with a few other choice expressions.

Then, just as quick as he appeared, he flung down his armful of books and reached to draw a gun.

Next thing, there's a pop and the horse rears again and the whole street is more silent than before.

I dismounted, easy does it, with my gun drawn and smoking and go over to the body. I'm still a little high from the draw, but already I'm getting that heavyhearted feeling and I know I won't sleep tonight if he dies. I feel ashamed.

He's lying still, but breathing very shallow. His hat came off as he fell. It lies in the snow a few steps away from him, among the books. He's much smaller than he seemed a minute earlier. It turns out he's a little Chinese boy. And instead of a gun, he was reaching for a dull Bowie knife on his hip that you'd struggle to cut cheese with.

Well done, Makepeace.

He comes to slightly, grunting with the pain, and tries to push me away from him. "Let me have a look at where you're hit. I can help you. I'm the constable here." But his clothes are too thick for me to examine him, and it's too dangerous to linger here, unarmed and dismounted, especially in daylight.

It's not going to be comfortable, but the only thing for it is to move him. Better get the books as well, so the whole escapade hasn't been fruitless. I toss them into a burlap sack. The boy weighs nothing. It's heartbreaking. What is he? Fourteen? I lift him onto the saddle and he rides in front of me, drifting in and out of consciousness until we get back.

The good news is he's still breathing. His arms reach feebly for my shoulders as I help him dismount. I know the pain is not so terrible for him yet. The body makes its own opium when it's been hit. But in the middle of that feeling, there's also a sensation of injustice. That you've broken something you don't know how to fix, and you won't be the same again.

Once down, the boy refused to let me near him. As much

as I tried to explain that I was sorry I'd hurt him and I wanted to help, he'd just slap my hand away. It was clear that we didn't have a common language. There are some tongues where you can get, say, one word in five or ten, and it's enough to make some sense of one another. We had nothing.

I gave him a pitcher of hot water on a tray, and some long tweezers, and gauze, and carbolic soap, and left him to it. And I locked him in, just to be safe.

The books from the burlap bag I put on the shelves in the living room. They were all odd sizes, so they didn't fit into neat rows like my parents' books. Some of them were picture books. I wondered if the boy was going to read them or burn them. I was pretty sure I knew the answer.

A burned book always makes my heart sink a little.

•

Every time I used a bullet, I made myself five more immediately. That had been my rule for a while. My bullets worked out pretty expensive, both in terms of time and the fuel it took to smelt them. It wasn't really economical to make them in such small quantities.

But what I figured was this: you can always find more fuel if you run out, chop out some hardwood and make charcoal— even burn the pianola, god help me, if you have to—but you must never let things slide, get casual, and run low on shells.

If you can find someone who'll trade with you, sure enough, a bullet has a market price. But say someone picks a fight with you, hunts you down with a posse of his friends. What price a bullet then? What price not to hear your gun go click on an empty chamber?

Plus, I liked making them. I like what happens to the metal as it melts down. I liked to crouch over the crucible, watching the flame through the smoked glass lenses that belonged to my father, watching the lead run like quicksilver. I liked the transformation and the cold, ugly slugs that I broke out of the sand in the molds in the morning.

The trouble, of course, is that my shells were none too clean. If I ever get shot again, I hope it's with a nice shiny bullet of surgical steel, not with one of my ugly things that looks like something someone dropped on a farrier's floor and carries god knows what dirt and germs in it.

After I'd made my five bullets, I carried up some food and water and a light for the spirit lamp by the boy's bedside. He was plainly feverish. Eyes closed but flickering under the lids. Short, bristly black lashes. His blue-black hair on the pillow put me in mind of a crow's wing. Muttering in that language of his.

The po was empty, but I took away the boy's stinking blue one-piece. He could have some of Charlo's old clothes if he lived.

·

At first light I took him up some breakfast.

There was nothing yellow about his skin. It was as white as bone. Faint black hair on his sideboards, but no beard or mustache to speak of.

He'd eaten all the food I'd left him, but as I cast around for the chamber pot he grew agitated. He was bashful. I knew then that I'd like him: I'd almost killed him, but he was shy for me to see his shit. How like a boy.

I tried to make clear as best I could in gestures that he was to stay in bed and rest. He still looked none too good. But I'd only just mucked out the horses when he appeared in the courtyard, looking even younger and smaller in Charlo's plaid jacket and his slippers. He was unsteady on his pins, but he made his way over to the stall to watch me giving the mare her feed, and the sight of the horse seemed to please him.

"Ma," he said, pointing at her.

I started to explain how I never named the animals, just called them the mare, the roan, the gray. It doesn't seem right to give a name to something you're going to kill and eat one day. And it goes down easier as plain horseflesh than as a chunk of Adamski or Daisy-May. But there was no way to make the boy understand, so from then on, the mare became "Ma."

And then he pointed to himself and the word he said sounded most of all like "Ping." That's right. Ping. Like the bell on a shop counter. Like a button popping off your shirt. Or a snapped banjo string. I wondered what kind of heathen name that was, or if there was a Saint Ping that no one had told me about.

But Ping he was. A name's a name. And so I introduced myself to him. I pointed to myself and I said my name. "Makepeace."

He looked all quizzical, squinted up his face as if he hadn't heard right, and he wasn't sure if he dared say the word. So I said it again. "Makepeace."

Now his face broke out in a broad grin "Make a piss?"

I looked at him careful, but he wasn't trying to poke fun at me, he just thought that was my name. And it seemed funny, since I had some laughs on account of his name, that he had made such a mess of mine.

.

There wasn't any point in having Ping in my home and not trusting him. I'm ornery and solitary and suspicious and that's how I've stayed alive so long. The last person other than me to sleep under that roof was Charlo, and that was more than ten years earlier. But it seemed to me then, it still does now, that if you let someone in, you should let them all the way in. Whenever I rode out of the courtyard, I took the view that everyone I met was, one way or another, planning to kill or rob me. But I couldn't live like that in my own home. I decided to trust Ping, not because I had a gut instinct about him—I didn't know him from the oriental Adam—but because that was the only way I could live.

And yet, I was still a little surprised when I rode back in at lunchtime to find my locks intact, and the firewood still stacked neatly, and the chickens pecking, and the cabbages and apples in the root cellar undisturbed. There was no sign of Ping, though, and I confess that at that moment, I felt sad at the thought that he might have left.

I clattered up to the second story in my boots, hallooing on the stairs. No sign of him. I burst into Charlo's room and was taken aback by the scene I found.

There was Ping, with a looking-glass in front of him, and my ma's old embroidery case, and the spirit lamp burning away, and he was taking the old steel needles one by one, waving them in the flame, and sticking them into the flesh of his ears.

He smiled to see me, and laughed at my consternation. His whole ear bristled like porcupine quills. It must have pained him dreadfully, but he didn't seem put out by it. In fact, he just went right on sticking them into his ears. And when he'd done that, he put one or two in his nose, and one or two in his shoulder for good measure.

I've a strong stomach. I have to. But the sight of that made me come over a bit queer. Ping gave me to understand that he wasn't crazy, that the needles were intended to do him some good for the wound in his shoulder. But what white or black magic that was, I'm afraid I can't tell you.

2

Ping had other strange habits. When the arm healed, he became an earlier riser than even me, and was up in the wintry darkness in the courtyard. It took me a while to catch him at it, but I finally stole down one morning and saw him out there, dancing.

He moved awful slow and straight up, as if there was a jug balanced on his head. Ten or fifteen minutes it went on, as he danced around the courtyard, waving his arms in the air, balancing on one leg at times, swooping down onto his haunches as well.

He didn't seem put out that I'd seen him when he'd finished. "What the hell was that?" I asked him.

"Gong foo. Gong foo." He said. And that was it. He tried to show me a few steps of his gong foo, but I didn't really take to it. It went so slowly I'd start thinking about what a fool I looked, and then pretty soon I start thinking about other things, my mind wandering all over the place, thinking about Charlo, and Anna, and my ma and pa, and by then I'd have my feet all in a tangle, and Ping would be laughing at me. But it didn't do me any harm. And to tell the truth, I had some good ideas while I was doing it.

Having Ping there had given me a notion to go traveling. There were caribou herders in the northern mountains who were happy to trade meat for whiskey. The trouble was their pastures were way up high and far off, across miles of boggy ground.

To get there in summer took a month, and even if I made it, the meat would spoil before I'd had a chance to bring any of it home. And in winter, I never liked to leave the house empty for too long. It was traveling weather, and there were desperate hungry people on the move.

But with Ping in the house, it would be a different matter. I could take a sled along the winter roads and bring back all the meat I could carry. It would stay deep-frozen and Ping and I could eat it until the thaw. My mouth watered at the thought of all that fresh meat. And Ping looked like he could use the iron. His face was all pale and washed-out.

Once a week, after Ping finished his dancing, he'd take my straight razor and shave his head. He had a cute touch with it, because I never once saw him cut himself.

A few days after the idea came to me, I went to him while he was shaving and used a piece of charcoal on the whitewashed wall of the pantry to show him what I was planning.

I hitched Ma to the old sled and loaded it with bottles of whiskey. How I came by those is another story.

I took a tent and bedroll. I ate so much the night before I set off that I began to sweat and had a stomachache. And in the morning, I left at first light along the frozen river that led out of town.

Naturally, I packed my guns and ammo and few other bits and pieces, and before I went I showed Ping how to use the rifle.

There was a bunch of dirty tents along the riverbank, and the stink of smoldering rubbish.

I passed a skinny woman gathering frozen berries on the edge of town. She was the first I'd seen in a while. She smiled at me and pulled open her coat to show me her lank titties, but I gee-upped the mare and kept moving.

Human beings are rat-cunning and will happily kill you twice over for a hot meal. That's what long observation has taught me. On the other hand, with a full belly, and a good harvest in the barn, and a fire in the hearth, there's nothing so charming, so generous, no one more decent than a well-fed man. But take away his food, make his future uncertain, let him know that no one's watching him, and he won't just kill you, he'll come up with a hundred and one reasons why you deserve it. You slighted him, you looked at his woman wrong, you wouldn't lend him a hatchet, you got more land than him, your beans have took and his didn't, and you know what else? You just never wrote to thank him when he gave you that hot meal that time. I heard that in the days when there were proper lawmen, and judges, and trials, and you could enter a plea when you were charged, people were fond of saying, "Your Honor, I acted in self-defense." But everyone acts in self-defense. That's the one certain thing. The man scalping you, the rowdies firing your corn, the gunman separating you from your cheap turnip watch.

There was a bed of fresh snow on top of the ice, which gave the mare's hooves something to bite into. I'd dismount and walk beside her for spells. There were a few last signs of human settlement along the riverside—a burned-out cabin, a wooden cross on a grave, some tumbledown walls—but then we were in the high country, nothing but trees as far as the eye could see, and the mountains behind. Isn't it strange that after so many years we never made a bigger dent on the land?

My heart lifted to have left the last of so-called civilization behind me. And just before sunset, I bagged a pair of snowy-white partridges for my supper. The first was a clean shot, the second fell, still fluttering, off his perch, and I gave him his quietus with my boot.

·

In the morning, I broke down the tent and we were off moving again before first light. My mind started to wander in the half-dark. I wondered what Ping was doing. And I thought of my life in that godforsaken place, doing a job that I hadn't been paid to do for years, for a citizenry that was determined to take each other to hell as soon as possible, and I wondered why I still bothered with it. I was enough of a frontiersman to live well outside the town. I didn't need to plunder, or steal food, or kidnap, to stay alive. I went through it a few times in my head, and it seemed to me that the only thing keeping me there was that house, that I was still keeping a part of the old life alive, in the hope that one day Ma and Pa and Charlo and Anna would come back to it. How lucky we are when we don't know we're lucky. Not to live among desperate people. Getting paid. Worrying about roof slates and why the bread won't rise. I thought about the woman in the woods, with her titties and her broken teeth.

What might she have been if things had turned out different. When she was a babe in arms, her father never thought she'll end up picking frozen berries and pleasuring strangers for food. That's why I say we live in a broken age.

·

It was five days traveling before I reached the mountains.

The caribou herders have been in those mountains for thousands of years, way before any of the white men got here. They always lived a simple life, following their herds up to the summer pastures and back down in winter, and it's stood them in good stead.

My father always preferred to do his work by hand, even when there were plenty of machines to make the work easier. We were always pushing him to get newer things, because like all children we were in love with what's new, but he wouldn't be told. "More things to go wrong. Just another thing to break."

The more complicated a thing is, the more badly it breaks down. He was certainly right about that.

The caribou people, on the other hand, they kept things simple: followed the seasons, never used anything they couldn't fix themselves. No engines to break down. Eat, ride, and wear the same animal. I couldn't live like them for any length of time. I like to sleep on a sprung mattress, between sheets, in a nightshirt. I like milled flour when I can get it, fresh vegetables. But more and more I had begun to think I was the last of my kind, and my children, if I ever had any, would have to be more like the caribou people if they were to raise any children of their own.

In the old days, the caribou herders were trappers, too, back when there was a call for fur and it fetched high prices out west. The winter roads were busy in those days, and traders were up and down them as soon as they'd frozen in November, and kept on traveling until the thaw. It was ghostly deserted now, but right where the river described a sharp bend back on itself, on the fringe of caribou country, just on that knuckle of land overlooking the frozen river, stood a hut, and, judging by the plume of smoke coming out of the tin pipe in its roof, an occupied one.

There were half-built sleds worked out of larch all round the yard. A big caribou carcass, skinned and frozen, dangled off the stoop, and a half dozen skins were tanning on a frame behind the hut. A dog came out of a little lean-to, pulling itself tight on its chain, and barked itself silly as soon as it heard our runners scraping along the ice.

The hut door banged open and a tall Tungus fellow hailed me from his porch with a raised hand. I could see the hut was emptyish, because there was only one coat on the stoop.

It was always my plan to get the trading over with as soon as I could, without going any deeper into the mountain country than I needed to, so this suited me just fine.

In I went to the hut, which was dirty but warm and, by the looks of things, home to four or five herders, all, save my host, out at that moment with the herd.

He boiled up some tea and fried some caribou meat for me, which tasted fine after that long journey, and I told him my business. His name was Solomon and he was the camp cook, he said. He told me to bide my time with him and the other fellows would be home presently. He was sure they'd be keen to trade.

Up on a shelf in the hut was a dead three-legged wolf, wrapped up in string and parcel paper. Solomon said it had been preying on the herd for months, and had been a sonofabitch to catch. In the end, they had put down poison to get him, which they weren't proud of, being hunting people. They were intending on carrying it back to the village with them, because their headman paid a bounty for wolves.

One by one, the herders trailed in as sun set, banging through the hut door and sitting down at the filthy table without a word for some food. Solomon served them hunks of caribou, which they cut into thin shreds with their own knives and dipped in salt before they ate it. Then he gave them a soup of caribou tripe, which smelled vile to me, but I guess it's the closest they had to greens in the winter months.

As soon as one had finished eating, he would wipe the crumbs off the oilcloth with his hands and onto the floor, and get up to make way for the next one in.

One stretched out on his ragged bed with a battered old guitar and sang a song to himself.

I'd eaten a heap, traveled a long way, and the stove was pumping out heat, so I soon found myself drifting off to sleep on the cot they'd let me have. But I woke up in the middle of the night with the guitar player standing over me, asking me if I wanted to make him a trade for one or both of my guns. I let him know plainly that the only way he'd be getting one of my bullets was in his head, and very shortly if he didn't back off.

He shrank back, complaining that I was being unfair. I said he should know better than to trouble someone when they're sleeping, and that we would talk about trade in the morning.

First thing after breakfast, I showed them a bottle of my whiskey. They were keen for it, I could see immediately, but they tried to play it off, in their simple way, as though they weren't too impressed with it. I knew otherwise, but I indulged them so they wouldn't lose face.

We haggled for a while over the price of the meat. I had

been thinking that the smart thing for me would be to take the caribou live. I could hitch them to the cart, they'd travel under their own steam, eating lichen from under the snow, and I could butcher them whenever I wanted, but the herders were adamant that in that case I'd have to pay for the skins as well. So we fixed on a price, spat and shook hands on it, and drank a tot of whiskey together.

Then they brought four caribou out of the herd and butchered them. They killed them one by one out behind the hut, gentling them until the last minute so the fear wouldn't taint the meat and make it stiff. The animals' eyes rolled as their throats were cut, and blood sprayed onto the snow. Then they dragged the carcasses away to flay the skins off and gut them, steam rising up from their innards as their eyes glazed. I let the herders keep the tripe since they were so keen on it.

The butchering was done, the sled was loaded up, and I was ready to leave by mid-morning. I had no desire to stick around there while those fellows binged on the whiskey. If they had sense, they would trade it on, but I wasn't sure they did, and the guitar-playing fellow, whose name was Gustav, looked like he was fixing to go on a holy bender.

.

It turned out he was much smarter than that. And I must have let my guard down, thinking that there was no one within fifty miles but a dead wolf and a half-dozen drunk caribou herders. Because after leaving the hut, and traveling all day, I broke my journey to make camp. And when I woke up in the morning, I found that someone had lifted my guns as I slept. My rifle, both my sidearms, and a great box of shells that had taken a great slice of my life to cast, all gone.

I cursed heaven for my being idiot simple, and my mother for raising a fool, and the reindeer herders for their criminal cunning, and a good many other curses, none of which in the least succeeded in bringing my guns back to me. I had one old shotgun back at home and the rifle which I'd left for Ping to use, but nothing else.

There was no doubt that without my weapons I was dead, so I was left with a simple choice.

I saddled the mare and followed the tracks. Gustav had made no effort to hide them, figuring that I would hesitate before I went in pursuit of an armed man. I knew I had a faster mount, since he was riding a caribou, but he had god knows how many hours head start over me.

I was careful not to catch him too quick. I knew my best chance was to creep up on him at nighttime, as he had me. And when I sensed I was getting close, I dismounted and went on foot.

His cooking fire was what I spied first, and his tent beside it. There was no point approaching him until dark, so I bided my time.

Now, I had been running a few plans in my head, but as soon as I saw how he had left his camp, I knew what it was to be.

I crept up in the darkness and set his tent alight with embers of his cooking. The floor of his tent was a reindeer skin, but under that he had packed dry branches so as to sleep more soft. It caught quick, and the smoke and heat must have made him more dozy for a while—or perhaps he had been drinking—because it was a while before he appeared, like a drowsy bee staggering away from a smoked-out hive, happy to have saved his skin, then less happy when he realized the fix he was in.

Traveling in the Far North in winter, it's always best to hang your coat outside your tent. The Tungus are pretty strict about it. Mainly it's for the sake of the fur: it molts less and stays in better shape. But there's another reason also. It's a hundred to one chance, but it's worth considering, that if you're caught short in the night or you have to go outside for something, and by sheer bad luck or otherwise you kick your stove over, your tent will go up and so will everything in it.

And just after you've finished congratulating yourself for not burning to death, you'll look up at the star-filled sky, and you'll hear the ice crystals in your breath tinkling together, making the sound they call "the whisper of angels," and you'll rub your shirtsleeved arms, and a bad feeling will come over you.

If I'd been that herder, I would have put one of the bullets from the stolen guns through my own head before I froze to death, because freezing to death is a terrible way to go. There were forty degrees of frost that night, and it took him almost two hours to die.

The last thing that happens to you when you freeze is your body feels like it's burning up. Your heart pumps the last of your hot blood to your skin as your organs shut down. That's why you'll tear off your clothes even as your liver is turning to ice.

I found him in the morning, followed the trail of his clothes deeper into the woods, and came upon him, naked, bluish, with rime on his hair and his johnson frozen. Luckily, he still had on my guns.

3

Killing always sits heavy with me.

Whether that's because of my being a woman, or because my disposition is naturally softhearted for another reason, I don't know.

I've had to fight the womanish things in my nature for almost as long as I can remember. These are not softhearted, womanish times.

Being tall, and broad in the shoulders, and deep-voiced, it's been easy enough to pass for a man, but I still shed some tears over that lousy herder, though I railed against myself for the weeping, because I knew he would have shed none for me.

Softness—and conscience and good faith—is like the pianola, or the books in the old gun store on Mercer Street. They have no place in these times. Yet, just because I don't eat dainty, and I don't scruple to kill, and I can't dance or read music, that doesn't mean I don't hanker after doing so.

Wild dogs had took some of the meat from the sled, but there was still a good quantity of it left, so I guess you could call the journey a success. I had fresh food, and I still had my guns, and when I called to the mare she came out from the stand of larches where I'd left her hobbled.

We were slower on the journey back on account of the extra weight. It was a week's traveling instead of five days, and I pulled into town beat and smelling pretty ripe.

When I knocked on the gate, Ping peeked out of an upper window with the rifle, and his face lit up to see me. We hung the meat out back, out of the sunlight. And then I got to thinking I would like to clean myself up properly.

It had got colder since I'd been away and the water in the well had frozen. Ping had been making do somehow, not knowing any better, but I hated to go short of water.

There was still some light left in the day, so I took Ping out to the lake on the cart with the ice saw and we cut blocks for a couple of hours, until we had a load. The blocks sparkled in the lengthening yellow light, like outsize sugar candy, or pale blue Turkish delight dusted with powdered sugar. We took them home with us and stacked them in the courtyard.

I lit a fire in the stove in the bathhouse. My pa had built it of cedarwood and the air inside smelled sweet even when it was cold, but when it got hot the perfume seemed to seep out of the wood and crackle in your nostrils. I heated a little water in a copper kettle on the stove, and when it was near to boiling I heaved in one of the ice blocks. It hissed and cracked on the heat.

It took a good hour for the bathhouse to get hot enough for a steam, and by then the sun had set, and the stars pricked the navy blue of night like needlepoints. I bundled myself up in a thick robe with towels and slippers as I crossed the yard. The smoke rose lazily on the freezing air, dropping as it cooled, until it spread sideways across the sky like a clothesline.

I hung my things up on the hooks outside the hot room and went through that creaky door to face the wall of dry heat. The dirt seemed to leach out of me, making grubby pools in the folds of skin on my belly.

Ping was clattering outside in the yard, maybe hesitant about coming in, so I called his name. There was the squeak of tight wood and his face appeared in the crack of the door. I didn't want to lose any heat, and the blood beating in my ears had made me fierce, so I yelled at him to get inside or shut the door, and the next thing is he's standing inside, done up tight to his neck in Charlo's old dressing gown and a few rolled towels, not an inch of skin showing.

He was looking at me wide-eyed. And I realized, of course, that he was staring at my tits, which had dropped out of the towel, and below that my bush. It must have been a shock, since he was expecting to see a fellow, to see a rawboned girl in the buff, but it wasn't going to make any difference to me: I knew what I was, and I didn't know how I was going to break it to him otherwise.

But he stared for a long time. And then his mouth opened as though he was about to say something. And then his hands trembled on the knot of the dressing gown and he tugged at it, as though he was in a hurry to get it off. And it passed through my mind that he'd seen something he liked and wanted a piece of, which was not my intention at all. So I'd bunched my fist to give him the lights out if he took one step closer, but the next thing is, he's dropped that old gown and half-doubled up with sobs.

And strangest of all, it seems that Ping is a woman.

There's no mistaking it: the pinch at the top of the hips, and the small oriental bosoms, and coal-black thatch of her bush. And that's not the end of it: by the swell of her belly it appears to me that she's not three or four months with child.

I let my hands drop and I felt Ping's arms round me, and the rasp of her bald head on my cheek, and she howls into my ear like a soul that has lost its body.

Being a woman in these times, I know some of what she's crying for. The world fighting itself like cats in a bag. The ordinary cruelty. The piles of unburied bones bleaching at the western edge of the town. And then there's her relief. She must have been worrying days how to tell me.

With a shudder I recalled that shot in her shoulder, and thanked god I never slung her belly-down over the saddle.

She let me touch her stomach. There was a line down the middle of it like the seam on a broad bean, only dark. And her nipples were chocolate brown and wide.

I began to wonder how I ever could have thought she was a man. The truth is, save me, I never encountered a woman in the last ten years who wasn't more or less some man's wife or property. I wondered how she was living, where she came from, who the father is, but there are no words that would make her understand my questions.

Right then, she felt so small in my arms that it seemed like I was the mother and she my child. I held her and caressed her baby-bald head, until her sobs were just sniffles, and I couldn't tell if she was sleeping or waking.

There was a stillness in the house the next day. Ping came down the stairs sleepily much later than usual, and looked at me almost shyly after the surprises of the night before, and the world felt a little different that morning with the idea of new life in it.

4

It was late January when I came back from my visit to the caribou herders and learned Ping was with child. With the help of a calendar and some drawings of the moon, I got her to show me the likeliest time of conception, and we calculated that the baby was due to arrive around midsummer.

As spring got closer, I started thinking about cultivating some more land, since there was going to be more of us. The one thing I had in abundance was packet seeds. Almost everything useful had been plundered from the stores downtown over the years, but a few oddments of things had got left behind, and in the farm supply on Willow Street there were boxes and boxes of packet seeds that no one had thought to touch. It stands to reason that if you're chiefly concerned just to live until tomorrow, you must think how to fill your belly today and find a way to defend yourself. Those two are tasks enough, believe me, so no one paid too much mind to planting a crop.

Those packets were stamped with dates in the past when they were supposed to go bad, but I knew that was just nonsense. A seed keeps its power. There are plants in the desert south where the seed just bides its time for a hundred or so years in the sand, waiting for the rain. Just waiting for a moment to bloom again. I've never seen it, but I've heard that every century or so the rain comes and that whole bare stretch of rock and sand is a mess of flowers and plants.

On top of the firehouse is a lookout tower they used to use for spotting blazes in the forest. One day, after I'd been collecting seeds from the store, I clattered up the rungs and peered along the highway, east and west, watching it fold through the trees in the distance like a ribbon of white silk.

The city looked emptier than I had ever known. I tried to be thankful for it. I missed what it used to be, but between me and then stood an impassable gulf—a river of blood and fire.

It's habits that keep you straight when everything around you is falling apart. Calling myself constable, keeping the tack clean and the horses in shape for the morning ride was all that stood between me and hopelessness—at least, until Ping came. I knew I hadn't been constable in anything more than name since Charlo died.

It occurred to me for the first time that maybe I was the last. Maybe me and Ping were all that was left. Up to a month or two before, I knew of at least three families scraping by in different sections of the city. But at that moment, looking down from the old tower, I couldn't see a sign of any of them.

The mist had lifted from that morning and it was a gray,

frosty day of about twenty below, but there wasn't so much as a curl of smoke from a household fire.

This place had been my life for as long as I could remember. I thought of the time before I was born when my parents had come to that city, along with all the other pioneer families. And in half a lifetime or so, it had emptied out again. From where I was standing I could see trees growing out of the bleachers round the softball field, which itself was a maze of scrubby bushes. The billboards along Main Street had shriveled in the weather. The drugstore where I used to drink malted milk was a hive of blackened glass and wood. The train station that the line had never reached remained half built and now would never be finished. All those hours and days of human struggle, thousands, millions of them, spent building up this place, only to have it kicked down like an anthill by a spoiled child.

This place had promised the first settlers everything. Now what was it? A ghost town, decaying back into wilderness.

•

There wasn't a soul left in the whole place save us, I grew surer of it by the day. Imagine: a city of thirty thousand souls reduced to two women and a bump. And yet, the odd thing was, I liked it a whole lot better. I started going round it by foot. Something I hadn't done for years. It made me feel closer to the place somehow, crunching the broken glass and paper underfoot, spying the discarded things—a filthy doll, some spectacles, broken shoes—that told the story of my city.

The houses where the Challoners and the Velazquezes had been living were abandoned. I put a ladder up to their outside walls and had a look in. There was a pitiful scrawny tabby in the Challoners' yard but no sign of a person. At the Velazquez house, I could see the place had been left orderly, with its furniture intact, and some sign that the garden had been dug, but there was no doubt they were elsewhere too. That killer Rudi and his brute of a son, Emil.

With the last humans gone, it seemed like nature decided to reclaim everything. On Considine Avenue, I came upon a herd of wild pigs, at least twelve of them, rooting around the old garbage heaps. The adults were black and square, like steamer trunks. I emptied both pistols from horseback and managed to hit two of them while the rest ran off squealing. I butchered them then and there on the street and dragged them home, chucking the lights and offal into the Challoners' yard for the tabby.

Once I reached home and glanced back at the long smears of blood on the ice in the roadway, a strange feeling came over me. I unbuckled my empty guns and laid them on the kitchen table. It occurred to me that that was the first time in fifteen years I'd been anywhere in the city without a loaded weapon.

We ate to bursting for days, smoked a flitch for the summer, and tried not to think too hard about what they might have fattened on.

I later regretted my generosity to the cat, because Ping knew a way to make dried sausage with intestines.

The other thing I noticed was the birds. By April, the birdsong was so raucous in the mornings that it was waking me up in the dark. And the types of them had got so various. I know my eating birds, but the smaller ones—I can name a sparrow and a robin, and that's it. But I could see we had a whole new menagerie. The circumstances had changed so much. They had all the windfall and the berries to themselves. So many new places to roost.

Ping and I were beginning to find ways to talk to each other. I never had much of an ear for her language, but we had "chai" for tea, and "dinner" for pretty much every mealtime, and a bunch of other words that helped simplify our life together, though we were a way off discussing politics or sharing our life stories—which suited me, in fact.

The first time she felt the baby move, a look of astonishment came across her face and she gabbled in her tongue and put my hand on her stomach; but I couldn't feel a darn thing, even though she was tapping my arm with her finger, trying to let me know what I was supposed to be feeling for. Six or eight weeks later, I was able to feel something stirring in that little melon belly of hers, and by April, I could make out distinct shapes; but I was never too sure if it was a foot, or a buttock, or a tiny head that I was feeling.

Ping was sure it was a girl. I don't know how. She spent evenings cutting patterns for her tiny dresses. That little thing seemed to like the pianola. She got very lively after I had played one of my rolls. I hoped she'd be musical and maybe figure out how to tune it, because the songs didn't sound much like they'd used to sound.

That whole spring was one of the great times in my life. Ping bloomed and she let her hair grow, and her belly swelled and swelled. I spent some happy hours in the farmers' supply choosing seeds for the garden. They gave me a great feeling of hope for the future, those little brown packets: beans, and corn, spinach, squash, and rutabaga, radish, melons, peas, tomatoes, zucchini, cabbage, and chard. I started turning the soil with ash and horseshit as soon as the thaw began, and I thought, Hell, let's plant some flowers as well so I got a whole bunch of them: cotoneasters, candytuft, marigolds, pansies. Waking early every day to that chorus of birdsong and planning my garden, it really felt to me that some sanity and color and orderliness had come back into my world.

•

Late in April I was up the lookout again with a spyglass and I caught something moving out on the roadway far to the east: first dust, then a column of people moving out of the horizon and toward us. It's eerie the silence when you look at a thing like that from far off through the glass. You know there are sounds: horses laboring under a heavy load, whips and sticks, chains clanking, men cussing out the stragglers, but you can't hear them. And the spyglass flattens it all out like a tableau in a picture book.

The thing it called to mind as it came into view was the big color picture of Moses parting the Red Sea in my children's Bible. It showed how the walls of water on either side were smooth like glass, and between them, on the dry seabed, fish lay flapping and dying under the feet of the fleeing Israelites. Way in back, Pharaoh's army was just about preparing to go between those high blue walls. Pharaoh's chariot was pulled by a pair of big snorting black horses and I had nightmares where I could hear their hooves as they gained on me, and I'd fall on my knees among the gasping fish, thinking, Let it be quick, let it be quick—before I woke up to the sound of Charlo's openmouthed breathing and the room still filled with that watery early morning light.

I wouldn't normally have put myself in the way of trouble, but since Ping came with her baby, I felt less careful about my own life. I was, after all, the sole representative of the law in the municipality, and it didn't feel right for me to be skulking round like a thief at a wedding while this huge caravan of people moved past right outside my city.

The highway skirted the north side of the town. A metaled

road ran up to it, but ten years of freezing and thawing had broken it into rubble. I didn't like to risk the mare's legs on it, so I galloped across the open ground instead. The whole column must have had close to two hundred souls in it, and the whole thing slowed to a halt as they saw me coming. I wasn't minded to get too close, so I stopped short about fifty yards away from them and waited to see if anybody would come.

My horse pawed at the dirt while I waited. I could feel hot eyes on me. There were five or six men on horseback bossing the prisoners. I counted at least three rifles and I was beginning to regret my boldness. Then a tall lean fellow rode out of the line, coming in close beside me, and tipped his hat. He had a sharp, leathery face, blue eyes, and the fingers that held his bunched reins were long and thin.

He licked his cracked narrow lips and spat into the dirt. "Looks like the rain is going to hold off."

"Depends how long you're on the road," I said.

"About four more weeks."

The gun he was wearing on his hip had a long silver barrel as thin and dainty as one of his fingers. I sensed he was afraid there was more of me, dug in somewhere around. He seemed cool and relaxed, of course, as a Pharaoh should be, but what gave him away was the eyes of his men, fidgety, flicking around to see who was lying in wait.

"What are you trading?" I asked him.

Those blue eyes of his narrowed into steel splinters. He said nothing.

I looked at the sullen faces in the line, all those filthy clothes, taking the chance of a stop to rest on their haunches: peasant girls, some Chinese, some with chapped red cheeks; some darker, asiatic-looking natives.

"First time I've seen you come by here," I said. I knew if he was silent again it spelled trouble.

He gazed down at his hands, which were folded on the saddle pommel, and looked up slowly, as though to let me know he was in no hurry to answer my question.

"We came through here in January."

"How about that," I said, to fill his pause. I was calculating how quick I could draw on him and then spur on the mare to get away from there. My heart was hammering, time seemed to be slowing down, and my eyes had that keenness that comes as your body dumps those fight chemicals into your blood. I could pick out individual grinning faces on horseback behind him.

"As a matter of fact," he went on, "I lost a girl somewhere around here. You didn't happen to come across a stray, did you?"

I shook my head.

"Too bad. I'd taken a shine to her." Leather creaked as he shifted in his saddle. "Nice visiting with you." He tipped his hat and spurred his horse back the way he'd come, and his men roused the sitting prisoners into moving again.

I stayed for a long time without turning my back on them—partly out of curiosity, wondering about all those people, masters and slaves, and where they'd come from, and what lives they'd been leading, but also in case any of them were minded to take a potshot when my eye was off them.

There were times when I wondered if I had done the right thing staying behind when everyone else had left or died. That day, watching the column of people vanish into the dust raised by their own feet, I was struck by a fear about what had happened to the world in my absence.

5

I showed Ping a map of the town and pointed out my house on it, and where we'd met, and asked her to show me where she'd been living before that.

She turned the map around and around to get a fix on it and then put a cross just behind the old fire station on Malahide Avenue. There was something in her face when she looked back up at me—trepidation, I'd call it, even though it was just lines on paper—so I smiled and stroked her cheek to reassure her that she wasn't going back there.

The fire station stood at the north end of town right off the highway that ran west to the old gas and gold fields and east into the empty tundra country, where it dwindled to nothing a thousand miles short of the sea.

Sometimes travelers would bed down there for a night. The sheds where the water trucks had stood were empty, but the building was a sturdy one, and the old walls were as good a windbreak as any. There were scorch marks against the bricks, and discarded cans where people had passed through. I gave it a wide berth in general. You never wanted to get mixed up with the kind of characters that traveled that empty road for the reasons they did. In the old days, living on the road was a boon, because it brought in trade. You got the lowest prices and the freshest news of anyone. But after a time the news was only bad. First people turned up hungry, then desperate and begging. Finally they'd just arrive quietly in the night, cut your throat while you were sleeping, take everything they could carry, and vanish like smoke before first light. Even the worst of our town learned to shun that road after a time.

I had stopped getting orders from anyone a long time before that, but I had always hoped that in the other towns to the east there was still some kind of lawful life being led. That was my consolation as first I buried Pa, and Ma, and Anna, and then Charlo, and the life we had known seemed to pass and be forgotten like an old tune nobody sings anymore. Maybe here it's especially bad, I used to think. Or someone's forgotten about us. But away from here, the old life continues.

Except the pitiful caravan of women in chains, and their hard-faced masters on horseback, none of that was part of the old life. That would almost lead you to believe the opposite: that away from here it's even worse.

•

Sure enough, there was an old manhole near where Ping had marked her *X* on the map. It would have had a cover on it in the old days, but someone must have rolled it away to melt and cast tools or blades. It was small enough to miss if you weren't looking for it, and I supposed that Ping had happened on it by chance.

I took a good look around me, but the town seemed quiet, so I climbed out of the saddle and crouched down by the hole to investigate. Behind me, the mare wandered off toward a tuft of grass at the side of the firehouse. I never hitched her anywhere away from home. I didn't like the idea of her being tethered. I trusted her to have the good sense to run away from trouble and to come back to me if I called.

"Anybody down there?" The empty hole returned the sound of my voice with a flat, booming echo when I yelled into it.

I holstered my gun and dropped down.

The drain ran ten, twenty yards in the darkness. I lit a tallow candle from my tinder box and shielded the flame from my eyes with my hand. Amazing, the construction of my poor old city. A storm drain you could almost stand upright in. Poured concrete for the walls, laid in sections. And down the center, a runnel of twigs and leaf mulch soft underfoot from the last fall rains.

In an alcove up on the sides I found what looked like an animal's nest: twigs, gnawed bones, rags, and scrunched paper. I turned over a blackened book with my toe. Ping's home. Living in the dark like a groundhog under a porch and sneaking out to gather books for fire. I knew then for certain there wasn't any love story behind her bump.

I hauled myself out of the drain and clucked my tongue to bring the mare back from out of the sheds. They must have berthed the caravan here when they came through in January, corralling the women in, out of the weather.

One of the slave masters must have cast his eye over the footsore and weary women. Your turn.

I liked to think she stabbed him with that blunt knife of hers. Most probably he fell asleep on the straw and she took her chance to run. Pitched into the hole and lay there in the darkness.

Close to three months she must have hidden here, wretched with hunger and cold. I hated to think how she lived, what she ate.

I found it hard to meet Ping's eye when I saw her back at the house. Her happiness filled the place like the sound of something tinkling and bright, but I knew what she'd suffered and I couldn't stop thinking of the bad thing that had happened to me.

6

I can't dwell on what happened next, because it pains me too much to write it, but in June, Ping died and the baby died with her.

It went very hard with me after that and the purpose vanished out of my life. My bad thing and every other bad thing that had happened in the years before seemed like nothing compared to that.

I buried them together in a grave I dug to the south of the city. The place sits in a ring of birches where the old Fourways Crossing used to be. I set them there in a larch-wood box and rolled a white rock over it for a headstone, but I couldn't bring myself to write words on it.

It was close to midsummer, light round the clock, and the insects and birds loud enough to drive you crazy.

I felt I couldn't live in the town any longer, and I rode away into the mountains. For two months of that summer, I lived in an abandoned cabin on a lake. There was an old skiff and I set nets in the water for fish, but looking back, the rest of that time is lost to me. All I know is that sometime in late August, when the long nightless summer days were drawing to a close, and the mosquitoes had died off, I ate my supper, pulled on my boots, and went outside to drown myself.

The boat sat on an outhaul because the lake was big enough to get choppy at times and I didn't want to risk her near the rocks. I pulled her in and then set off for the middle of the lake.

I loved the sounds of the moving water, the plop and drip of the oars, the gurgling from the stern, and the occasional slap of a small wave; and I loved the smell which rose off the warm larches like cinnamon off a baked bun.

In my mind, those moments between summer and the start of winter shared the sadness of my own middle age. I knew that in a few weeks, the first snow would fall and dust the horseshoe of mountains that ringed the valley. Then the mercury would plummet, down to where only an alcohol thermometer could gauge how cold it was: sixty and seventy below. The lake would be locked under six feet of ice. Soon there would be nothing to smell on the freezing air, and the lake, until it broke up with loud cracks the following May, would be silent.

About a hundred yards out, I shipped the oars and drifted. The sky above me was turning purple. When I got to the fishing nets, I hauled them in. *The last time*, I thought, and there was a sense of peace inside me that I hadn't known for years.

A couple of grayling fell from the net with fat thunks onto

the floor of the boat. I felt sorry for the poor creatures. I grabbed one. It bucked in my hand and then slipped over the rail of the boat. I threw the other one after it and there was a flash of silver as it vanished in the inky water.

Alone in the gathering darkness, I yanked off my boots, stood upright in the teetering boat, pinched my nostrils shut, and got ready to jump.

I'd thought about this moment so many times that I almost felt I'd done it before. As I went, I gave the boat a kick to send it far away from me. The shock of the cold water knocked the breath out of my body. Suddenly, I was fighting for my life. The thick padded sleeves of my summer jacket filled with water and dragged against me like lead wings, but my face kept on upwards, looking toward the sky. I shut my eyes and tried to force myself deeper into the water, but my body was struggling against me. It felt like I wasn't killing myself but some poor, unwilling fellow who wanted nothing of it. His legs were keeping me up and his sharp, shallow breaths were putting air in my lungs.

Gradually, I figured, my legs would weaken, and the fight would go out of me. That idea kind of relaxed me. Water began trickling into my mouth and nostrils. I peed myself and a cloud of warmth spread out around me. I waited for a flood of final images to fill my brain as my whole sorry life folded up like a telescope into that moment. As I floated on my back in the lake, I could still hear the rasp of my breathing, but behind that now was another note, like the deep bowed string of a contrabass, drawing me in toward it: the sound of my quietus.

I forced my head under again. The water bubbled and closed over my ears, muffling the noise. My body began to shake. It seemed like death was close. That throbbing bass sound grew louder and my eyelids flickered open for one last look at the valley.

There was a tiny silhouette above me, banking steeply toward the farthest northern slope. An airplane.

I watched amazed as the silhouette dipped down below the top of the ridge. Then there was a faint pop, followed by louder cracks as trees broke under the weight of the plane. The noise echoed around the valley for a time. Then it all went quiet again.

My fingers were so numb and cold that it took me a while to unlatch the buttons of my jacket. I let it sink in the water and struck out for the boat. By the time I got to her, I was too weak to crawl in, so I just clung on to her stern, sicking up water and flailing my legs to bring her in to shore.

•

It was midnight by the time I reached the wreck. It had been so long since I saw anything like it that it seemed like an apparition, and I half thought that I was on the lake bottom already, dreaming these things.

She was a biplane, fitted with wheels for summer flying, in a red and white livery. The starboard wing had sheared off at impact. I ran my fingers over the jags in the metal.

Most of all what struck me was the smell in those woods: it seemed to belong to an old childhood dream. It came back to me in waves. I kept thinking of when Pa put his auto on blocks for the last time and he gave me the job of draining the fuel tank with a length of hose into a can. I sucked so hard I took down a gulp of gasoline. I wanted to be sick but couldn't and my shit turned tarry and dark the next day.

Gasoline. That was the smell in those trees. It was so strong, you felt you could have got drunk off it. It had that shimmering, sharp feeling you get when you put your nose over a glass of warm whiskey.

And then suddenly the whole wood was lit up for a second brighter than noontime, as though a flash of lightning had hit. The thunder followed a second later, and the boom knocked me back off my feet and down into the darkness I'd glimpsed at the lake bottom.

7

The Tungus have a story that, who knows how many years ago, when the first pilots were opening up the east, one named Sigizmund Levanevskii flew out to reconnoiter a Far Northern route.

In those early days, the craft they had were small and spindly, with no fancy instruments, and they were forced to fly low without stopping, hugging the earth, and getting all mixed up in the weather.

Two or three days out, Levanevskii and his crew ran into trouble. They lost power from their engines. They had no parachutes and the land below them was nothing but an ocean of trees.

Knowing that it was too late to save his aircraft, Levanevskii gambled that at least some of his men would survive the crash if he could bring the plane down in a lake. But the plane smacked into the water and sank in seconds, leaving an oily stain and a hiss of steam behind it.

The government of the time searched and searched for the wreck and the dead men, but couldn't find them.

But the Tungus will tell you that someone *did* see that plane go down. The great-great-great granddaddy of one of them was herding reindeer by the lake as that doomed thing came plummeting out of the sky.

This man, who was just a boy at the time, watched it slap into the water, break up, and sink almost immediately. Seconds later, the valley was silent again, but the face of the lake was all shaken up by the impact, and waves splashed over the boy's boots.

Then the boy lit a fire so that when the men finally appeared he could welcome them with a cup of tea.

The herder who told me this story the first time found it so funny, he almost wept with laughter as he recounted it. He put on a big performance, pretending he was kindling a fire while greasy bubbles rose to the lake top.

Imagine! The boy was so in awe of the white man's fancy gizmos he thought that was how a plane was supposed to land!

The story seems to be making fun of the boy's simpleness, but the real butt of the joke is Levanevskii and his broken plane.

The idea of looking up at that aircraft, that miracle, must have made the Tungus feel pretty small. They like to say their shamans know how to fly. But I've met some shamans and they could certainly drink, but not one of them could fly worth a damn.

Levanevskii's plane was like a boast from on high; it was the white people saying, Look what we can do! And everyone likes to see a braggart humbled.

The story seemed to tell the Tungus what they knew from their own lives and, from dealing with people like me, the remnant of the other way of doing things: time has a way of evening things out, the simple ways endure, and the fancy pants with his smart new way falls by the roadside. The best way to tell how long a thing will last is ask how long it's been around for. The newest things end soonest. And things that have been around for a good long while will last awhile to come.

Those herders took it in the neck for years from people who claimed to be better, to know more. From the little I know of history, I understand that their holy men got killed, and their villages broken up, and their ways of doing things beaten out of them, all in the name of progress. So if they came across a trifle smug in telling their story, you can understand it.

But whenever I heard that story I felt something different. I thought: What a piece of work man is! What can't we do when we have a mind to? I feel a kind of awe at my ancestors, living surrounded by more kinds of knowledge than will fit inside any one man's head. You can say, as the herders do, that they overcomplicated their lives and that made them weak. Or you can just marvel at their ingenuity and hope that what they did once can be done once more.

When I came to, the woods were burning, and my eyebrows and a good part of my hair had been singed off. My collarbone was broken, and I could hardly hear on account of going deaf from the boom.

I lay on my back in a pile of brush, watching a plume of black smoke coil into the sky, masking the stars as it went up, and I thought: Glory, hallelujah, we've come again.

·

The mare looked at me with a kind of reproach in her eyes when I got back to the cabin. I hooked omul from the lakeshore and watched as the hillside burned. The woods were in flames for three days, and it was almost a week before I was able to get anywhere near the wreck. By then there wasn't much at all to see: a skeleton of blackened metal, propellers, a few charred boxes that had been tossed into the air from the blast and damn nearly taken my head off.

The heat had been so fierce it was hard to say how many people the plane had been carrying, but I guessed five or six. I buried what I could find at the approach to the woods so animals wouldn't get at the bones, and marked the place with a simple cross that I pounded into the ground with a rock.

When I reflected on it, it seemed to me that the best monument to those people was the plane they had died in. I knew I had never seen anything so beautiful, in all my years, as that plane arcing through the sky over the valley.

I'm not superstitious, but I took it as a kind of sign—from God, or the gods, or the ancestors, or whoever is up there—not to abandon myself to my despair. It does seem strange to take comfort from death and disaster, but the appearance of the plane in the sky told me I was no longer alone. The people who flew in her had died, but I knew she must have been built somewhere, that someone had fueled her, prepared her for her journey through the air. Of course, I still mourned Ping and the child, but whereas I'd thought that the three of us were the last of the old world I'd cared about, it seemed now that there was more than a remnant of that world out there, working as it ought to, as it had in the past, performing its miracles, putting men and who knew what else in the air, and I set my heart on finding it.

8

Since the plane was flying roughly west when it went down, my first thought was that it had been sent out of one of the cities between here and the Bering Sea. Five had been built during the waves of settlement that had brought my parents from Chicago: Plymouth, New Providence, Homerton, Esperanza, and Evangeline—the first to be settled and the farthest west by some two hundred miles.

I felt certain that one of them had scraped up fuel and a plane and gone to scout out the others. In that position, I'd have done the same. There was me, so there might well be more than me: Makepeaces all over, still scratching out a solitary life, longing for contact but afraid to move, like a person lost in a wood, in case they miss the search party when it comes.

There'd been no word between the towns for years. Even at the best of times, the links between us were slender. The settlers were inward-looking on principle. They didn't come here to be social, or to re-create the bustling trade and business of the world they'd left behind. But even so, there was a sense of cousinhood with the other cities. They were the closest we had to a nation.

.

My father used to say he decided to leave America when he noticed that the poor had all begun to look alike.

He didn't mean their faces, and he didn't mean only the poor of the United States. He meant poor people everywhere.

It stands to reason that the poor of each country should differ more from each other than other men do. Their roots are in the soil. What they eat, how they dress, their homes, their customs—all grow out of the ground. Thatch, palm, or caribou skin. Rice, wheat, or manioc. Fur, cotton, or worsted. Their whole lives are fixed by the character and habits of the land.

He said it hit him traveling one time in the year or so before he met my mother. Whatever country of the world it was—Persia, Siam, or the Indies, Europe or the South Seas or Mesopotamia—the poor were starting to look alike, live alike, eat alike, and dress alike in the same kind of clothes all made in the same part of China.

To him, it was a sign that the people had got severed from the land. I can't say if he was right or wrong. By the time I was old enough to take an interest in his world, it was already passing away.

He liked to say that ever since we slid out of the primeval mud on our bellies, we had been shaped by scarcity. Whatever you took—cheese, churches, good manners, thrift, beer, soap,

patience, families, murder, fences—it had all come about because there was never enough, sometimes not quite enough,
and sometimes not nearly enough, to go round. The story of
the mass of humanity was the story of people struggling and
failing to get the wherewithal for life.

The pain of that struggle taught people forbearance.

And yet, my father said he was born into a world of abundance. It was a world upside down, in which the rich were
skinny and the poor were fat. In one single day of his youth,
there were more people alive on earth than had lived on it in all
the years since Noah parked his boat on Ararat.

You don't need to be any more than normally superstitious
or even a Bible reader to guess that lean years will follow fat
ones. Milliards of people who want feeding will make a rumble
that shakes the planet. But my father's concerns weren't practical ones. He believed that one way or another, these people
would be fed, but that the price of this abundance was an im-
poverished spirit. He wanted to turn his back on a world that he
felt was debased and graceless.

It must have been strange for the Tungus to think anyone
looked at their difficult lives with envy. But men and women
like my father dreamed of quitting their cities, putting fresh
roots in the soil, and growing up again in the patched, hand-
made world of their ancestors. They chose that instead of—
instead of what, I don't know—whatever dreams of speed, and
glass, and luxury drive men who know they will never go hungry.

In centuries before, they would have obtained a warrant
from a king and set sail to found a colony in some emptier place.
But the earth was full. There was no place to start again. Even
the moon had a flag on it in those days.

I believe Siberia was suggested to them as a joke. People
thought of the place as a land of ice, a desert of rocks and snow,

with the wind blasting it ten months a year from the Urals to the Pacific Ocean. Lucky for us they did.

Short of any other ideas, the church sent my father and another man on a mission to visit. They flew to Moscow and traveled out by train to Irkutsk.

Nothing I've known in the Far North resembles the land of ice that people expected him to find here.

The farthest north I went in my life was with my father when I was fifteen up to the Chukchi people in tundra country. He took me instead of Charlo, not just because I was older, but because he was expecting a difficult journey. I know that he valued my hard and practical nature, seeing that the rest of them were all talkers and thinkers. That's some comfort to me now, since I wished for so many years that I could be more scholarly and soft, a daughter he could be proud of.

Even where the Chukchi lived it was nothing like a frosty desert.

It was summer and the land was purple and brown. There was tiny arctic willow and rhododendron growing in the boggy ground. They bred dogs for fur and travel. The water heaved with salmon and they had crabs you could eat with legs a foot long. I saw seals, and ate walrus, and watched whales breach the cold green water of the bay and spout. There was nothing barren or poor about that land. And that was up at the lip of the arctic circle.

My father would say later that by the time he stepped off the train, he had fallen in love with the land. Day after day, birches and pines swished past the window, and little wooden villages, and churches with gilded onion domes. He said he felt as though he'd come back to a place he had seen in a dream. It looked like the storybooks of his childhood.

I have a sense what he meant, but I've never known another landscape. I grew up with bears in the woods behind our house, and wolves, and poisoned toadstools, and a rotten bridge that might well have had a troll under it, so the storybooks never seemed that far-fetched to me. What seems far-fetched is life in a city, or my father's tales of Chicago, or the plane which I saw with my own eyes breaking up on that hillside.

.

The land was leased to us by the Russian government to build and farm on. Why had they let us in? Simple. Their leaders wanted us to fill up the empty spaces of their country. We were a graft from a strong and youthful plant. The people here were sick and depleted and the Chinese across the border were looking on Russia's empty regions with a hungry eye.

By leasing small tracts of the Far North to us, the Russians got to restock the land with European settlers. The settlers got more land than they knew what to do with. And it seemed like a smart bet to us. Our summers in the north were getting longer and our winters milder. No one was overly concerned that what was easing the cold of our winters was making the crowded parts of the globe hot and hungry and restless.

I was born in the false dawn of those early years. The dawn that was really a sunset.

But in those peaceful times, four or five cities followed ours, drawing their citizens from people like my father, who'd never fired a shot in anger or known a hungry day.

To them, the cold and hardship of their new world felt bracing and good, like rolling in snow after a steam bath. This life was a novelty to them and something freely chosen.

"Aren't you glad," they'd say, "that you live here in this

beautiful place and don't travel miles by bus to eat plastic food in a school cafeteria?" I'd answer yes, but only to please them. They painted a picture to us of the world they'd left: rootless, money-crazed people enfeebled by soft living, trapped in violent cities of night and rain.

Not knowing the world they left, I can't say if it was like that or not. But I don't share their view of the merits of scarcity. We come out of the dark, as frail and tender as the furry buds on an antler. Why turn your back on anything that will make life easier? Why spurn cities and machines, diesel, plastic, medicine?

It was a matter of faith with them. I suppose all settlers must be zealots first. Those first colonists who went to Roanoke or Plymouth, what did they think as night fell for the first time over their strange anchorage? Behind them were playhouses, and libraries, and stone churches, and the well-kept graves of their ancestors. In front of them were the forests of their weird Canaan, birds and plants they couldn't recognize, and the unwelcoming spears of their new neighbors. How did they know the land could even support life?

·

We had had to renounce our old countries as a condition of settling here.

At the time, this land was almost as empty as it is now. Even so, the settlers had to pay twice for it: they handed over cash for the title to the land, and they gave up the rights they had as citizens of other nations. What's more, they had no right to what lay under it: oil, diamonds, or gas. The government kept that for itself. We owned nothing below the thin topsoil.

My father kept his old navy-blue passport along with his birth and marriage certificate in a tin box up in the attic, but it was a worthless document, and all those like me who were born here were born stateless.

It was a high price, and many balked at paying it. Some had pointed to the empty spaces of Canada and said we should settle there instead. But the land in Canada that suited them belonged to its native people, while on the other side of the straits the Tungus had no such claim.

It never seemed to matter too much at first. The most religious among us regarded nationhood as a fiction. But by coming here, we made ourselves into orphans.

The Russian government never looked upon us as real citizens. Eventually they would grow to hate us, but first there were many years of official indifference. Once or twice, they sent bigwigs to see that all was in order, but soon those visits stopped. No one paid us much heed, tucked up in the empty north of this huge country. We were left to ourselves.

Seventy thousand people, all told, had come in three waves of settlement that lasted over ten years. Most of them were Quakers like my father and mother who had turned late to their faith. Others were believers of a different strain who held that we stood in the last days and the chosen would shortly be snatched up to heaven in the Rapture. A few had no fixed faith at all but worshipped nature or reason or just believed that the old crowded cities they had grown up in were hopelessly out of whack with how life ought to be. The chief thing they had in common was the shared belief that the old world was going to hell in a handbasket. None was fleeing poverty; if anything, they were fleeing its opposites: money, greed, idolaters. Some left the old lives happily and some left with a great sadness, feeling it was a defeat and an abandonment. But all of them believed that in the space and stillness of the Far North, they would recover the quiet music of life as it ought to be—austere, rugged, shaped by the seasons and the knowledge of hardship—and contact with others like them.

The settlers were hardworking folk. The cities thrived. The winters grew milder. There were hot springs to the north of our city which we piped to heat our glasshouses. We raised tomatoes in the arctic and talked about growing oranges.

Gradually, over time, it became clear that the settlers had less in common than they imagined. The absence from the world made their differences bigger. And try as you might to begin afresh, pretty soon people fall into old ways of doing things. A lot of life is habits. Start everyone off equal, some still wind up with more and want to protect it, some wind up with less and cry foul.

But I think in those first years there was a sense of promise about the place, and a sense of mission and hopefulness around what the people were doing.

When war broke out, the government demanded oaths of loyalty. The many Quakers among us were barred by their faith from swearing to anything. They could *affirm* their loyalty, but not *swear* it. It was too nice a point for our new government. The idea was that Quakers told the truth all the time, hand on holy book or no. Funny when you think what thieves and liars they all turned out to be. The government took it ill. It sounded like a refusal to them. And when we told them our young men wouldn't serve in their army, either, they withdrew the little they'd granted us: cheap fuel, medicines, the teachers who had traveled here to school us in our new mother tongue. But we'd come here to be left alone. There was nothing they had that we wanted. If anything, it bound us together a little more.

•

I took a sliver of blackened wing from the wreckage and made a keepsake out of it, working it into a tiny cross and wearing it on a string round my neck. From the depth of my sadness about Ping arose a new hope in the shape of that plane.

The more I thought of it, the more it seemed right: out had gone the plane, from one of the sister cities or some scratched-out dirt airstrip on the Bering Sea. There would be some broken hearts when it didn't return. I knew how that felt: days spent waiting for a key to turn in the front door, or to hear a familiar voice in the courtyard. But these ones weren't coming back. And when they didn't, what then? Would they send another plane? Did they have one?

Whatever their loss, I reasoned that any place with the know-how to put together and fly a plane was in better shape than I was. I imagined even their grieving would have an orderliness to it.

•

Right here in front of me is the world of the real. The pencil in my hand. The old exercise books I'm filling. The plum-black pinch on my thumbnail I put there hanging a bird feeder. The backs of my hands, more wrinkled-looking than they were the last time I checked. I see it pretty clearly, because I don't need things to be otherwise. Just like when I'm tracking game, I don't go after what I hope to find but only what's there.

But when it came to that plane, and the lives I imagined behind it, I let go of my reason too. Everything I needed to believe about the world came between me and a clear sight of reality. I clung to the few facts that fit with my preferred way of looking at things, and the rest I kicked under the rug.

Careening out of my grief in any case, I wasn't in my right wits. A kind of frenzy took hold of me. The world, which had seemed so desolate after Ping's death, now seemed so full of possibilities that I was fidgety with hope and couldn't sleep. After so many years in the Far North, I should have recognized the signs. The arctic year is nine months of cold and three of living hell-for-leather. Grief and the change from the long dark months of winter could bounce anyone into lunacy.

.

It took the best part of a month to get back to town and close up the house to my satisfaction.

I shuttered every window and barred them across the inside with wooden braces. I fastened the door with three different locks and buried the keys in a waxed bag at the foot of the pear tree in the garden. My father had grown it from a cutting he brought with him at the time of the first settlement from America. It grew small and stunted, like the willow in the tundra, but it grew all the same. And once in a while it fruited: tiny, thick-skinned pears that appeared so rarely they seemed more like talismans than fruit. Try as he might, my father was never able to coax more than a couple a year off that spindly tree: he cropped it, fertilized its roots with potash, dabbed pollen from flower to flower with a paintbrush. But if he was disappointed that his hard work yielded such meager harvests year after year, he never showed it.

As I buried the keys, it crossed my mind that I might never be coming back; but my zeal for the journey, and the twisted hold I'd got on the facts, turned what might have been a sober and thoughtful farewell into a breathless dash for the exit. I practically galloped out of there with the second horse in tow. It was certainly stimulating, after all those years of caution, to rip out onto the highway.

That brought me to my senses a little. I'd never once traveled that long, straight road alone. Its condition was good enough to surprise me. The gravel was well laid and pretty flat. What I hadn't expected was how I'd feel standing above the weird straight flatness of it, running from horizon to horizon. The paleness of the gravel and the bend in the earth made it seem like the road floated slightly above the ground. It seemed to roll on forever, forward and back, and not a soul to be seen either this way or that. And the next settler city lay two hundred miles to the east.

The laid roads here were built not by machine but by the gangs of slave workers who were sent by the commissars. Millions died here: starved or frozen, worked to death in mines, shot by the guards trying to escape, shot by the Tungus when they had escaped, killed and eaten when whoever they escaped with had run out of food. Numberless dead. You can look up on an August evening and see the sky throbbing with mosquitoes. Imagine every one with a man's head, and it's still too few.

You wonder if the land itself ever forgets a curse like that.

There's an old prison factory at Buktygachak that I visited on horseback as a little girl.

Buktygachak: even the name has the air of no good about it. The main factory building was still standing, and a block of punishment cells. In summer, the tall grass and the warmth took the sting out of it, but the Tungus guide who took us there slapped the water out of my hand when I filled my canteen from a stream and told me it would make me sick.

He said so much blood had soaked into the land, the stream was undrinkable. I didn't know why he was trying to scare me. The Tungus were superstitious about everything.

My pa let his horse drink, but he didn't touch it himself. Later he said the prisoners had been digging uranium ore for power stations and bombs and the radiation had leached back into the ground. I imagined the taste of the water furring my tongue with iron, or maybe reeking slightly of sulphur, and I felt my stomach turn.

The truth is that not many people besides us have ever chosen to live here. The Tungus wound up here centuries ago, starting off in Mongolia in colder times and then following the reindeer north. Then some came out from the west, following the fur. Most of the rest were prisoners and exiles. People had to be bribed into coming east, with big wages for working in the mines and wells. And once they had done their time, they usually went home. You could imagine them waking up again in apartments back wherever they had come from, with the noise of an old city around them, and their money in the bank, and this strange, cold, bloodstained empty land just a memory.

But we settled here out of conviction, as a handful of people had done in the past, because the land was empty and our parents wanted the freedom to create their world new. What an old story that is. You'd think people would be done believing in a fresh start by now, in thinking they can escape their own nature. The proof of it was all around us at Buktygachak: the slave armies that had been building a new dawn, the grim chimney stacks. But no, the godless commissars had had the wrong idea and we had the right one. This time the bright new future was really just around the corner, and with god on our side and a collective determination to do good, we'd put a bunch of New Jerusalems right here in the frozen north. What hooey.

This world is a scaly old snake. She is a cunning old woman, and I'm growing to be a cunning old woman, and the last human being that draws a breath on this planet will be a cunning old woman who raises chickens and cabbages, has no illusions, and has outlived all her children. The world is not sentimental but pitiless. I've given it to myself to know her mind. I flatter myself that I understand her a little. Maybe I've grown to resemble her. Only, she's going to go on forever, and I won't.

•

So it was getting close to October and I was traveling again. It always feels good to move, and this time I had a dose of hope in my soul.

Every now and again along the highway, I'd pass a tree tied with faded strips of cloth, glass beads and old coins round its base. That was a Tungus custom. Some trees and places are holy to them.

And back in the old days, when there was real traffic on this road, before people piled into their creaky buses for their long, jarring drives, they'd fix swatches of fabric and drop pennies here for a safe return. Strange what survives of us. Beads, a random footprint, some papers. How would anyone make sense of it?

At Buktygachak, in the punishment cells, there were patches of writing scraped into the walls: dates, maybe a name, or curses, as if they needed to leave proof that they'd really lived.

I vaguely remember Dad's auto, but I don't recall if I ever traveled in a bus. Maybe it was fearful. Giving yourself up to it. Something else's motion. Like me in that lake. What would anyone have found of me?

The road was good. I counted on ten or twelve days for the journey, but I could have halved the time if I pushed it. I was happy with the horses at a walk, covering fifteen or twenty miles a day. Sometimes I would doze as we went, slumped into the saddle, eyes half shut. In that half-sleep, I'd see visions. It always went back to me as a child. What seems like a good time to you, you figure must be a good time for the world. But in those years that I remember as either lit with sunshine or the comforting crackle of split logs in winter, there were already shadows gathering.

•

When I was seven years old, I was drinking a soda with my father at the grocery shop that used to belong to Walter Perryman, who came from a very old Quaker family someplace. I look back at it as part of the good times, because I don't recall going without anything. I remember us as all pretty contented and well fed, and houses still going up, and a general kind of orderliness to things.

It was a hot flyblown summer day. Walter was wiping down the countertop and chatting with my father. Then they stopped talking and walked together out onto the porch.

I followed them out with my soda, which was in one of those bottles we used to have that closed with a glass ball. Walter made different flavors, but the best one was flavored with birch syrup.

Walter and my father were staring at a wraith, a stick-thin form in rags, in bare feet that were soft and spreading like caribou hooves.

Someone called to her, but she moved like a person in a trance, big glassy eyes unblinking. She must have been walking for weeks. Walter touched her shoulder and she crumpled into a heap at his feet, panting. My father carried her into Walter's store and laid her on the counter. They propped her head up and tried to get her to eat something. Her head shook and she pushed them away from her, her skinny shoulders heaving.

Then her eyelids fluttered shut and she died right there in front of us.

She was the first. On the outskirts of town, they found her baby. They buried them in the town cemetery, under a plain wooden cross that said: *Mother and Son, Known to God.* But the ones that came after her were just too many in number to get the same treatment. It wasn't lack of consideration. Some of the townsfolk who buried them ended up unburied themselves.

•

Snow started coming down toward the end of my first day on the road. I never minded riding through the weather, but the visibility had been cut down to no more than ten yards front and back. I liked to be able to see what was lying in wait for me, so the next chance I got, I ducked off the road to a clearing at one side behind a screen of trees. The snow covered my tracks. And I decided against laying a fire, on account of the smoke. By the time I pitched the tent, I was even too tired to eat, which saved me some food; but I woke in the middle of the night, hungry as a bear and still dreaming of the smell of frying bacon.

9

And for ten days or so that was pretty much the size of it. Ambling along, morning to dusk, keeping my eyes peeled for places to feed and water the animals. As we went, the ice got thicker, until it was no longer enough to give the top of a frozen stream a smart rap with a branch, I had to dig out a hatchet and chop right through the crust.

Most nights I risked a fire. I hadn't seen a soul on the road all day, and besides, I kept my loaded guns in my lap.

The first clear frosty night I saw the Lights, billowing across the sky like god shaking out his laundered sheets—if the Almighty sleeps on green gauze. Later in the season, the Lights would have more colors in them, but they looked pretty good to me now. There's something comforting in movement, and that easy, flowing pattern of lights overhead felt like someone stroking my hair.

About a week in, I shot a moose, and camped for two nights in one place so as to butcher it properly. The skin I had to leave, the offal I don't care for, but just about everything else I was able to smoke or let freeze and carry with me.

I had a strange thought while I was cutting her up, which seemed to come to me out of nowhere. Once in my life, I said to myself, I'd like to taste an orange. That word: "orange." It seemed impossibly beautiful. I thought of how an orange sky looked and tried to imagine its flavor: somewhere between caramel and strawberries, I guessed.

Under the Lights, with the planet gently rocking and a week or so of food curing over the smoke, I felt hopeful that whoever had sent the plane would be waiting for me at the end of the journey. Sometimes I fell asleep and dreamed of arriving somewhere and being met by a woman something like my mother, who was pleased enough to see me but a little bit disdainful of my shabby clothes and the food I ate. She'd offer me a basket of oranges in the dream, and with a pleased-with-herself smile I'd say, "We've been saving these for you." But however many times I dreamed it, I always woke up just at the moment when I was putting one in my mouth.

·

I got to Esperanza after a couple of weeks. I had the sensation from the road that this wasn't the place I was looking for, but I rode into her anyway, just to be sure.

It was a copycat version of the town I'd left, without a soul in it, never mind someone who could fly a plane. That was the first time since I'd hauled myself out of the water that I felt a glimmer of doubt about what I was doing. All that time on that dangerous road just to get to a place worse than the one I'd come from. I thought, What if this is all there is between here and Alaska, or beyond?

But the plane I'd seen was real, no doubt about it, and I'd buried her crew and passengers with my own hands. I tried to console myself by asking myself how I'd feel if normal life had been going on here all this time. That would sting, wouldn't it? Me living like a cockroach in a cellar, and them here with, I don't know what, schools, and funerals, and Christmas, and oranges.

In the old days I heard there were wars where soldiers disappeared into the forest, only to come out decades later and find the fighting had been over for years, and their families enjoying peace and plenty while they'd been drinking water out of tree stumps and chewing leeches to live.

That thought was a painful one. The idea that I'd just got separated from my proper world, and time was passing, and the other world moving on, and when I found it, I'd be showing up, like a savage in a loincloth, to a city of sparkling glass.

But I think I would have preferred almost anything to the burned-out houses, and trash, and the decay that just told another ten thousand times the story I'd been living in for so long.

And that night when I saw the Lights, they hadn't a jot of consolation in them. They rolled coldly on overhead, like they will for another million years.

•

That disappointment sobered me a little, but I kept on my way. The days were shortening and getting colder. Beyond Homerton, I was pretty sure the laid road ended and it was all ice roads between there and the sea. I had to put on my hunting furs to keep warm—Tungus stuff that I had to battle every summer to keep from becoming moth food: a wolverine jacket, snow-sheep pants and gloves, and soft boots of reindeer skin.

On clear nights, which they mostly were, the snow doubled the moonlight, and I went on, following the glow through the darkness. I tried to be merciful to the horses, but it was a task to keep both fed. They'd both gotten skinnier and I knew in the back of my mind that sooner or later I would have to slow up or get new mounts. There were Yakut ponies out in the bush, but finding them and breaking them might take until spring. It wasn't so much that I couldn't afford the time, though that's what I said to myself, but that the idea of slackening my pace was frightening to me. Forward, forward, said the hooves on the snow. I only wanted to go one way. Behind me, too close for comfort, was that dark shadow in the lake, and the recollection of Ping and her child, which I still didn't have the courage to face.

·

Then one day in early November, in the gloom of mid-morning, I came upon a felled tree by the roadside. When I saw it at a distance, I thought it had toppled of its own accord, but up close there was no mistaking the axe marks in the trunk or the freshness of the cuts. It had been taken down recently. And further along, another. And another.

Still, just because someone's smart enough for axe work, doesn't make them a friend. So I swung myself down off my horse, and I led them on foot through the thicker trees. I stumbled in the fresh drifts and sweated into my furs. It was slower going, but there was less chance of being surprised. And bit by bit I homed in on an unmistakable sound: the zip of a wood saw working back and forth through timber.

I tied up the horses and went on alone, crawling on my belly under the branches, until I could just make out the feet of the two men working. They were wearing felt boots, which meant they weren't Tungus.

Lying there with a pile of snow in my face, gazing at their feet, I thought: This is what we've got to. In the Far North, walking up on a man is fraught with peril. The constant fear between people is like a fog that makes them seem larger than they are and all their gestures threatening.

·

My intention was to stand up and approach them as slow and friendly as possible, but with one hand on my gun nonetheless.

The trouble was I got caught up in the thick brush at the edge of the roadside on my way out of the wood. My boot was trapped in the fork of a branch. They heard me struggling in it and stopped sawing.

When I tried to untangle myself, I ended up crashing out of the brush onto the highway, waving my gun in the air because I had lost my balance. The two men panicked and dropped their saw on the log with a clang. And then I noticed a third with a rifle who had been standing too far off for me to see. He turned and lifted his gun to squeeze off a shot.

I was lying on my back in the road with both guns aimed at his head, but I spoke as slow and deliberate as I could, telling him not to shoot.

He said to drop the gun, and there was a break in his voice that told me just how much he meant it. I kept on, calm and slow, saying that if I'd wanted to kill them, I could have done it easy before they had even seen me.

The clang of the saw seemed to be stretching out into the silence.

I knew he didn't want to shoot me. Some people have a talent for violent deeds, and I could tell that he didn't, but I was afraid he'd kill me as much out of fear as design.

So I holstered my guns and waited for him to come over.

It seemed to take an age for him to pluck up the courage to approach, and by the time he was standing over me with his rifle up my nose, my behind was getting cold and I was starting to regret putting away my weapons.

Now the others inched up, too, their eyes beady and curious, but not daring to come as near as their companion.

He had a startled look on him. And he was older than I expected—not as strong as those other two, I supposed, so more use with a gun than a saw. He was wrapped more warmly than them, as though he'd been expecting to stand guard while they worked. He had a sharp-cornered frontier face that had been frost-pinched more than once, and a big gristly nose which was pink at the tip from the cold.

"What's your business?" he asked. "Where you from? Who you with? How many of you are there?"

I asked him to take the gun out of my face, and told him that I was alone, and a constabulary officer from the incorporated city of Evangeline, and therefore licensed to bear arms.

He had some trouble digesting that information. "Evangeline?" he said. "There's no one alive there. Where are you really from?"

There was real indignation in his voice, as though I had told him I was from the moon and expected him to believe it. But the more I think of it, the more I'm certain the indignation he felt arose from shame. Catching him there, with his patched-up clothes and old gun—to a man old enough to remember how things used to be, it was like opening the door on him in the outhouse.

"I really am from Evangeline," I said. And his confusion was so great that he actually put down the gun. I told you he was no soldier.

The other two were on his shoulder with a "What's he say?"

"He says he's from Evangeline."

That they took me for a man suited me fine. Those weeks of traveling certainly hadn't made me any prettier.

I asked if anyone minded if I stood up, and one of the two woodcutters gave me a hand to my feet. Then I introduced myself by name, but didn't get any kind of response out of them. They were staring at me in silence, so to prod them into conversation I asked where they were from. The woodcutter who'd helped me up said, "Horeb."

So now it was my turn to be puzzled. By their appearance and their English, I took them for settlers, but there was no settlement in the whole of the Far North I knew of that went by that name. And the notion that anyone alive now could have dredged up the will and the strength to settle a new place—that was almost beyond my comprehension.

I had the feeling of something inside me that flipped like a fish in a net. It was hope. As much as I bad-mouth people in general and think the worst of them, I'm secretly waiting for them to surprise me. Try as I might, I haven't been able to give up on them wholly. Even though they are nine and nine-tenths dirt, now and again they are capable of something angelic. I can't say that it restores my faith, because I really had none in the first place, but when it happens it does confuse you.

Still, my new friends weren't in any hurry to weigh me

down with their hospitality. I couldn't help feeling that they wished I would disappear much as I'd arrived. I explained to them that I had two horses with me, that I'd been traveling for weeks, and I'd be grateful to water my animals and wash, if it wasn't putting them to any trouble.

They weren't as quick to agree or as cordial as you might expect, and a number of doubtful glances passed between them before the man with the gun nodded, and the friendlier of the two woodcutters came with me while I fetched the animals.

Then I waited beside the old man while the other two finished their job of cutting. He couldn't but have been curious about me, or at least where I'd come from. And I had plenty of questions I wanted to put to him, but each time I asked him something he wandered off to poke his gun into the woods, as if at any minute he was expecting us to be surrounded.

We didn't leave that place for another hour at least. The men loaded their sled with their logs and put themselves into harness to tow it. They were a somber bunch, hardly sharing a word with each other, and I wondered if they always talked this little or if it was my being there that had made them so shy.

I walked my horses, so as to keep the men company, and finally one of the two in harness asked me what it was bringing me to New Judea. It had been so long since I'd heard anybody call it that that it took me a second to figure out what he meant.

It almost made me laugh to see these men barely perching on their piece of the world and still calling it by the old name.

I told him his question put me in mind of the old story about the hunter who goes to stay with his friend in the woods and on the way he gets mauled by a bear.

He shook his head at me to say the story rang no bells with him. Our little walk together was pretty short on entertainment, so I decided to tell them how it happens.

The hunter's going through the woods. It's winter, and the bear's what the Russians here used to call a shatoon—which is to say, a bear that's woken up out of his winter sleep because he couldn't lay down enough fat in summer on account of food being short, salmon not running, no berries, and so forth.

Their eyes were all big and fixed me on now, and it felt like I was telling the story to children. The one in particular who'd asked me the question had a pair of blue eyes that were as round and trusting as a couple of open mouths. His face spurred me to pad the story out with details, because I liked the way he was drinking it all in.

Well, I said, you can imagine, there's nothing ornerier than a skinny, wakeful bear in February, with its fur hanging all baggy from starvation. What should this bear see but a juicy hunter making his way through the forest. Now, the bear's drooling with hunger at the idea of eating this man, and it leaps out and takes a big bite of him.

The hunter and the bear struggle for a while, but the bear's more hungry, more strong, and more desperate. Then, just as those big jaws are about to crush the hunter's head like a pine-conc, he manages somehow to wriggle free and sprint away to freedom.

Now, you can picture for yourselves how battered and raggedy he is when he shows up at his friend's cabin. He's more or less alive, but the bear has taken a big chunk of his arm and scratched up his face with its claws. Add to which, he's dizzy with blood loss. So he's banging on the door, in need of water and bandages to stanch the bleeding.

Now his friend opens up, takes one look at him, and says, in his gravelly deadpan way: "I see you already met Flossie."

Maybe I had just lost my knack of telling a story. I certainly hadn't had the opportunity to visit with anyone for any length of time lately. There was a silence after I stopped speaking that reminded me of the clang when the two of them put down the saw on the tree trunk.

And then the man with the gun said: "It's bad for bears round here. Seems like the fewer of us there is, the more there is of them."

And the man with the round blue eyes said nothing at all but looked a little disappointed, as if he'd been expecting some other kind of story.

I explained that I'd told them this because they'd called the place New Judea.

They still looked at me puzzled.

"I guess I'm saying," I said, "that when a thing is terrible and dangerous, a man needs to find a pretty name for it to let himself sleep a little easier at night."

That didn't make it any plainer for them, and my spelling it out bled any drop of humor from the story altogether.

"What do you call this place, then?" said the round-eyed man.

I couldn't answer him. In my mind, I didn't gave it a name at all. I wasn't like the Tungus, who had been there so long that all the places meant something to them. To me it was just the city, the land, the snow, the sky, the bears. If it was any place, to me it was the Far North.

My father had an expression for a thing that turned out bad. He'd say it had gone west. But going west always sounded pretty good to me. After all, westwards is the path of the sun. And through as much history as I know of, people have moved west to settle and find freedom. But our world had gone north, truly gone north, and just how far north I was beginning to learn.

Our way turned off the road and onto a narrow track

through the forest. We'd been going for about fifteen minutes. I said, "You gentlemen are awful choosy about the wood you cut."

The man with the gun knew what I was getting at, so at least he wasn't simple. "We don't like to fell it too near the town. We live quiet and we don't like to be bothered none."

That made sense to me. I'd been lucky so far, but that road could bring you no end of trouble.

We picked our way a little further through the forest until finally we drew near to the place they called Horeb.

It wasn't anything like I'd been expecting. They had put a lot of work into her, no doubt, but it wasn't a settlement our parents would have thought too highly of.

The narrow path wound into a clearing about an acre square, and smack in the middle was a five-sided stockade with a gateway let in to it. It must have enclosed about a quarter of an acre of land. I guessed there were a number of buildings inside it, because there were separate plumes of smoke rising up.

The men asked me to wait and then disappeared inside with their logs.

They were a long time coming out, and I could see eyes peering at me through chinks in the palings, so that I began to wonder if some kind of ambush was being set for me. It must have been close to twenty minutes that passed before the front gate was raised up, and out came half a dozen men, led by one in a long black robe, and what was stranger, beside him a woman of about my own age, who laid a basket at my feet that had some gray salt in it and the smallest loaf of bread I had ever seen.

It was a strange little welcoming party, and a couple of the faces in it were not exactly friendly. The man in black who led them stared at me with a holy look that made me want to giggle.

He embraced me, and I stiffened in spite of myself, because I didn't like to be touched that way by a man, and I noticed that he had some kind of perfume on. "Welcome, brother," he said. "Our remnant. Remnant of a remnant."

And before I could think of anything to reply to him, they were all on their knees and he was leading them in a prayer of thanksgiving. I stood there, feeling foolish, but knowing I'd feel more foolish if I joined them, so I snatched off my hat as a mark of respect and waited for them to finish. And now instead of just feeling foolish, I felt foolish and my ears were beginning to freeze.

When the prayer was over, they stood up again and there was a pause as if they were expecting something from me. It reminded me that for all the hardships I put up with in my life, awkward silences weren't generally one of them. I looked at them all and recognized the faces of the three men I'd encountered in the forest, and they were all of them waiting for me to speak.

I cleared my throat and told them my name, and where I'd come from, and thanked them for their kindness. They still seemed to want more, so I added that, though I had never heard of a settlement called Horeb until just this day, they were a credit to their folk.

"Amen," said the perfumed man in black, and he took my arm to lead me in, nodding at the woman to gather up the bread and salt.

"Brother," he said, "we can stable your horses with ours. But, as a sign of peace, I ask you to surrender those guns you're carrying while you're our guest."

He could see me hesitate. "I'll vouch personally for them." What it was that made me trust him, I can't say for sure, but there was something about him that reminded me of one of my uncles. He must have been around fifty. I could see that he wasn't all seriousness, and I liked the way he bossed them all without ever raising his voice.

I unbuckled the belt and handed it to him, and we went inside.

·

The settlement seemed bigger inside than out. It had a number of dwellings in the yard, and smaller shacks built right against the wall. There must have been thirty to forty people there altogether, including children, at least one babe in arms, and several barely old enough to walk. It had been a long time since I'd seen a child—at least, a living one. Their eyes followed me as I followed my host across the yard to the largest of all the dwellings. They all looked well enough, if a little grubby and underfed.

We shucked off our footwear and our outdoor clothes on the porch and went into a long, plain room that reminded me of the old meetinghouse at home, except it had a cross at one end, and some Mary-and-Child pictures, none of which they would have stood for where I came from.

Reverend Boathwaite, which is what I came to know him as, invited me to sit with my legs under a low round table that had a kettle of hot charcoals beneath it and a thick cotton cover, somewhat of an asiatic style. Six or seven of us as sat there, with our feet under the cloth, warm enough over that brazier. The Reverend locked my guns in a box that he put back under the altar, and then he joined us.

The man with the frost-pinched nose set down a battered urn and a dish of hard candy that looked like it was ten years old. The Reverend poured out the tea and passed it around the table.

"I won't pretend that these are good times for my flock," he said.

"No," I said, "but compared to elsewhere, you're thriving." The enamel mug they gave me had been part cleaned at best and smelled of caribou stew.

"Are things bad in Evangeline?"

The men round the table stopped fighting over the candies and waited for me to say something.

"What things?" I said. "There's no one there." I told him what he pretty nearly must have known himself. The years of calamity and migration as starving people came out of the south. The hungry and the desperate who came to prey on a people gone soft with compassion. I said how we'd belatedly designated a few of us constables and set us to keep the peace, but by then we were overrun. "In any case, the townsfolk themselves were among the worst of them. It turns out that goodness only lives when the times permit it."

"Well, we allow more hope than that, Mr. Makepeace."

"Esperanza's the same," I went on. "I passed through on my way here. Homerton, too, I expect."

"If that's where you're headed, I can save you a journey. All that you see here is what's left of the place."

I told him that I thought the name of this place was Horeb.

"Or New Homerton, you could call it." His grin hadn't an ounce of humor in it. He rubbed his tired, unslept eyes. Looking round at all their dark, smoked meat faces, I thought how much they resembled Tungus. It was as though they'd come here with their European faces as blank as bars of white soap and had new asiatic ones carved out of them by the cold and the wind.

"What happened to the city?"

Boathwaite shook his head. I felt such a weariness in him. "Much like you said. Rather late in the day, we had to adopt a more muscular variant of our beliefs. We had to let go of a lot of things that were precious to us."

I tried to imagine my father saying it. But to him that would have been total defeat. In his mouth it would have meant: "We came here and lost everything."

"Things have a life built into them," said Boathwaite. "You just never expect to be in at the end of anything. You never expect to be among the last."

Around him, the men nodded or sucked tea through their candy, rather untroubled, like children whose father was doing their fretting for them.

Boathwaite went on: "The great blessing is that as our life becomes harder and simpler, I feel such closeness with my God."

The round-eyed man sucked up his tea in time to cap the Reverend's words with an "Amen," which the others followed.

Then the Reverend stood up and told me I was welcome to stay as long as I wanted.

·

I felt light round my hips without my guns, like you do when you take off heavy boots after a long day walking.

They gave me a bed in one of the shacks that belonged to a woman called Violet. She served me a dish of cold potatoes with a bit of fatty meat and watched over me while I ate it. The shack had a funky smell which put me off eating at first, but after a while I got used to it.

I thought it was just the two of us, but a cracked old voice suddenly called out from behind a sheet that cut off one corner of the shack. "I'm dying!" it said.

Violet lifted the sheet and went in behind it. "Shut up, Mother," she said "We've got a visitor. A young man."

Which was wrong on both counts.

I went round the sheet out of politeness. A tiny toothless old woman was sitting up in her sour bed linen. She looked like a bag of sticks. "I'm dying!" she cried out at me.

Violet rolled her eyes at me and let the sheet drop back. "Don't mind her," she said.

The bed she gave me was hers—no more than a cot slung just above the floor, and it creaked when I sank into it. Violet got into the bed with her mother, who kept it up all night, moaning and crying out.

Violet woke me in the middle of the night when she got up to put a log in the stove. The stove door squeaked and the light in the shack sat up a little as the log took. She didn't shut it immediately but came and stood over me. I pretended to be asleep. The fire from the stove lit my eyelids orange. I could hear her breath sighing through her nostrils as she stood there a while, gazing down at me.

Then I felt something like a tickle and I realized she was touching my head. It was gentle, but I didn't feel altogether comfortable with it.

"What are you doing?" I said.

She didn't startle but kept on. "What happened to your face?" she asked.

"Someone burned it," I said.

"You poor thing," she said. She stroked my head for a bit longer, then she shut the door of the stove and padded back to bed with the old woman.

I never feel sorry for myself—never—but that small tenderness upset me in a way I hadn't been for a long time, and I was awake for a while with thoughts of Ping and the baby roiling in my brain, and every hour like a cuckoo clock the old woman would cry out "I'm dying!" in her high, cracked voice that seemed like it was speaking for all of us.

10

Look at it how you like, there was something strange about Horeb and I wasn't minded to stay, but my horses got colicky in the night and there was no chance of my leaving the next morning, or in the days that followed.

I didn't much like bunking with Violet and her mother, either. Something about the heat and the feety smell in their hut, and the old woman's crying, gave me bad dreams.

One night it was women and babies, tumbling out of one another in an endless squalling chain of red bodies, all linked up with their belly cords, like one of those families you might snip out of paper. But this one went on forever, and the babies were women themselves, with babies of their own, so that if you stretched it all out, it would reach back to Creation and the first woman, with her pinched monkey face, who ever walked upright.

You never expect to be in at the end of anything. That was what Boathwaite had said.

Ping's child had been a girl too. Choked with her own belly cord as she lay wrong-side up in her mother's womb. So that line perished with her. And as for my line, I was the last of it, and there would be no slippery little women dropping out of me.

•

I thought life back home was hardscrabble, but Horeb was even worse, grubbing in the woods for ferns and burdock; thin, watery soups at mealtimes; and a taste of meat at most twice a week. The only thing they got to fill up on was religion. They had big helpings of church three times a day. Morning, lunchtime, and evening, they would troop into that building and have Boathwaite read or preach at them for up to an hour. It struck me early on that if they prayed less, they'd eat better; but as a guest, I felt bound to keep my thoughts to myself.

From the second day, I decided I'd give the sermons a miss and went off to the woods for a scout around. I'd not gone farther than five hundred yards from the stockade when I came upon half a dozen wild caribou nosing through the forest, scratching up lichen to feed on. Boathwaite still had my guns, so there was nothing I could do but watch. It was too much for me to take. All those fools sat in church with their bellies grumbling, and here there was breakfast, lunch, and dinner wandering about on four legs, just daring you to put it in your mouth.

I ran back to the stockade. There was one man on guard at all times and he let me in. I went straight to the little chapel and burst in, breathless. I begged them to excuse my interruption, I told them about the caribou, and I said that if the Reverend would be willing to return one of my firearms, I'd put more than enough meat on the table to repay their hospitality to me.

The Reverend's face hardened into a hatchet while I was speaking, and as soon as I had finished, he told the congregation that, just as many of them had not yet made the acquaintance of Cousin Makepeace, neither had Cousin Makepeace had the opportunity to acquaint himself with the customs of Horeb, in particular that the service of God came above all other works. The appetite for sanctity surpassed mere carnal appetite.

If I'd been a little smarter, I would have stopped there. Everything was counseling me to bite my tongue, from the angry sparkle in Boathwaite's eye to the dumbstruck faces of his congregation. But living alone for so long had made me stubborn.

I said I was sorry for bursting in so loud and unmannerly, and I would never have done it in the ordinary way. I didn't mean that they should stop their praying or the Reverend should stop his preaching. But since I wasn't much of a churchgoer myself, I'd be happy to make myself useful to them. And I said that even Jesus let the disciples gather ears of corn on the Sabbath. So how about it? Could I have one of my guns?

By now I saw that I'd made myself as unwelcome as a juggler at a funeral. The Reverend hissed at me that there would be no further discussion until the service was over. Then he turned his back on me and prayed in a loud voice for ten minutes. Most of the congregation turned their faces with him, but one or two of the children stared at me and had to be cajoled into looking away again.

I was so angry I barely heard a word he said. My mind was

fixed on the caribou, snuffling away through the forest. I was hungry myself, of course, but I also thought of those pale, skinny children in the chapel, with their streams of yellow snot and dirt-streaked faces, and how much better off they would be with a plate of meat than a bellyful of words.

They grumbled away in their prayers and I stalked out furious.

The Reverend didn't speak to me for the next couple of days. I mean, he greeted me when he saw me, but very cool and offish, and most of the others in Horeb followed his lead. It didn't bother me any. I had enough to do with nursing my horses, and when I wasn't I doing that, I liked to be outside. Still, I never saw any more caribou, and that was a pity.

Every time Violet came back from the chapel in her head scarf—her mother was too feeble to leave their shack—I asked her what the Reverend preached on. Most of the time he told them to keep close to Christ in these difficult moments, hold him like a match flame in their hearts, and other such bunkum. But he also warned them of false prophets, and the dangers of a divided kingdom, in ways that made me certain he didn't much like having a mutineer in his midst.

Partly I was flattered to give him a text for his sermons, but I didn't mean to offend him, and I think we were both glad when my horses took a turn for the better and my thoughts began to shift to moving onwards.

I went to him in his quarters a few days before I was set to leave. It was evening, an hour or so after his last service. He was writing by lamplight. The room was comfortable, and there was a plate of food on the table beside him.

He put his pen down as I came in, and closed the book.

"Nice digs you've got, Reverend," I said, meaning to be friendly.

"My flock are happy to see me comfortable," he said, as if I'd meant to put his back up a little.

I told him I was getting ready to move on, and wanted to provision myself for the journey. None of that came as much of a surprise to him. Then I said that I needed my guns back so that I could hunt before I left, and that out of gratitude to the people of Horeb, I hoped he would let me share whatever I took with them.

The Reverend said there was a very strict ordinance on no weapons in the stockade, but he would hand over my guns when I rode out, on the understanding that I would put them back in his safekeeping when I returned.

I told him that would be fine with me.

Before I left, he asked me in a schoolmasterly way what had happened to my own impetus towards religion. As a child of settlers, I must have been brought up in the church.

I said that, speaking personally, I couldn't find much in it. I said that religion made people soft with love or think they were better than other people. I said I'd read the Bible cover to cover and I thought it was a scam. It seemed obvious to me that the whole thing was cooked up by the Levites so the other tribes would feed them. That it was good stories, but that there was stables of horseshit in it: the Urim and the Thummim. That no one was bigger sinners than the kings of the Old Testament.

"Interesting," he murmured. "Very interesting."

I said I apologized if my speaking plainly gave him offense, but that he would find me a straight-dealing person, and I'd come to collect my guns in the morning.

As I turned to leave, he called me by my name.

"Sometimes," he said, "our imperative is survival. We are much reduced. But this community coheres. You are the last of your whole city. Ask yourself, by what grace did this settlement survive, where yours and others collapsed?"

I said I had always had the utmost faith in the power of dumb luck.

"Yes," he said. "Perhaps."

But walking back to Violet's shack in the twilight, I did think that maybe he had a point. Boathwaite had kept his little flock together somehow. And even if Moses and Mohammed were charlatans, maybe that was better than inflicting the naked truth on people: we are all out here in the desert, and we are alone, and all of us will die. Even if it's true, maybe it's not the kindest or most practical thing to tell anyone.

And lying in bed, listening to Violet's mother again ("I'm dying! I'm dying!"), I thought, Am I angry with Boathwaite because I want to believe him so much—because I want to settle like a kitten in the crook of the Almighty's arm, and surrender to His wisdom?

That night I had another of those weird dreams again. This time it was about thousands of people on a quayside, embarking on a huge ship. For a while there were hordes of us at the dock, waiting to go on, and then there were much fewer, and suddenly it seemed that almost everyone was on board, apart from myself and couple of stragglers, like some queer-looking animals that Noah had left behind, doomed, irrelevant, because we had arrived too late.

The Rev was as good as his word about the guns. He walked me outside the stockade and handed them over before his morning service. I told him I'd be back in a day or so, depending on the hunting.

We were never friendlier with each other than at the moment when we knew we'd be apart for a while. He was so pleased to be rid of me that he came over quite warm toward me. "I can continue to respect a man while differing with him," he said. "There's a lot of good feeling toward you here, Make-peace."

I thought he was referring to the gaggle of children who followed me around because I had gotten into the habit of giving food scraps to them, but he seemed to be talking about himself.

"Surely you won't miss me, Reverend?" I said as I heaved up into the saddle. He didn't reply, but he winked up into the light at me, his lips parted in a big toothy smile, and I felt his eyes on me all the way into the forest.

11

I am one of those who need motion. Sometimes my body barks at me like a dog that wants walking. I was always that way. My father would say the devil had got into my legs the way they'd kick and fidget if I went to bed after an evening when I'd done nothing except sit and write homework. My mother said I was the same as a baby, always pedaling, and wriggling, and waving my arms. I think better when I'm moving.

If only they'd let me pace in the classroom, I could have taken in a heap of science and learning. But after twenty minutes in my seat, my knees would be hopping up and down, battering my desk, spilling ink, getting me into trouble.

Constabulary School was different. I was older. There were

only a half dozen of us, and the time in the classroom didn't seem endless. We had to study so quick. And there was something exciting about it. Sitting in school felt obedient. But we were disobeying so much just by being there. There was still so much anger towards us, even from our own families.

We were police. We were being trained to use violence. And our parents had come here because most of them were against the idea of using force, ever. My own family was too ashamed of what had happened to me to say anything about it, but of the others who were training with me, I knew how hard it was for them.

Me, I was a cuckoo. I never belonged in that world. I mean, I believe in being good. But so many of those people were wedded to appearing good. Like the Crashaws and the Steadmans, who had given up eating meat because it was ungodly.

And because of my nature, and my being a good shot, and because of everything that had happened to me, people in the city seemed pretty accepting of me.

The man who trained us was called Bill Evans. He came out from Alaska and they gave him a classroom above the bank to teach us in.

I loved Bill Evans. He was fat and crusty. He smoked and swore, and he had no patience with city and their anxiety about being true to their founding principles and the long arguments about what to call us.

"Too few, too late," he said. "Little Quaker village at the end of the world. You don't need a police force. You need an army."

Some families would have no truck with it. In spite of what was happening to their city, they preferred to move away. In spite of being robbed by hungry people. In spite of what happened to their daughters.

We provoked hate from people who said they didn't believe in hate. Some would spit at us when we patrolled the town. The key was not to take it personal. They could feel the world they'd created slipping away, and we had become the symbol of it. The city was unsafe and they blamed us, the hated lawmen.

Now all that was ancient history. The towns were gone and the people that preyed on them had moved elsewhere. The Far North looked like it was me, and Horeb, and the scattered Tungus, and the ghost of a hope that tickled my chest with that piece of broken wing.

When Noah sends the birds out onto the flooded earth and one brings back a leaf—that was what the plane was to me. It meant we weren't forgotten. Someone else had survived the flood. Someone was beached on Ararat and the waters were in retreat.

Sometimes I couldn't help myself and I built a life in my head, planning what this new world would be like. And that's when I felt I understood my father a little, because the world I wanted resembled the place he must have had in mind when he moved out to the Far North. And I realized that it wasn't his fault. It was in the nature of the times. It was in the nature of the calamities that had struck our planet. People had all those possibilities in them, devil and angel, depending on how the times moved them. Like the seed that splits concrete, it was the appetite for life in them that made them so destructive. It was just everyone's misfortune to be born in times when the wherewithal for living had got so scarce.

Well, it's a fact with me that I like people more the less I see of them. And after two days of thinking like this, I was almost ready to give the Reverend Boathwaite a hug. It may not seem it, but I have a soft heart. There's a streak of fond soil in me that Ping put roots into, and they tore me up when she went.

•

I didn't see any game the first day, but by a stroke of luck I stumbled onto some caribou on the morning of the second. They weren't skittish, as you'd expect. In fact when I held out my bare hand and yelled "Makh, makh," as though I had brought salt for them to lick, they came nosing up to find it. I knew from this they'd belonged to someone once. It seemed to me the best thing of all would be to bring them back alive.

Though they came up close, they soon dropped back when they learned there was no salt to be had, and they were leery of being roped. I could have chased around all day and not caught a one of them, so I decided to work a little sideways.

I dropped my pants and crouched down, shuffling a little in my boots, to spread the piss around in the snow. You can't keep caribou away from fresh piss. The heat and the salt in it is like apple pie to them. And while they were jostling each other to get to the freshest patches, I pulled up my pants and roped six of them.

It still wasn't the easiest thing in the world to get them moving as a team. Every now and again, one or two would fix on a patch of lichen and I would have to tether the others while I tried to shift them, because I just wasn't strong enough manhandle all six. But it was gratifying to have gathered so much food, and I knew that with the hunger there was in Horeb, there would be nothing wasted and they'd get eaten up hooves and all.

So we made our slow way back and arrived at the stockade toward late afternoon on the third day.

The gatekeeper slid open his spyhole and called for me to wait while he fetched the Reverend.

I greeted Boathwaite all friendly: though I was tired, I was proud of my haul, and the hard work seemed to have got the life flowing through me again. "I expect you'll be wanting these," I said, and waved my guns at him. He flinched, then saw I meant no harm, and smiled as he took them from me.

They must have fallen on me just as soon as I entered the gate, though my recollection of it is not clear. There was a heavy blow on my shoulders as though a branch had fallen on me, and a dull pain which made me sink to my knees.

I couldn't tell you how many of them attacked me, or even what they used. The only face I remember belonged to the round-eyed boy I had met that first time in the woods, but now it was all snarled up with hate, and I could hear him screaming "Traitor!" as he broke my arm with a club. I thought to myself, So this is how it is, and curled up, limp, on the ground, since there was no way to fight all of them. But once I was down the beating eased and they dragged me by my feet into a lean-to by the wall of the stockade that was not much bigger than a doghouse.

They gave me a few kicks as they squeezed me in it, and I lashed back at them, and called them foul names, saving my best expressions for the two-faced Reverend. Then someone had the idea of throwing a bucket of water on me to shut me up. It was still afternoon, but the air was cold enough that my damp clothes seemed to leach out all the heat in my bones. Still, I kept cursing them through clenched blue lips, knowing that if I fell unconscious now the cold might well finish me off. Luckily, the water had hit me at an angle and enough of my body was dry to keep me alive. But when they finally pulled me out, toward nightfall, I had ice in my hair and I was shivering as though racked with a fever.

Boathwaite and a few of the elders had set up chairs in the chapel. They sat me on a stool in the middle of them, lower than the others and placed so I had to twist according to who was addressing me. My hands and feet had been tied with rawhide thongs hard enough to cut into the skin, and I had to half hop, half shuffle into their presence. And the break in my arm ached like hell every time I jarred it.

The Reverend had a somber face on him and he told me he'd had no choice but to submit to the will of his flock in having me arrested.

I asked what possible reason they had for thinking that this was fair dealing toward me, and one of the elders stood up in a rage and said what right had a deceitful bitch like me to expect fair dealing? I said he was very brave in threatening me, bound as I was, but I still had no idea what I might have done to earn this hatred from them.

Boathwaite said they had a number of charges to examine against me, of which the most serious was spying, but that they were also concerned to find out for what reason I had tried to pass myself off as a man.

I said I never passed myself off as anything, but that if people were minded to think of me as a man, I never felt the need to correct them. Think of me as you like, I said.

And the old man who had abused me before leaped up and said he would think of me as a deceitful, disfigured bitch.

I could tell that Boathwaite thought that this was taking things too far, and he told the man to be seated.

"What is more serious," he went on, "is that among your possessions we found certain notebooks written in cipher. Show her the book, Dr. Pritchard."

Dr. Pritchard was a ginger man of about fifty who had so far been silent but who I recognized as being the man who had thrown the water on me. He held a battered old book about the size of a hymnal under my nose and opened it up. Its frayed pages were covered with letters or signs that had been inked by hand. Someone had taken great pains to write it, but it wasn't me, since I had never seen it before in my life and I told them so.

"Then how did it come to be among your possessions?"

I said they ought to know that better than me since they put it there.

"Do you deny that this is your work?"

"I do," I said.

They seemed almost pleased with my answer, although they could have expected no other. I said nothing more to them that evening and they soon took me away to a cellar in another part of the stockade.

.

For the most part of two weeks, they kept me in the cellar, fed me slops, and hauled me out for questioning at odd hours of the night or early morning. Dr. Pritchard was sometimes the questioner, and sometimes Boathwaite.

Aside from the lack of sleep and the bad food, there was no terrible hardship. Each time they questioned me, they produced more fake books that they said I had been carrying until it seemed they must have thought I was a traveling library.

They asked me about all sorts of things: where I was from, why I was dressed as a man, about my face. I answered them as straight as I could.

The bell went off in my head when they started talking about accomplices, and mentioning names of people in Horeb who I had never even heard of. Jacob Vetch was one that came up over and over again. And when I said I didn't know him, they snorted and grew impatient with me.

It turned out that I was the liar that time. They brought me in the next day, hooded, and told me that I would now meet Jacob Vetch face-to-face.

They pulled off the hood and I stood blinking in the light for a moment. There were more of them in the chapel this time. Boathwaite sat apart from us, making notes.

Jacob Vetch sat slumped on a stool in front of them. Of course I had met him before: he was the old man with the gun who had been guarding the woodcutters the first day I ever clapped eyes on Horeb.

That wasn't the surprise. They had given him a proper working over. One of his ears was torn and he had a raw stump for a thumb.

It seemed like my coming had been a boon to Vetch's enemies. I've often wondered what the poor man had done to deserve such usage. I've seen enough cruelty to know it lights on the unlucky more often than the guilty. Horeb was a place staring into the twilight, as my city had been once. Those last days were the worst for us too.

Boathwaite's eye met mine and I felt a flash of understanding pass between us. Bill Evans used to call that the cold reading. He said that in detective work, sometimes the very best can slip into a man's skin and know everything that he knows, feel everything that he feels. It's hard to hate someone you've cold read. You see there is a reason behind their actions. And that even people with as much front as the Rev are split inside of themselves.

In that moment I could see that Boathwaite lived in fear of the people he led. Love and mercy wouldn't guarantee their obedience. They were disappointed and hungry. Boathwaite had to use the patterns of older gods to keep them cowed: terror and mercy, like twin shadows of an old totem that gets fed with blood. Poor Vetch would die to terrify those half-starved people. And all of this I sensed Boathwaite knew as plain as I did.

That look told me too that a part of Boathwaite held himself in contempt for what he'd sunk to. But it was no consolation to me. Something in him was of the utmost dark and I knew he would want to stub me out for having seen it.

·

They built a gallows that evening and at dawn they marched us out. There were four of us. I don't know where they'd kept the other three, but they were in much worse shape than I was.

Vetch's hand and ear had been patched up, but his face was grayer than boiled beef.

Boathwaite said as ringleader of a treasonous plot against the people of Horeb, he could expect no sympathy, but he was entitled to his last words.

Vetch mumbled a prayer and then they pushed him off the scaffold. The drop was too short and he kicked until he strangled.

Time slowed down as they came to me. I must remember all of this, I thought. Odd thoughts were taking shape in my head. How strange to be hanged as a traitor. How strange to be hanged just when my broken arm was beginning to knit.

Boathwaite said I had been found guilty of conspiring, too, and sentenced to death and what did I have to say?

All their eyes were on me, waiting for me to speak, but no words came. I looked at their dingy clothes, and the colors of all of them that seemed like the colors of the earth that would swallow me up.

That time at the lake I hadn't been in my right mind. My brain was all mixed up, as though I hadn't slept for a month, and the pain of leaving the world had seemed less sharp. But now I felt sad. Even out here in the cold, six weeks at least away from spring, the sky still had some beauty in it, and the light on the melted ice looked moist and clear as a child's eye.

There was a creak as Jacob Vetch's body twisted on the rope beside me.

With the practice I've had at last words, you'd think I'd be better at it. In fact, my intention was to face them out with silence and a look of loathing, but at the last moment, something blurted out my mouth that makes even less sense now that I've had all these years to think about it.

"What you take from me is not mine," I said, and the pause stretched out afterward as they waited for something else, but I was wise enough to know that it would be even worse to add to it.

"The death penalty has a biblical sanction," said Boathwaite. His voice was loud and it had a hoarseness to it that grated like an ice saw. "For a long time, our people preached against it. But Jesus came to fulfill the prophecies of his Father in the Old Testament. Jesus himself is God. And the one thing He cannot do is contradict himself. He never scrupled to punish with death the enemies of the Holy Spirit." There was a muttered amen from the people.

Good night, Makepeace, I thought. I prepared for the push in the small of the back, the panic, and the choking heat of blood in my throat. You have to lie back and breathe, I said to myself. I figured that submission would lessen the pain better than going tight and kicking.

"Even so," he said, "the blood of Jesus himself was spilled in mercy, and that mercy can in some instances countermand the sternness of chastisement. In this case, since the condemned is a

female, we have decided to commute the sentence to one of in-
definite servitude."

The Reverend like to lard his talk with jaw-breaking words
that were hardly English. But I understood that they were giving me a break for being a woman. It was the first time that
things had ever shaken down like that for me.

The landscape in front of my eyes began to fizz and bubble
as they cut me down. I hadn't ever passed out in my life before,
and I was damned if I would now, but my legs trailed on the
ground behind me like a pair of limp sausages as they carried me
back to the cell.

.

They let me sit in the dark for days after the sentence was passed,
because I told them my arm was still too damaged for heavy
work. A few of them didn't like that, saying that my other arm
looked good enough, and what was the point feeding a layabout
and a traitor when plenty of honest people were going hungry?
I managed an inward smile at that, because it reminded me of so
many arguments we'd had at home about the incomers.

I was told my rations would be cut until I made myself useful to them. They gave me moldy pickled cabbage the first day
and a chunk of bread.

The bread was stale and heavy. I turned it over in my hand.
It was the first I'd seen for a while. In its way, almost as much as
the plane, that sour old crust gave me a jolt of hope. The summers had grown warmer in the north, but there was still no
wheat planted at our latitude.

So much of Horeb remained a mystery to me, but they had
flour, and they must have been getting it from somewhere. The
thought hadn't struck me before. But once I started turning it

over in my mind, I saw other ways that those people were linked to a wider world. Boathwaite's letters, or whatever he'd been working on when I went to see him in his quarters. Even his suspicion of me, and the fake conspiracy, meant that in his head I fit into something larger and more populated than Horeb and the wilderness around it.

•

Until it came staggering into the drugstore, I'd never given much of a thought to the world outside my town. Charlo, yes. He was buried in maps and atlases, and he had the tongue and memory for other languages.

Me, I was an outdoors girl. I was restless and impulsive. The trees outside the city were the world, and the house was home, and the highway running east to west led I didn't care where.

To say we were an inward-looking people was like saying that the Tungus found the reindeer useful, or that the Siberian winter could be chilly. My mother had grown up in a house that was warmed in winter and cooled in summer. But when she followed my father to settle this new world, she left all that behind. She wasn't the only one. Many people saw a kind of virtue in what was simple and homespun and patched in the days before that became the only thing there was.

My mother despaired sometimes that I was not a girly girl, not fair and curving like her, but tall and lean, with a chest as flat as Charlo's. I was like Dad: all angles, hard red elbows, and a big nose to cap it. She'd try to interest me in household things, knitting and wickerwork and caning chair seats, but without much luck.

One gray spring day when I was out of school with croup, she let me lie in their bed, the wrought-iron one with brass balls at the corners that they'd brought with them from Chicago and which had loose joints that made it jingle when you moved on it.

I was scratchy and restless. I must have been ten at the time. My mother brought me basins of hot water with lavender in it to ease my breathing. She took the lavender from a chest in her cupboard. She was so patient with my griping.

"Here, M," she said, which was as close as she had to a pet name for me, "I want to show you something. But you've got to swear not to tell your father."

That immediately made me forget my sore throat. I think of her turning, half out of the cupboard, her long, fair hair almost at her waist and some mischief in her eye—which, if you knew my mother at all, you would hardly believe.

"Swear?" That one word struck me as extraordinary. As Quakers, we were held to such a high standard of rectitude that to swear to anything was against our religion. We told the truth all the time, hand on the holy book or not, and to suggest otherwise was considered an attack on our dignity.

"This is something for the two of us only. Understand?"

I nodded and she brought out of the cupboard the carved lacquer box that she kept the little vial of lavender oil in.

She put the box down on the bedclothes and let me investigate it myself.

It was of a kind of Chinese design, round shaped, with a big carved wooden handle that stood proud of it.

The handle was dark red and the lid black, and on it was a faint drawing in chipped gold paint of a man under a willow tree. The lid was worked on tight and she had to help me to shunt it off.

Thinking back, it must have been a sewing box because of

its shape and the way it was built in layers. The topmost layer held ointments and dressings and little glass ampoules of medicine. I could tell that wasn't her reason for showing it to me. Her eyes had a sly laugh in them, and she was quick to help raise the tray and open the lower part of the box.

My first feeling was one of disappointment, as the contents were drab. The first layer had had a touch of the forbidden about it, but this looked like what I cleaned out of my school desk at the end of each year: pencil shavings, crumpled paper, elastic bands.

"These are a few things from before I met your father," she said, and took one of the pieces of crumpled paper and set it in front of me. Inside it was a silver stone, about the size of an apple, but flatter and hard and cold. It lay there, dead and unresponsive.

"Not working," she said. She took it out of the room and put it somewhere, then came back, and we went through the other things in the box together. Trinkets really. A leaving card. A lock of hair. A broken watch that she said had belonged to her father. Nothing that was really equal to the sense of mischief she'd brought to our conspiracy. I felt deflated and my throat was hurting again.

She went out of the room and brought the stone back. "I just hope there's enough sun today," she said as she set it back down in front of me.

It was warm to the touch now from having laid out in the sun, and on the skin of it you could see little shapes in light, like the outline of stars in the dark, but green. I was almost afraid to handle it.

"Go ahead," said my mother. "It won't bite."

I prodded it again and the stone seemed to leap into life. A picture appeared on it, not flat and painted but lit up on one whole side of it, and moving, and speaking.

It was of girls, six or seven of them, and a bit drunk. "We all think you're crazy," said one of them. "But we still love you."

Then one of them sang off-key: "The only one who could ever reach me, was the son of a preacher man."

And another said, "Not a preacher, dumb-ass, a Quaker."

Then the picture froze and faded away.

"It's a memory stone," my mother said.

"Who are they?

"Friends from before."

"Before what?"

"Before I met your father."

I don't think my mother was prepared for what that stone made her feel. She was curt with me afterward. I remember what the stone says so well because I used to go up and listen to it on my own sometimes.

The stone was like no other object in our house—or our town, for that matter. So flat and smooth, there was no workmanship in it. It was perfect, like a thing that had grown up from a seed. And yet, somehow it held a piece of my mother's own past, a fragment of the life she had left behind her to come with my father.

Those girls in the memory stone are all dead by now. And everything they had is dust. One of them has lipstick on that's smudged, and it looks like she's been kissing. I wonder about that kiss. Was it a he or a she? Is that him, standing just out of view but casting a shadow over the wineglasses and getting a sidelong glance from her, a twinkling look, right before the stone goes dark? I can't begin to contemplate everything that's been lost. It's too much for one small brain to take in, but I think about that kiss.

12

My parents never spoke of the past, and me, I never took much interest in it. The past had nothing to teach me. The beginning of the world and my birth seemed like the same event. For me, the world began with water dripping off wet sheets in the sunlight. I was the creator, blinking my eyes to make night and day. And I was Noah, arranging my chipped hardwood animals in the dust of the arctic summer. I taught my family language, and I was the first human to set foot in the wilderness at the bottom of our vegetable patch.

But now I know different.

I thought I was born into a young world which was aging before my eyes. But my family came here when the world was already old. I was born into the oldest world there was. It was a world like a beaten horse, limping with old injuries and set on throwing its rider. And my parents, who claimed to love plain workmanship and the clean forthright language of the Bible— behind them was a world of memory stones, and planes, and cities of glass that they wanted to unknow.

There's plenty of things I'd like to unknow, but you can't fake innocence. Not knowing is one thing; pretending not to know is deception. While me and Charlo and Anna were playing in the dirt like fools that think they've found Eden, and the other settlers were congratulating themselves on having the foresight to land up in a perfect corner of our damaged planet, the world they left behind was unraveling. What arrogance made us think we were far enough to be safe?

·

We didn't know it at first, when that first starving woman fell dead outside the grocery store, but it seemed like half the world was on the move.

By the time I was fourteen, our city had close to doubled in size and there were shanties on the outskirts that seemed to grow every day with new arrivals who brought stories of flood, pestilence, and war. Our city felt like the hub of a world in chaos instead of somewhere obscure and insignificant, way out on the spinning rim of a calamity we had no power to control.

Only the desperate traveled in summertime. It meant they'd given up all hope of a harvest and were traveling in the heat and dust, trying to scavenge food as they went. Some of them were settler families who had been flooded out of homesteads to the south, but most were from much further away: Russians, Uighurs, Chinese, Uzbeks, all rail thin, with ancient, withered faces, even their little ones. Some were too sick to be helped. The things these people were fleeing made the world my parents had left seem like paradise.

In those early days, my father and the largest number of the settlers saw these peoples' coming as a test of their doctrine. They welcomed the incomers like lost kin. I remember one exhausted Uzbek family who were billeted at our house when I was nine or ten. The parents scolded their children for snatching at the food as it was set down on the table. The mother picked at her meal in a restrained, delicate way, as though she was too proud to admit to her hunger.

She could speak English and she translated for the others as my mother made small talk about the life she had left. It was things I had heard a thousand times and never paid any heed to—about the rich hiding behind a wall of money, and street lamps blocking out the starlight, and strawberries in the cooler in February, and noise, and dirt, and incivility. And I'll never forget the look on that man's face as he listened: there was reproach, and incredulity, and a yearning like you might see in the face of a stray animal when he catches the smell of barbecue at dusk. They must have thought we were mad.

·

The people who came at first were not of a bad kind at all. They were placid with hunger and eager to work. What was strange was how resentment got stoked up by our charity. With nothing at all, the first incomers threw themselves on our mercy. When the edge was off their hunger, they looked around and wondered about our spare rooms and the food that was being kept by for trading and planting, and it rankled with them.

The more dangerous ones began to show up later. They

were fewer in number and traveled in wintertime. That was only common sense. The winter roads made for better going and you had summer and fall to provision yourself for the trip. They arrived in better shape. One or two had cars. Most had guns. That was common sense, too, but it didn't make them any more welcome. They tended to squat the outskirts of the city. At night you could see their cooking fires. Many of them were deserters. They were young, and even the best were changeable and still smarting from the indignities of the battlefield.

So there we were, settlers who had forsworn the old world, only to have it fetch up on our doorstep. Us on the one side, and the desperate and dangerous on the other. It was like two different species colliding: the world that had a choice, and the world that had none. The strains between us were ratcheting up in secret. And even those who noticed it didn't like to admit to it. The trouble lit slow, like one of those lazy damp leaf fires in autumn.

·

The summer I was fourteen, some Russian boys were squatting a barn that belonged to a settler family called the Tumiltys. Mr. Tumilty had said two of them could stay, but ten came, and they ended up in dispute over it.

One night in August, the barn went up in flames and eight of the boys were killed. They'd been drinking and cooking shashlik among the hay bales, but a rumor went round the fire had been set on purpose. The dead boys' angry friends went round to Tumilty's farm and broke his windows. When he came outside to speak with them, they roughed him up. He had a weak heart and died on the spot.

The boys lit out, but the ill will stayed round the place. Settlers complained they felt unsafe. Incomers were spat at, and some shopkeepers refused to take the little tickets that were doled out to the poorest of them to buy food.

Families that had been friends for years fell out over the way the incomers were getting treated. People dropped away from church or set up rival meetings. It became clear that our city was tearing itself in two.

My father, as a leading man in the city, was looked to as someone who ought to give guidance. He called a gathering of the heads of families in the meetinghouse—the same one where I later found the fingers.

So many came that the meeting had to be held outside. It was a rowdy gathering. Tumilty's son and widow were there. Mrs. Tumilty made a passionate speech, naming the murderers and asking for justice. There were plenty that sided with her. But there was another faction, too, who felt the call for punishment and revenge would alter the spirit of our settlement utterly. At that time we had no police, no courts, no judges, no penal code. There had been deaths before now, but no crimes of violence. This was our Cain and Abel.

Many were waiting for my father to speak. He took his time, rising slowly to his feet to speak against revenge. Pa was steeped in the Bible and he wanted us to be moved only by love and compassion. He pointed to the feeding of the multitudes as a sign for how we should behave.

Tumilty's widow shouted from her place in the crowd that we didn't have six magic loaves that could feed five thousand.

Dad tried to handle her gently, but he pointed out to her that the loaves weren't magic. The miracle was human nature, behaving in a spirit of goodwill, that multiplied in the act. In simple words, he said, when each of the five thousand saw the fish and bread coming out, they reached into their robes and pulled out the food they'd been keeping for themselves. "Fear breeds fear," Pa said. "We have to offer our guests selfless support and expect nothing in return. We have enough food. The land around us is empty and big enough to absorb all that have come and more. We have to be soft enough to yield to what's inevitable, but strong enough to hold tight to our doctrine."

Tumilty's widow and son took his words very badly. It seemed my father was blaming the dead man for being ungenerous. "They are not people like us," said Tumilty's son, Eric. "Give them an inch and they take a yard. They're laughing up their sleeves at us and think we're fools for parting with what we've sweated for. They'll pay us back all right. You'll each get what my father got: six feet of ground for every one of you."

Then a man called Michael Callard spoke up.

The Callards—Michael, Freya, and their twins, Eben and Liesl—were one of the settler families who had left their home further south. The Callards had arrived with almost nothing and had lived with us for a few months before Michael Callard put up a house of their own on the other side of Delamere Street. They were devout and hardworking and well liked by the other settlers.

Eben and Liesl were eighteen. Liesl was shy and handsome like her mother. Eben farmed with his dad. He was proud of his strong shoulders and lean brown body. Sometimes after a day of work in summer, he would wander downtown and brave the midges with his shirt off. He was a good rider, too, and once or twice we had raced ponies on the fields outside the city. A rumor found its way back to me that we were sweet on each other. But he had always struck me as ruthless and quick-tempered, and the truth is I have never liked a man who was too much like me.

Michael Callard spoke of how his farm in the south had been attacked by armed men, how they'd been rounded up at gunpoint and given an hour to leave. He said he, like the rest of us, had come here to live in a new way, free of the threat of violence, as equals. But he was damned if he thought that meant accepting the threat of being hounded out of his own home, or having his food taken or his wife and children hurt. He called on the able-bodied of us to form and arm a militia to keep the streets safe, and eject or punish anyone who broke the codes of the town.

You could see that many were moved by his words—even those who had persuaded themselves that all forms of violence were wrong.

I watched my father as Michael Callard was speaking and I saw trouble flit across his face. I loved my father, but I was not like him. I never needed to believe the best of people. I took them as they were: two-faced, desperate, kind—perhaps all at once. But to Pa, they were all children of God, poor troubled sheep, who only wanted love and an even break. He needed the world to back up what his religion told him about people. And when it came down to a choice between reason and faith, he let go of his reason.

They held a vote that time, and my father carried the day, but that was the start of two factions in the town. The one, led by Callard, was warm for the militia and us getting armed to defend ourselves. The other, which looked upon my pa as its head, wanted us to stick to the original spirit of the settlement.

Thinking of my pa just now, I see something childish in his need for things to be perfect. He was a clumsy workman and could labor for days over something that would get tossed out if he marred it. A thing would be worthless if it wasn't just so. And that childishness fed his intolerance of people. He loved ideas more than men because they were less contradictory. And Pa sometimes seemed to be able to forgive a thief or a murderer more easily than he could forgive lateness or back talk. Murder or theft was less troubling because wholly bad. Variety and contradiction bothered him. He was like the god of the Methodists: one word could put you out of the Elect forever.

I think in his love for the arctic you see the same hunger for simple truths: sky, snow, mountain, trees. What I found in a city—when I finally saw a real one—was disquieting. Nothing matched. It was a weird assemblage of things, but there was beauty in the oddness of it, and the thought that it was all man's doing.

But the doctrine my father chose, like our landscape, had a crystal order to it: peace, self-reliance, love, submission to the will of god. The simple shape of it had a power to persuade. People were drawn to him. The force of his conviction made them trust him.

It puts me in mind of a piece of block ice, with its glassy sides shirred from the saw teeth. When you melt one for water, for the longest time the block stays perfect. It just sighs and shrinks a little. But as soon as the heat finds out a bubble of air in it, it swells and bursts the whole thing into tiny pieces.

That year was one in a cluster of hot summers. The city was splitting at the seams like a fat man in his wedding suit: so many incomers, Quaker people and others, pouring up out of the scorched south, fleeing the famines. There had been squabbles all through July: people filching food from gardens or squatting empty properties and refusing to go. And as it turned out, what happened to me was the tinder that set the haystack blazing.

Callard and Tumilty put their militia together, with weapons they bought off the incomers themselves in spite of the vote going against them.

The settlers who opposed them—which was the majority, led by my father—dogged them throughout the summer, followed their patrols shouting and ringing bells, and sat down in the streets so their horses couldn't pass.

Over the coming weeks, the arguments went on, in the meetinghouses, in stores, on the sidewalks, and between husbands and wives at dinner tables. Family by family, people were won over to Callard's side. In our house, I was the cuckoo who spoke up against my own father. I had a simpler notion of right than he did. I think I was relieved when Michael Callard spoke: he gave voice to feelings I had had all my life. I said if someone slapped my face, I slapped back, no matter what the Bible said. My father went thin-lipped with disapproval and ordered me up to my room. He felt the mood going against him in the town, and it was too much to have mutiny at his own table.

Those weeks were the worst I ever got on with him. The pressure he was under made him angry and bitter. He raged at Callard. He still had support among the settlers, but day by day it was ebbing away from him, and it didn't take a wild leap of the imagination to foresee a day when he stood alone. He was losing authority and he was losing the city that he had struggled to build. He warned anyone that would listen what would happen if we followed Callard, but the number who would listen grew smaller and smaller every hour.

What had started out as a quarrel over interpreting our laws was turning into a straight fight for the mastery of the city.

In late August, my mother and father left the city for a few days. He liked to hunt and fish and took her when he could for company. Whenever they went away together, I would sneak into their room to sleep. I loved their deep mattress and the jingling bed frame they had brought from America.

Past midnight I heard the door open and the sound of breathing. I called out Charlo's name. It was half a dozen men with pillowcases over their heads.

They had holes cut out for their eyes and mouths. There was was froth on their lips as they shouted names at me.

I ran to the window to jump but they dragged me off it. Two of them held me down on the bed. I wriggled a hand free and slashed at my attacker with a water glass. "Jezebel," he said. I felt something wet on my face and I thought he had cut me, but it was lye they'd picked up from our kitchen.

The mind is merciful in what it leaves you with. I don't remember much of what followed and less still of the aftermath, but they left me alive for my parents to find, and apparently I told them Eben Callard had been the leader.

I've since wondered how I knew—and even why he would have done such a thing—but the years have taught me not to wonder too much at the dark things men do. Strange how it is that men never act crueler than when they're fighting for the sake of an idea. We've been killing since Cain over who stands closer to god. It seems to me that cruelty is just in the way of things. You drive yourself mad if you take it all personal. Those who hurt you don't have the power over you they would like. That's why they do what they do. And I'm not going to give them that power now. But it was a cruel thing that they did, and when they had finished hurting me, a splinter of loneliness seemed to break off and stay inside me forever. Nowadays, I don't think of it much, but I can never hear the bedframe jingling without a sense of disquiet.

What happened to me killed the hope of our city and it killed my father too. He took a straight razor and cut his own throat in the forest. I was too badly hurt to see him buried.

For three weeks, I had to lay in bed with a wet cloth on my face to keep the skin moist and lessen the scarring. The pain was bad, but what I remember was the noise of rioting in the street outside the window. The Callards were driven out of the city and in the upheaval many houses burned.

When the bandages came off, the skin was raw and my whole face was pulled out of true: left eye drooping, mouth awry. I'm not saying I was a looker before, but I wasn't unhandsome and I had my good days when I could feel men respond a little quicker to me. But after that, I started wearing my hair short and mannish. When the city fathers agreed to start a militia, mine was the first name on the list.

·

Our police rode armed and had powers of arrest. We had a code that our magistrates were supposed to enforce, and cells to remand offenders. But all we had as actual punishments were orders of interdiction, which meant in practice being evicted beyond the city limits if you were found guilty of a crime. The city fathers didn't have the stomach for anything stronger; an armed police force was bad enough.

At the beginning we were able to stand in the way of mayhem, but as time wore on there was just too much of it. And we were in the crazy position of a man finding mice in his larder who picks them up by the tail, carries them outside, and then waits for them to dig their way back in.

Try how we might, the disorder multiplied. Once, there had been an understanding between us about how disputes should be settled. People were direct and approached each other boldly. They had staked their futures on this experiment. We didn't all like each other, but we knew each other. Now there was a gap between us and our neighbors, and it filled with fear and resentment. No one wanted to be the last unarmed man in the city. And if you looked for justification to arm yourself, there was plenty of it. If the Callards were capable of what they'd done, then no one could be trusted. "'If the salt has lost its savor, wherewith shall it be salted?'" people said. With my father dead, there was no one to speak up for the old ways. They junked the ideals they'd come with and bought guns. The city changed out of all recognition.

The chaos seemed to draw in a particular kind of vagrant. Everything was up for grabs. In peaceful times, the steady and patient thrive. But it takes a quick and ruthless type to flourish amid disorder. And we, the citizens of our own city, were co-conspirators with them.

The thing is, to people brought up on a diet of the Bible and the thought of their special place in God's plan, a global disaster is something they've secretly been longing for. We'd been talking about the millennium for centuries. Now it seemed the end-time had arrived. Men like to meet a crisis head-on, wallop straight into it as though it's a test of strength. Why? Surely it's better to edge round it, fade into the background with the things you need. Spring will come again next year. There's food in the woods if you're sharp enough to know where to look.

The scriptures were certainly fulfilled, though, just not in the way anyone had expected. There was no Second Coming, no lion and lamb lying down together. No. An orderly, modern city descended into a bunch of hungry tribes fighting over a desert. So I guess you could call the Bible a prophetic book in that sense.

Bill Evans had finished his work and was looking to find a way to travel back to his home in Alaska when he got killed breaking up a fight. But that was a long time later. It took a couple of years for things to descend to that.

13

They kept me in the dark in that hole above two weeks. It was cold enough not to stink too bad, but that was the best you could say for it. I kept myself sane by letting my mind wander. I built up a world in my head where things had gone otherwise and I spent my time there, instead of on the dirty blankets in the darkness. I liked to think of Ping's child growing up strong. I could see her face and her straight black hair like her mother's. I took her bathing at the lake in the mountains, and though her chin trembled in the cold water, she had a strong kick like a little frog.

The food improved after the first ten days. The soup was thicker, with a little meat in it, and potatoes. I figured that they were trying to build me up for my hard labor. I wondered if they would be stupid enough to let anything resembling a weapon into my hands. Boathwaite didn't look like a person who would underestimate somebody, but there was no harm in hoping.

Finally, one morning they opened the door, and instead of sliding in a tin plate of food, in came a man in a farrier's apron holding a set of manacles and a length of chain. He was followed by two men with cudgels who held me down while the first man fastened me into the restraints.

I resisted a little, but just to keep the men occupied. One called me an ugly bitch and waved his cudgel at me, but it wasn't heartfelt. He was just showing off to his friend, and though I was wriggling, what I really wanted was to get a good look at the locks on the manacles.

Unluckily for me, the men knew their work. They put me into a leather belt, and the chain passed through a loop in it to join the handcuffs with another set of restraints on my ankles.

When they left me alone again, I shuffled into the brightest part of my cell and pulled a clanking length of chain into the light so I could examine it better.

It was of good-quality steel, heavy and well made, and it looked new. For all the hardship in Horeb, it was clear that Boathwaite wasn't cutting any corners where his enemies were concerned.

I wondered about that steel, its provenance. Like the wheat flour in their stale bread, it was beyond what the people in the town seemed capable of. The farrier must have shortened it by a link or two, and worked the loop into the leather belt, but his handiwork seemed gross beside the fine workmanship of the steelmaker. It seemed an awful waste of metal to me, but then, Boathwaite and I had different priorities.

•

Sometimes, when you've suffered a lot, it turns out to be the small thing that breaks you. That chain almost finished me. It wasn't so much the weight as the cold of it, drawing the heat out of me and clanking when I moved. I started to reminisce about the good old days: I don't mean at home, I mean before the chain, when the cell was still stinking and cold, and the food bad, but at least I had the freedom to move. Gradually, it felt more and more burdensome. And to stay comfortable, I had to slump, hunched up in the dirt in a posture of defeat, and too tired to budge.

All my dreams of escape came back to mock at me now. They seemed as unreal as my dreams of Ping and her child living. I am nothing when I can't move. I refused to eat, and I'm stubborn enough to have starved myself, except that after two days more, one of the jailers swung the door open and told me it was time to leave.

Someone threw me a ragged quilted jacket, a hat, and a pair of greasy mittens. I thought of my warm snow-sheep gloves and my wolverine pants. I wondered who was wearing them now.

I put on the clothes and shuffled forward into the light, blinking like a thing that lives in darkness. The main square of Horeb was smaller than I recalled, barely the size of our backyard at home.

The gates were open and the people of the town drawn up in two rows, making a corridor for me to pass through. They stood in silence, watching me shuffle past, chains clanking.

I searched their faces for some clue to where I was headed, but they were all gray and stony. Finally, I caught sight of Violet among them. "She'll wish she'd been hanged after all," she announced to the crowd, and there was a murmur of agreement.

Boathwaite stood on a ledge high up on the wall of the stockade. He was dressed in a black surplice and he had his Bible tucked under his arm.

Just through the gateway, I could see men on horseback waiting for me.

Boathwaite never met my eye. He called on my guards to stop and he led his people in a prayer, entrusting me into god's care and calling on him to be merciful to me.

As their voices mumbled away, I took a good look around me. It was coming up to April and you could smell the world coming back to life after winter. The floor of the stockade was melted to slush. It seemed a long way since all the hope of the spring before.

They finished their prayer with a throaty "Amen."

"And god have mercy on *you*," I cried. It had been boiling up inside me throughout the prayer and it burst out in a crazed howl. It was so loud, it split the air like a rifle crack, and those nearest to me flinched. But others muttered "How dare she?" and pushed toward me, not so much violently, but with the steady menace of a herd of cows that could trample you to death.

The guards dragged me on and I staggered, falling to my knees in the mud. They heaved me up and pushed me forward, through the gateway, and stopped, leaving me to walk on alone.

One of the men on horseback swung down from his saddle and slipped a rope through the loop on my belt.

He was practiced and indifferent, as though he was wrangling livestock or shoeing horses. Then he was back in the saddle and gave his horse a whistle.

I worried that I wouldn't be able to keep up, that I would fall in the slush and be dragged, but they walked on slowly. Even then it was hard work to stay with them.

They rode along the track through the woods, to where it broke out onto the main road—the place I'd come upon the men logging a lifetime earlier.

I was weak from bad food and being cooped up in one place, and after each set of a dozen paces I'd think I wasn't going to be able to make another. "The flesh is weak," they say. Me, I say the flesh is strong but the mind is weak. It's the mind that hisses at you to give up, lay in the snow. Only women know what the body is capable of. Pain that feels like it will tear you in half, but doesn't.

So while my muscles cried out at me, I staggered on, counting my breaths, trying to rise out of my mind. At first I tried too desperately, and my thoughts had a sense of panic about them and wouldn't settle in one place, because I was snatching at anything.

But then a kind of peace came over me. I lost track of my footsteps and gave myself up to the motion.

The woods were silent except for the tick of melting snow, and I thought we were alone; but as we turned onto the road, we came upon a big crowd of people camped right there on the highway.

They were crouched down on their haunches, trying to rest and hold their clothing clear of the slush. One or two you could see were more hopeless and lay flat-out exhausted in the wet, not caring how they would feel about it later.

Around them, a dozen men slouched on horseback.

The captives were chained together in groups of ten.

One of my guards gave a whistle, and the group nearest to me stood up. The rider hopped down and padlocked me to the last man in the group, a fellow of about fifty with a matted beard and a worn rabbit-fur cap. No one spoke.

The riders made the other prisoners stand and then positioned themselves along the flanks of the line and waited.

Finally, someone broke off from the front and rode up and down the line, checking that everything was to his satisfaction. He barely glanced at me, but as he turned to ride up the other flank, I saw his face and recognized him as the man I had encountered on the highway outside my own city.

He galloped fast to the front of the caravan, which lay almost sixty yards away from where I stood.

My companion turned to me as though he wanted to say something, but with a shout we were in motion, and we saved all our breath for walking.

TWO

1

The place they called the base lay almost a thousand miles west of Evangeline, close to a tributary of the Lena.

We didn't reach it until past midsummer. All that time we were just banging down the road, minding our blisters.

If anything, it was more desolate than the road to the East. We didn't see a soul, just bleached bones on the road and deserted settlements beyond it.

They lightened our chains to keep us moving quicker and to save on food: each link of chain cost something in flour to carry.

The caravan traveled with its own food. The covered wagons carried sacks of flour, which they mixed into porridge or cooked into griddle cakes for the prisoners.

Our guards broke off to hunt sometimes, and at night the smell of their meat cooking kept us awake, teasing our noses with the smell of burned flesh.

If you were quick enough at the reveille, there might be some scraps to chew on, bones or gristle to remind you what real food tasted of.

The man beside me was a Mohammedan called Shamsudin. Five times a day he'd crouch, wash his hands in the dust, and aim himself to pray at Mecca, or where it used to be.

He'd been pals with a fellow called Zulfugar, but when any prisoners looked like they were getting too friendly, the guards separated them to different ends of the line. How they thought any of us would survive with our bare hands, carrying twenty pounds of chain in that wilderness, I don't know, but they put me next to Shamsudin to break the two of them up.

The guards watched us pretty closely, so I had to glean information out of him a piece at a time. One day, crouching down beside him in the dust at one of the water stops, I found out that he was forty-six and that he had been born in Bokhara, one of the old silk cities in the south. He left to train as a surgeon in the Far East and returned to work at a hospital back in his hometown.

He had been a wealthy man and had managed to bribe his way north when the troubles started.

I told him that from what I had observed, it only took three days before desperation and hunger overturned all civilized instinct in a person. He smiled and said I had a bleak view of human nature, and that in his experience it was nearer to four days.

His chains clanked as he scooped up the water in his hands.

I asked him what kind of surgery he had done.

"Noses," he said, and there was just the trace of a smile.

"You were a nose surgeon?"

"I made women more beautiful."

"Don't muslim women go covered up anyway?" I said, and he laughed.

The guards rode past, and chivied us to move on. We ambled on, all eighty of us, getting into motion slowly like one big reluctant animal.

"I don't suppose you could do anything for me," I whispered to him with a wink.

"There is nothing wrong with your nose."

"I wasn't thinking of my nose."

"What were you thinking of?" he asked, deadpan.

"You're very gallant," I said.

He looked me over carefully, as though it was the first time he had noticed anything odd about me. "An acid burn, I think?"

"It was lye, but you were close."

"Yes, this is easy to treat. We use chemicals to restructure the epidermis. I would take skin from your thigh to reconstruct the eyelid. I could make you even more beautiful."

That was the nearest I came to laughing. You could see how he'd got rich: charming the cash out of wealthy women. It meant something to me that he knew I wasn't a man.

There was a gentlemanly way about Shamsudin. He wore his rags well, and when he ate, he didn't wolf his food the way we all did, tearing at it and burping. He ate elegantly, breaking off morsels of food with his long fingers, rolling it into little balls and eating them one by one. I started to do the same: apart from anything, the food went slower that way, and so there seemed to be more of it.

The little I told him of my life struck him as insane. He couldn't believe that my parents had willingly abandoned lives of comfort for the cold of the Far North.

Shamsudin's own family were all dead, and he had left

Bokhara with two companions. They'd been hoping to get to the coast to find a boat that would take them south to Japan or even up to Alaska. They'd come across very few living settlements in their travels, and fewer still who'd help them. One of his companions died of dysentery and the other was shot dead when they broke into a farmstead to steal food. Shamsudin arrived at his destination alone, almost starving, and all the banknotes in his pockets already worthless paper.

He said there was still the occasional boat on the Pacific coast, but the only trade as such was in men and women. About two-thirds of our fellow prisoners had arrived as cargo from Peter-Paul in Kamchatka. Shamsudin had watched on the quayside as they disembarked in manacles. If he was aghast at first, he soon got to noticing that the slaves were better fed than he was.

When night fell, he could smell the food cooking over in the slave camp. His guts ached with hunger and his muscles were wasting from slow starvation. He just handed himself over to the guards and begged them to take him. He said he sobbed over his first bowl of food with the shame of what he had done, and he thanked god his parents weren't alive to see his weakness.

I told him he was being hard on himself. He wasn't the only one. For every two that were bought, there was another that had enslaved himself because he couldn't stand it any longer as a free man.

.

Shamsudin aside, the self-enslaved tended to have a harder time of it. There were beast-people among us. One man called Hansom killed a man with a rock one night and strangled someone the second. The guards stripped their bodies of their clothes and left their gray corpses by the roadside.

Hansom went unpunished. The guards let him walk and sleep alone so they didn't lose any more men.

.

We were backtracking on the same road I'd ridden on through the fall, the commissars' highway. It all looked different with the snow gone, but now and again I'd see places that I seemed to remember from my journey north. We passed Evangeline toward mid-morning around the fourth week of the march. I'd known it was coming for days, and as we drew closer to it, my chains seemed to hang a little lighter on me. Just to be close to home was a comfort to me. I hoped we'd pass the night there. Like the rabbit in the storybook, I felt my chance of freedom would be greater in a place I knew well. I could slip away like Ping had, vanish into the storm drains until the men driving us grew impatient and moved on.

I could feel my heart lifting as the tower on the firehouse loomed proud of the trees and the line slowed to a stop. We were there ten minutes in all as the guards doled out water. There was one tin mug for all of us, but most of the prisoners, me included, had made our own cups of birch bark like the Tungus did. It was cleaner than sharing, and the birch sap sweetened the water. More than that, just to have something of your own, however small, gave you some of your dignity back.

But at that instant, standing on the edge of the town that had once been my whole world, I felt—not for the last time—like the ghost of the woman I'd been. I thought I could hear a voice calling to me from a distant part of the city, but the sound was drowned out by the shouts of the guards riding along the line and yelling at us all to move on.

.

There was no rain for weeks after the thaw, and the dust raised up by all those feet meant we were marching through a choking cloud. It coated the trees beside us and turned the prisoners' faces gray. Our eyes were wet and bloodshot in masks of ash.

The guards were reluctant to ride at the back of the line, where the dust was worst, so for those of us in the rear, discipline slackened somewhat, and we were able to talk more freely to one another, and I got to know Zulfugar a little.

He was an old thirty-five, a full head shorter than me but tough as the devil, and stringy and brown as though they'd made him out of walnut and rawhide. He prayed even more than Shamsudin.

One night, the guards killed a couple of wild pigs and threw us the leftovers, not out of kindness, but to see us fight over the scraps. A big chunk of haunch landed at Zulfugar's feet, but he didn't so much as budge.

I wasn't too proud to stoop for food, so I grabbed it and ate. It was part burned, part raw, and very bloody because it wasn't killed right, but my spit still runs when I remember it. I offered Zulfugar a piece but he wouldn't take it: he said his religion forbade it.

Zulfugar had been a soldier, and he was very particular about the state of his feet. He washed and dried his foot cloths each night if he could. Some of the prisoners would rib him about it, as though it was sissy of him to be so concerned about such an unmanly thing, but I soon saw the wisdom of it. One of the men who mocked hardest at him got an abscess on his foot that made his toes goes black. He hobbled so badly that the guards cut his chains off to give him a chance to keep up, but he drifted further and further behind, till one day there was just one fewer at the evening muster. A lot more of us started taking care of our feet after that.

·

Another time we passed the outskirts of a town on a river which must have flooded some years earlier. You could see the high-tide stains on the buildings that were still standing. There was silt across the highway, and we came across an automobile all crusted with dried mud that looked like it had been swallowed and spat out by a whale. Its windows were all blurred with mud, but it still had an odd poise, like something squat and powerful. It put me in mind of one of those low, broad men with sloping shoulders. The rubber of its tires was ripped and splayed out.

Zulfugar was drawn to it. He caressed its rear window with his dirty hand and muttered something in Russian to Shamsudin. The two of them laughed.

"He says as a child he dreamed of having such a machine," said Shamsudin.

Zulfugar tried the door but couldn't budge it. The sound of him snubbing that lock seemed almighty loud in the silence. He was so insistent on getting in that I thought one of our guards would shoot him.

I took hold of his elbow and his arm went slack in my hand, the way it does when you pull someone away from a fight he doesn't really fancy, and he came along with me, but not without turning to look at the car as it grew smaller behind us. And when we stopped ten minutes later to fill up from the river, he was still full of his car, banging away in Russian and shaking his head, like a hunter who just missed bagging a white moose.

There's always those moments with the loss of someone close when the pang just grabs you and doubles you up. Other times, it's just another of the facts you live with, like the time of sunrise, or the color of the windowsill. In different ways, all of us confronted the facts of what we lost when the world our ancestors bequeathed to us hit the buffers. I had things which triggered it for me: laundry was one; there was something so sedate and ordinary about the routines of washing linen. But we didn't come across too much clean linen on our march. In some strange way, for Zulfugar it was all about that ancient car.

•

We lost eleven men on our trek. That includes the two that Hansom killed, a guard who was thrown by his horse, the man who got left behind, and four of the other prisoners: a heart attack, snakebite, malaria, and an older man called Christopher something-or-other who just didn't wake up one morning. I envied him a little.

To be honest, I was surprised that we didn't lose more, but the gang master knew his work: He knew when to push us hard, and he knew when to ease off when we were floundering. He kept discipline among the guards, and though there was drinking among them, they never went beyond common or garden rowdy.

He rode up beside me one day and started speaking in a low voice and without any introduction. "I hear you fell out with my brother Silas."

He was ambling just slightly in back of me, so I had to turn at an odd angle and look up into the sun to see his face. I told him he must have been mistaken, as I didn't know anyone of that name.

"I'm Caleb Boathwaite," he said. "My brother Silas is who sent you here." He had a kerchief pulled round his nose against the dust and now he lowered it.

I said nothing.

"He tells me you're a woman too. I took you for a man that time we met outside the city limits of—now what place was it now?"

"Evangeline."

"That's right. I've been racking my brains to think why you left that place. Someone like you, on the move, getting mixed up with my brother. It makes me nervous." He smiled as though to say that nothing in the wide world could ever make a man like him lose his cool.

I could feel my cheeks burning behind their layer of dust, but I stayed silent.

He looked at me for a few moments and then spurred his horse to the front of the line. He never spoke to me again after that, but I noticed now and then that he would watch me; and when he wasn't, he had detailed one of the guards to give me closer attention.

·

Once I knew they were related, I saw lots of likenesses between Caleb and his brother, the Reverend. They both had the same thin noses and those smart eyes that weigh you up in a second. If anything, I preferred Caleb of the two of them, since he wasn't apt to prettify what he was doing with the name of religion. He wasn't self-deceived. But I got to know him better in time, and I learned he was more dangerous. That look he had I've seen on few men, and it never boded well. In other times, it would have been the look of a sea captain or an explorer pushing his men into an unknown latitude, or a military general, perhaps, of the most practical and ruthless kind. But in these times of ours, the material of conquest was much more limited, and he had turned out a trader in human flesh.

•

We all felt we had an idea where we headed for, but no one knew for sure. Rumors would pass through the line about our destination, a different one each day. Someone would say he'd overheard the guards saying we were going to fight in a war. Another would say that the base was a mine and we'd be working miles underground. I tried not to think that far ahead, just sticking to the moment at hand, keeping marching, holding my nose and eyes clear of the dust.

There wasn't a soul to be seen on that road, but now and again you'd see a place that looked like it might house someone: there'd be a couple of chickens, perhaps, or a row of beans in the garden. The guards would scoop up anything that could be eaten and we'd move on. I often wondered about whose meal they'd taken. I suppose whoever it was had learned to hide the moment they saw our dust on the road.

By the beginning of June there was a kind of laggardliness in the line that no amount of cajoling or threats of beating could cure us of. Something in our bones sensed the object of our journey growing nearer, and the fear of what was to come made our feet drag.

•

It was usual for us to stop and make camp toward the end of the day. Although you couldn't tell by looking at it because it seemed so straight, the road had been making a slow arc to the south. The trees had changed; there was more variety among them: walnuts as well as birches, elm, willow, limes. I'd never been this far south in my life before. I almost missed the arctic summer. In the Far North, there'd be no night at all by now—

only round-the-clock daytime—and that always gave me a jolt of energy that I enjoyed. But where we had fetched up, the day unraveled into darkness around nine.

We had been growing jumpier by the day. Whereas before, the spurs off the highway had been rare, now we passed more and more of them. There were road signs, too, blackened and twisted and not in any lettering I could understand, but still, keepsakes of something, mementos of the past.

I thought of all the other humans who had looked on these signs, arriving here from the West with a sense of wonder and hopefulness as they came to start lives in these cities—a late chapter in the story of humanity. How late, they could never have guessed.

And I thought of Ping. How lucky for her that she had been spared this. Sometimes I looked at the guards and wondered if one of them had fathered her child. I could have been fooling myself, but I felt that Boathwaite was too cold of a fish to have done a thing like that. Was it him? The horseman with the Tatar eyes? Or the older one in the patched jacket, who ate with his knife and whose slow movements breathed his contempt of us? Or the young one with the sweet face, the most junior of the whole crew, who gathered their plates after their mealtimes and fetched fire for their smokes?

We'd hear them talking and laughing in the evenings, but too far away to make any sense of it. All of them must have had stories like mine and Shamsudin's. Boathwaite was the child of settlers, like I was. One of the others was part Tungus. There were Russians and a couple of fellows who looked like they were from the Caucasus, reddish of hair with joined-up eyebrows, gold teeth, and big ears.

And I supposed it was just dumb luck that we were in chains

and they were on horseback. I told myself that they had had to unlearn their natural compassion, those who'd had any, just as Shamsudin had to overcome his squeamishness about slicing up a woman's face so that he could make her more beautiful. But it didn't make me hate them any less.

Then one evening, instead of stopping to camp for the night and two of us being sent on a detail to gather wood, we just kept going.

The mosquitoes were like hellfire in the evenings without any wood smoke to keep them off you, and there were big smears of blood on my arms when I killed them. "Damn it," I said, "they're eating better than we are."

"The first time in my life I am jealous of a mosquito," said Shamsudin.

There was only a crescent moon, but the sky was so clear you could see the part of it that was in shadow beside the tiny piece of it that had been gilded by the hidden sun.

Ahead of us, the road forked and we were herded off to the left.

The road ran down and then turned back on itself and up to a gate that was lit with a couple of oil lamps. This was a real gate—not like the gimcrack carpentry at Horeb but a vast door hung on concrete posts, with a chain fence stretching off into the darkness on either side.

It opened without a word from Boathwaite or the guards and we marched in two by two through the gate, across a large patch of gravel, and into a long low hut with three lines of steel bunks stretched along it.

And for the next five years that was my home.

2

There used to be a look on the faces of some of the Tungus who came into our town to trade, or pick up work, of naked, peasant astonishment.

Plenty of them, especially the older ones, had spend time in cities better than ours, but some of the younger ones had never traveled and knew of us only by hearsay.

Think of it: a child of the tundra who knew everything about the movements of the caribou, who knew ninety-seven things you could make out of willow and sinew, who could live forever on the stingy soil of the Far North; and now he's walking down a thoroughfare, gazing at a child holding a balloon, or a woman with a shopping basket, or the great glass panes of the bakery, pulled every which way by the sudden variety of what's around him, getting bumped and jostled by passersby and jeered at by rude kids.

That poor baffled Tungus was me in my first days at the base. The place had a vitality I had never known except in the town of my childhood. I was so fizzed up I could hardly take it in: the extraordinary powerful smell of unclean men and animals, the raised voices, the faces of every brown and yellow shade, and the press of bodies in the barracks and at mealtimes, surging together, tighter than a run of salmon.

It was days, maybe weeks, before my new life took any kind of shape in my poor overloaded brain, and until then I just kept my head down, did as the others did, and tried to stay out of trouble.

We were housed in two sets of barracks. There were some three hundred souls altogether. The barracks had been built for fewer, so the overspill had to fit in somehow. The old-timers had the best bunks. The new arrivals made do with common space on big raised wooden boards. For nearly three years, the planks of wood above my head were my whole private world. I shivered under them in winter, sweated there in the heat of summer or when fever gripped me. I could still draw every knot in those planks. I know them better than my mother's face.

Almost every one of the prisoners worked at farming—every aspect of it, from shoeing horses to milking cows, from sowing and reaping and preparing feed to salting cabbage and pickling grass in the silo for winter.

They mustered us for a head count morning and evening.

That first summer I baled hay in the hot sun all day and in the evening I milked cows in the byre. I hadn't seen anything on that scale for years. There had to be a couple thousand acres under cultivation. And the land was the good-looking rich black earth that the Russians used to tell jokes about: if you leave a spoon in the ground, they'd say, it grows into a shovel. Chernozom, I believe they called it.

There was a team that worked in the kitchens. Everyone wanted that. It was considered the softest labor: plenty of food, indoors all day. The jobs in there went to the most senior prisoners. But I never minded being outside. We had food in abundance. And I have to give it its due: the prison bakery made the softest loaf I have ever tasted.

In the first weeks, the new prisoners had that giddy sense of themselves that comes with eating, and a good day in the sun, and the relief that they had arrived at their destination, and it was no worse than this.

We came in from the fields around five for the second head count.

"My belly aches!" one said in wonder as he wiped his dish with a hunk of black bread.

There was a lot of contented snoring in the barracks, and when there were eggs for breakfast, those fools thought they had died and gone to heaven.

If we're living this soft, they thought, how can it be on the other side, where Boathwaite and his men live?

.

It was like a busy little village in that barracks at night. Most of the men knew at least one trade and they'd do odd jobs on the sly for the guards: a little tailoring or woodwork. One man built banjos out of scraps of wood and wire and sold them. Another, who had a reputation for cooking plov, was dragged out to make it for the guards on birthdays and always reeled back from the celebrations drunk. They would generally be paid in drink, or smokes, or bits of food.

There were rumors of women at the base, but I was the only one I knew of among the prisoners, and I didn't lay eyes on another for two years.

For those two years I was barely alone for one second. Even in the latrines you couldn't escape into your private self because there would be others in there constantly. At the same time there was nothing that I could call companionship.

I had hoped to stay friendly with Shamsudin, because I liked him and he seemed a decent man, but my friendships with him and Zulfugar didn't much outlast the march.

Now and again I'd have reason to work with one of them and there was a trace of the old warmth, but most of the time they were following a different road. There were other muslim prisoners at the base, and they all stuck together for prayers and mealtimes, and fasted together for forty days in the fall. My being a woman made any closeness with them impossible. And of the other prisoners, there were none that I wanted as friends.

·

The grimness of life at the base had no end. It doesn't make sense to number all the fistfights and the killings, and the drinking, and the bawdy talk. What struck me though was that, in all that time, we never had a man take his own life; and as for me, who had got so close to taking my own, it never entered my head to end it there.

When Ping and the baby died, my life had taken on a kind of looseness. It was a strange feeling for a person like me, who wakes up every day with a belly full of fight. It's hard to explain how it was. But back then, after she died, between this and that, there seemed to be no kind of meaningful difference. Not in anything. When I threw myself in the lake, I think I was already three-fifths dead and I just wanted to stop breathing.

And yet, when I remembered my life in the cabin from my stinking berth in the rack of bodies at the base, it seemed like the most beautiful part of it that had ever been: all the space, the music of the water, only myself to please. But that was where I had wanted to die. Now, here, I woke up each morning raging to live.

All my energy burned on living. How to eat better. How to keep myself strong. How to lay by warm clothes for the winter. When I dug, or baled hay, or humped potato sacks, I did it with the intensity of prayer, and my prayer said: Keep my body young, let me outlast this place, let me not die here in the stink of these men.

Many times I thought of escape. We had the chances. But the guards' best weapon in keeping order was the prisoners themselves. We lived so on top of one another that you could never have got hold of even the minimum of the things you'd need to survive outside the base without someone turning you in. There was a whole group of snitch prisoners who told tales to the guards to try to get in friendly with them. They would be paid for their tattle, but most of them would have done it for free. An oddity of our prison was that, once in a while, someone you'd got used to seeing in the bunkhouse, or working beside you, would disappear for a week or two and then turn up again, but this time holding a gun, perhaps on horseback, having been made a guard.

It was cunning on Boathwaite's part for many reasons. Men need hope. They need something to dream on. For the prisoners, this was better than heaven: they could come back, in this life, with all the rights and pleasures of a guard! That's one reason why there were so many eager snitches. It also meant that Boathwaite had men under him who knew the mood in the prison so well that any troublemaker could be rooted out and dealt with before he had time to organize. There didn't seem to be much rhyme or reason to the process. The prisoners who got the break weren't especially anything. But they never made into a guard a man who was too keen on prayer—and there were some of them—and they never chose a muslim.

I'd be lying if I said I was miserable every minute. If it were true I couldn't have lived. I had unfinished business outside there. I hadn't dreamed that plane.

And, the plane aside, it was still possible to find some joy in each day. I always liked farming, its colors and smells, and the miracle of the soil. We die forever, but a plant dies back to his root. That was also a kind of comfort to me. Nature favors the small and simple when times are hard.

I never got over the power of that land. We grew so much that each fall we didn't need to harvest it all. We left some fields to rot, and others we plowed back under. In August and September we had tomatoes coming out of our ears. Pumpkins, squash, corn, milk, butter. And that was with slaves working it—griping, hating it, goldbricking on principle, every chance we got. Imagine what free men would have made of the place.

None of the prisoners would say such a thing, of course. We had unwritten dos and don'ts that were stricter than the ten commandments. Only the greenest newcomer would let on that he was impressed by the food. The style was to gripe and complain, to fight your corner fiercely if someone was encroaching on you—maybe even if they weren't, so long as you could cut a good figure—never to express surprise or doubt, and never to be curious.

·

There was a pigsty at the base where they raised pork for the guards. One time Shamsudin and I were sent to lay shingles on part of its roof. It was filthy hot on the roof in midsummer, and as new prisoners, we got stuck with the worst jobs. Also, it was the guards' idea of a joke to have a woman and a muslim working on the pigsty together.

After about fifteen minutes, the fellows who were supposed to be watching us sloped off somewhere, leaving us alone. The sun was bright overhead and the smell of tar and shingles took me away from the place and made me think of home.

Shamsudin was working on a patch away to my left. I glanced over at him. He didn't look up. He was crouched down on the slope of the roof, studying something. I wondered why he was so quiet. It crossed my mind for some reason that he felt guilty about throwing me over as a friend. Then I noticed how slowly he was going. I moved over to him and asked if he was all right. His face was grayer and his hammer was shaking.

I was certain he was going to pass out. It was the height that was making him ill. We were twenty feet up. I wasn't strong enough to hold him if he slipped, so I cupped my palms to yell for the guards. Shamsudin laid his hand on my arm and pleaded with his eyes for me not to do it.

Even at ground level he would have struggled with the job. There was something in Shamsudin of my father. He was out of place in the rough-and-tumble of the Far North. His hands were more like a woman's than mine were.

In a decent world, there's no shame in weakness, but there was nothing decent about life at the base. Failing at his task would mean at the least a week in the punishment cells. At the worst, it would be the kind of small wound to his reputation that would encourage others to tear at him, perhaps fatally. That's how it was at the base.

I helped him up higher, where he could hold on to the peak of the roof, and gave him the nails to hold. He felt rigid and unsteady and I knew he was trying not to look down. I said we should talk to keep his mind off the height.

"What should we talk about?" he asked.

"I don't know," I said. "Tell me how we got into this fix." I meant how we got stuck up on the roof, but Shamsudin had a cast of mind that always leaned toward speculation, and he shared the interest of many of the other prisoners who liked nothing more than to talk about the disasters that had befallen us and why they'd come about.

It always seemed to me that nothing revealed the prisoners' ignorance as much as when they talked of these things. You came across as many explanations as people you asked, and most of them told fairy tales that would shame children: a piece of the moon had fallen into the sea and made a tidal wave; tiny atom machines had eaten up all the sunlight; and so forth.

Of course, I knew what I'd seen: desperate people pitching into and overwhelming our tiny city. And I could guess the things they were running from—failed crops, cities with no light or water, gangs of lawless men—but what lay behind those troubles I couldn't say.

So as he clung to the shingles with one hand, trying not to look down, and reached me nails from his apron with other, Shamsudin told me his own idea.

He said the earth was close to five milliard years old. He spoke of seeing it from space, surrounded by a blur of clouds, turning from blue to white and back again as the centuries pass. They were long summers in which the oceans teemed and winters when even seawater froze hard. He said five times in that span of years all life had been wiped from the planet when it grew too dark or too hot. It was one of those times—a big moon that whacked into Mexico from space—that did it for the dinosaurs.

It sounded like fairy tales to me, and I asked him if it was written in his holy book. He said not, and that it was science that said so.

After the fifth time, it was our turn. We crept out of the mud. We peopled the planet, living in every corner, never mind wet or ice or desert, steadily growing wiser and more resourceful.

Around four and half milliard years after it began, the earth started to alter. Looking at it from space, you'd have seen rocket ships and satellites burst out of it like corn from a popper. The earth was in one of its warm times—had been since before we mastered farming; we'd grown accustomed to predictable seasons and good growing weather. But now there were so many of us, all wanting so much, and all armed with the inventions of previous centuries. Once, we'd been so many naked apes, scratching for life on the foreshore of an African ocean. Now we were a vast army, a termite mound of giants, who could shake the planet if we stamped together, who could warm the air just by breathing.

Shamsudin said the planet had heated up. They turned off smokestacks and stopped flying. Some, like my parents, altered the way they lived. Factories were shut down. "You asked me about the Koran," he said. "But I understand it as a doctor. For all our knowledge, things happen that we do not understand. Sometimes the patient dies not from her illness but from the medicine."

As it turned out, the smoke from all the furnaces had been working like a sunshade, keeping the world a few degrees cooler than it would have been otherwise. He said that in trying to do the right thing, we had sawed off the branch we were sitting on. The droughts and storms that came in the years after put in motion all the things that followed.

Life in cities had ended.

I asked him about the world beyond the north, thinking of the plane, but he shrugged. "The whole world is a barer and less interesting place," he said. "Human misery has few varieties: tent camps, forced labor, hunger, violence, men taking food and sex by force. You yourself have seen them all."

I'd finished the roof before he came to the end of his talk, but we both stayed up there, resting on the peak in the sunshine. His vertigo had passed. We were still up there talking when the guards came and yelled at us to come for the evening head count.

·

For a while I passed in the camp as a man. I kept myself to myself, bathed alone, and rounded up the clean rags I needed each month discreetly. But sooner or later I knew the truth would come out. Living the way we did, there was no getting away from it forever. I was braced for a rough ride when it did. The men in there thrived off each other's weaknesses.

I was in the bathhouse when it finally happened. Two yahoos stumbled in and yanked my pants off me as a joke.

They were too stunned by what they saw to make anything of it, but when I came in from the fields that night, I could tell by the looks I got that my secret was out.

"Come and bunk with me, Makepeace," said the taller of the two who had found me. "I've got fourteen inches of kolbasa to share with you."

I could hear the snap of his trousers as he pulled out his johnson and waved it at me.

It seemed like the whole hut snickered with him.

I was mending my work gloves but I looked up when he spoke, and I guess my eyes betrayed the contempt I felt.

"Better cover her head. I've seen prettier faces on moose."

"I'll just turn her around . . ."

And so it went on. The two of them alternating menace and foolishness, saying how they'd do this and do that to me.

I felt a prickle of interest from around the hut as the others put down their work or folded their cards to watch. Over on the far side of bunks, where the muslim prisoners kept together, Shamsudin and Zulfugar were watching with grave, troubled faces.

Already, some of the other prisoners were joining in the sport, goading the others to make good on their boasts. These men who ordinarily feared and distrusted each other felt a little easier now they had baiting me as their common purpose.

I thought it was better to be silent. It didn't do to appear weak or craven, but equally too much tough talk was like buying things on tick and sooner or later you had to pay up. I bit off the thread and slipped on my glove to check the new seam.

The taller fellow was still bragging away. He was enjoying his new notoriety. But some of the other prisoners were getting bored with just words and were urging him to do what he was boasting of.

Slowly, to a chorus of jeers and whistles, he made his way across to the bunk where I sat. I was on the lowest bunk of three and he had to crouch down to it.

I told him he was blocking my light and to get out of the way.

Next thing is he reached in with his hand to grab me. It was awkward and cramped for a man of his height, and he came at me with a looping arm, so I went straight for the crotch of his pants with my gloved hand.

I don't know if he was as big down there as he claimed, or I just got a lucky hit, but I put enough darning needle into his khui to send him back howling to the far side of the hut. I heard later it went an inch deep. The laughter that followed him was so loud that I thought it would lift the roof off the place.

Only Shamsudin wasn't laughing. He had his eyes cast down at the floor, and when he raised them, I seemed to see only coldness in them.

I didn't feel he should have stuck up for me, but maybe he did. And we both knew that things being the way they were at the base, this wouldn't be the end of it.

·

The next evening after muster Shamsudin bumped me as we were walking in to eat. I was too surprised to say anything. He said sorry immediately and knelt down. "You dropped this," he said, and pressed something cold into my hand.

It was the haft of a trowel, snapped off at one end, and about six inches long. I appreciated what he'd done for me. The guards frisked us for knives at the muster, and if it had been found on him, they'd have made life hard for him.

I whet it on a rock and I made it a handle with rags and window putty. Each morning, I hid it in the corner of the outhouse. Each night, I'd pick it up and keep it under the balled coat I used for a pillow.

It was a strain on my nerves to have to wait up, keeping an ear on the whish of breathing in that cramped hut, but I took the same kind of pleasure in it that I used to take in hunting at night, or making a new firearm in the workshop, with all my awareness fixed on a single point. And more than once, in the course of those wakeful evenings, I regretted that I never had a shiv in my hand when Eben Callard and his friends had burst in on me, all those years before.

·

They waited over a week to try to catch me unawares, but when they made up their minds to come, I was ready.

I heard their feet slap on to the floor as they slid out of their bunks and came padding across to where I lay with my eyes shut.

They had shivs, too, of course, but I was soberer, and quicker and angrier, and I caught one of them in the throat and the other a bunch of times in the back and ass as he ran away squealing. When the guards ran with their lanterns, it turned out he'd cut his own finger half off in his panic.

The guards dragged me to a punishment cell, and as I went I cursed the lot of them and told them that anyone who tried that with me could expect the same. Both the men lived, which was a pity, but they couldn't save the finger.

·

They made me stay in the punishment cell a few nights, which was no hardship. I was pleased with how things had turned out and I expected to be left well enough alone after that. I understood that the guards wouldn't kill me because we were of some value to them: Why else drag us all that way and keep us fed and housed? And I was looking forward to getting back to the farmwork when they let me out.

The only upshot of it was one day when Boathwaite was making his rounds of the fields, he came up to the cart where I was baling hay and made conversation with me.

He said, "I gather you had a contretemps with Stavitsky and Maclennan."

I shrugged. I knew who he meant.

He told me about Maclennan losing his finger.

I couldn't pretend to be sorry about it. And nor did he.

Because I couldn't abide my companions in there, and Shamsudin didn't dare risk his position in his muslim family by being open about his friendship with me, I was always slower to hear the current rumors than the other prisoners. That didn't bother me at all, since most of what they talked about was nonsense. I gleaned enough overhearing conversations in the barracks where we slept. I realized early on that it made no sense for Boathwaite to go to all this trouble to round up farm labor, but because of my solitariness it was a while before I understood what was the real reason for our being there.

·

Six months after we arrived, sometime in February, they had reveille early and assembled us in the parade ground before breakfast.

It was still dark, and in the frosty silence you could see our breath rising and hear the muffled stamping of feet as the prisoners tried to keep warm.

Aside from the usual guards, there was another bunch, some of them newly created, all dressed for winter travel.

Each of them passed along the line and picked out a couple of prisoners. The leader of them was a fellow called Tolya who was half Russian and Boathwaite's deputy in the place. As he walked slowly past the prisoners, they strained slightly and swayed forward, as though they were desperate to be chosen.

Tolya stopped in front of me and paused. I could hear the men on either side of me groan and one muttered under his breath, "Me, Tolya." Tolya glanced at him, broke into a smile, and yanked him out of the line. The fellow was elated to be picked and looked back at us with a grin.

This went on until twenty prisoners had been chosen and marched off separately.

I asked the man who had been standing on my left what I'd missed out on. He looked at me, puzzled. "Why, those lucky so-and-sos are off to the Zone."

That was the first time I'd heard the place mentioned. Facts were like any other precious thing in there and hard to get hold of.

He told me it was a factory city to the northwest of the base. Just as some prisoners were promoted to guards, others were taken to the Zone, where they were trained to undertake industrial work. Only the ablest prisoners were chosen, he said.

I felt a stab of regret that I hadn't been picked, and the next time we were mustered I hoped that someone would stop in front of me and tap my shoulder, but I never came close to being picked again.

3

When the other prisoners sewed pants, or played cards, or
carved chess pieces, I tended a small garden in back of our barracks. I dug up wildflowers and planted them in it, and I took
cuttings from some flowering shrubs. Because of what happened to Stavitsky and Maclennan, people let me be. Besides,
there were always newcomers for them to pick on.

That chernozom was something else. And when the sweet
peas came up, one of the guards bought some for his wife, and
so did a couple of others. They paid me in clothes, some of
which fit, and those that didn't I was happy to stake and lose at
cards. It never hurts your popularity to lose at cards.

We had Sundays free. There was some worship but more drunkenness. The day I'm thinking of was a rainy day in July, which was the worst: hot and wet, and all of us stuck in our quarters making trouble. I lay on my bed, pretending to sleep, when a guard came in and called my name.

That wasn't in itself so unusual. From time to time people would be called out and told to bring their things. We didn't know where they got sent, but we mostly didn't see them again. No one ever refused, because of the chance you'd be made a guard.

I followed the man out, to where his companion was waiting, and the two of them led me to out of the palisade, the opposite way to when we went out to the fields. The gatekeepers let me through and frisked me in the lodge by the gate. By now my heart was hammering in my chest. I wasn't free, but I was breathing free air.

What had I expected? I don't know. But the place I saw was not different from countless others that I had seen in the north or that we had passed on the march there two years before. It was another abandoned town, emptied out and overgrown.

After about fifteen minutes we reached a street of bigger houses, and this time there were signs of life in them. The yards were better kept and curtains hung in the windows. There were dogs barking—but not wild dogs: dogs with collars and chains.

I knew of this place, because in winter some of the prisoners would be marched out here to shovel snow. It was where Boathwaite and the guards had their homes. And the rumored whorehouse was around here somewhere. This was the so-called town that our labor served.

The guards led me to the rear of the biggest house on the

street. It was ugly enough, built out of a kind of liverish brick, with no real shape to it, but it was a grand size, and big-boned.

I complimented one of the guards on the house, knowing it wasn't his but wondering what he would say.

He said nothing at all, just looked awkward, spat through his teeth, and scuffed it in with the toe of his boot.

"You're to work here this afternoon," said the other, cutting in to shut up any more of my questions.

I looked around the yard. It was unkempt and gloomy.

"What kind of work?" I asked.

"This garden. You're to make it like the one behind the barracks."

I kicked at the patchy turf. There was the makings of a lawn and some beds, but a lime tree at the far end was throwing shadow over the whole place. "It can't be done," I said. "It's too dark. The tree's robbing light. The best I could do would be to stick in a few bulbs, but there aren't any." It was the way I'd learned to be since coming in there: on principle, we dug our heels in when there was work to be done. I didn't want to let on what I was really feeling, standing on the brink of work I could do alone, and who knew what other privileges?

The lead guard said the other one would fetch me what I needed, so I told him to get me a rake, and a spade, and a barrow if he could find one.

The two of us waited about fifteen minutes until the other fellow showed up with a bunch of tools and a sack in place of a barrow, and I set to work.

•

From then on, my days took a whole different pattern. I worked with the prisoners in the morning, but two or three times a week the guards came in the afternoon to collect me for my work in the garden. The guards' names were Zhenia and Abelman. They watched over me while I was working, but though I was never entirely alone, it still felt like a taste of solitude.

Zhenia was the junior guard who was sent on errands and once in a while helped me wrangle a tree root out of the ground or carry cut branches while Abelman kept an eye on me. They were fierce and aloof inside the palisade, but once out they grew easier with me and occasionally made small talk about the weather or complimented my work. Abelman was a city fellow, but Zhenia was a country boy and he understood what I was doing.

My new duties also meant small freedoms inside the prison compound. I persuaded Abelman I needed a half-moon spade to edge the turf right. First it appeared there was no such thing to be had; then, when I drew him a sketch of what I wanted, he brought me one, but it had been badly made and broke apart the first time I used it. I showed him there was a cold shut in the blade and said that I could make a better one myself, if he would just let me into the smithy.

The smithy was outside the palisade and it was under constant watch because of what the prisoners could get up to there if they had a mind to.

It was a time before he gave me answer, but after a wait he came back with a yes.

From then on, I made my own tools when I needed them, and I enjoyed the work in the smithy almost as much as the solitary toil in the garden. I think, too, that the prison smiths, who were a kind of nobility among us, were impressed by the skills I had picked up from all those years swaging my own bullets, and their good opinion of me made life easier in the barracks.

I knew there would be less to do in the winter months, so I

saved myself jobs to last me through to spring: I talked them into letting me fell the lime, I cleared brush from around the edge of the garden, and I worked up tools for the planting season—anything to keep me out of the barracks and working on my own. The labor I spent on that garden kept me sane.

Now and again, while I was working there, I noticed someone in the house watching. I'd hear voices, too—women's voices, and the quick scattering sound of feet in the house. But the strangest thing was this: One day in the fall, when I had stayed longer than usual and I was gathering up my tools in the half-dark, I heard a humming sound. I turned around, and the windows of the house were blazing with yellow electric light.

In March the garden burst into life. It felt like winter had passed in a heartbeat. That was good for me, because spring meant more solitary work in the garden, but it made me think how things had altered.

Seeing the flowers in that garden bloom so early, and the trees bud so much sooner than they ought, it struck me that a change had happened deep down in the fiber of things, and it put me in mind of the Tungus, who said the world needs to sleep through the winter, or it wakes angry, like a shatoon, and tears up everything in its path.

•

Through spring and summer, I cut the grass of the lawn every other day with a push mower. It was old and rusty and the devil to roll. In the July heat, with all the bugs out, it was hard work, and I'd break from time to time to mop my face with a rag. It doesn't hurt me, but the salt in sweat makes my scarring flare up worse.

More and more, it was one or other of the guards, but not

both of them. Today it was Abelman, who I liked less, leaning up against the wall of the kitchen, his gun on his lap and using a twig to tease the housecat.

I heard the slap-bang of the screen door opening and suddenly Abelman shuffled to his feet, all simpering and friendly, like a dog that can smell sausages.

A little girl of about ten stood there in a blue check dress, holding a glass of water.

She handed me the glass. She was brave enough not to startle when she saw my face, but her hand shook a little as she lifted the glass, and something clinked in it.

"We've got a refrigerator," she said.

The water was almost too cold to drink. The ringing came from the ice cubes bobbling against the sides of the glass.

"Are you a boy or a girl?" she said.

I sipped the water. She was a pretty thing, not a tomboy like me. "I'm a girl," I said.

"What happened to your face?"

"Isn't it rude to be always asking questions?" I said.

"Do you want some more ice?"

"Yes, please."

She came back out of the house with a whole tray of ice cubes. I had to help her break them out of there. The metal was furred with ice crystals, and it stuck to the wet on my hand. When the cubes were free, she handed them to me and Abelman like candy. Abelman held his in his hand until they melted and dripped out.

A low woman's voice yelled through the screen door for Natasha to come back inside now. Natasha took the glass and the ice tray and skipped back into the house. "Bye, Natasha," Abelman called out in his sickly buttery voice.

When the door slapped shut for the last time, I turned to him. "Where do they get power for a refrigerator?" I asked. But he was back to fooling the cat again. There was no more butter in his voice and he threw my words back at me: "Isn't it rude to be always asking questions?"

•

The next time I came back, I saw they'd put a bench in the garden and hung a swing. Natasha came out to me that time carrying a bowl with something in it.

"I saved this for you," she said.

It was canned peaches, four slices of them. I grabbed a piece. The flesh wobbled like something living and naked.

She watched me eat it, the way you would if you'd brought home a wounded bird to feed and pet.

It was as gold as sunset and sweeter than honey. "Thank you," I said, and I wiped my fingers clean on my pant leg.

She giggled delightedly and ran back into the house. After that, she was always bringing me little things.

Another time when I was working in the heat, Abelman dropped off to sleep and began to snore. The first thing that went through my head was the thought of escape. I let my rake drop and walked toward the rear of the house to see if the road in front was clear both ways. I moved with that all-purpose prison shuffle, nothing urgent about it, but already my mind was haring off, figuring out if it would be possible to break off my chains, maybe steal a knife, hustle together enough food to start the long trek north, until I came level with the back of the house and I heard the tinkle of a child's laughter.

I followed the sound to the window and peered in: Natasha was sitting at the kitchen table with her hair wet and a sheet over her shoulders while her mother moved around her with a pair of scissors, snipping off a little here, a little there—tiny tufts like powder which she let fall to the floor. The mother had her back to me and I couldn't hear what they were saying, but every now and again it seemed like the two of them shared a joke, and one or other of them fell about laughing.

There was nothing special about the place. I mean, I must have been in fifty different kitchens in my life and all of them looked pretty much like that, but something about the scene just glued me there, until the next thing I knew, Abelman was pressing his piece in the small of my back and telling me to get back to work.

.

The next few times that Natasha came out to me, her mother hung back in the kitchen, just sticking her head round the door to call her daughter back in so I could get down to some work. But toward the end of summer, in late August, when most of the flowers had blown, she came out to visit with me in the garden.

She was a tall, lean, handsome woman, a little younger than me.

"Natasha and I are very grateful for the work you've done here," she said. "You've made this place beautiful."

I never count myself inferior to anyone, but something in me went squirming and servile while I was with her. I was conscious of my smell, and my filthy torn clothes, and the earth ground into my hands and fingernails—and there she was, all clean, and sweeter than a spray of apple blossom.

"Well, it's been its own reward," I said.

We were both stuck there for a while, her with a million questions that she didn't know how to ask, and me desperate to get back to my pruning—just so long as I didn't have to stand there, facing the ghost of what might have been, and mired in the shame of what I'd become.

I stared at the ground and watched her scrunching the long brown toes of her bare feet in the grass.

"Well, thank you again," she said finally, and went inside.

·

At reveille the next morning, I refused to move and stayed put in bed. Men had been flogged for less, but I told the guards it was my monthly time and for some reason this made them leave me be.

After lunch I went to the byre, and when Abelman came for me, I told him I didn't care what they did to me, but I wasn't doing any more gardening. He tried to talk me round, but I wasn't having any of it, so he went to get a couple more guards and they frog-marched me to a punishment cell and tossed me inside. I beat on the door for a while, and then I fell asleep. I didn't know what craziness had got into me.

It happened now and again that a kind of madness descended on a man and they would lock him up and beat him till his head went straight again. I was almost looking forward to their coming in, but when the door finally opened, who should walk in but Boathwaite himself.

Boathwaite signaled to the guard to help me to my feet and told me to follow him. He had a wide-kneed, horseman's swagger.

I went with him to a two-story building on the other side of the parade ground. Most of its windows still had their glass in them. "This used to be a military base," he said. "I expect you knew that."

His office was up on the second floor. It had a big desk at one end. A map hung on the wall behind his chair. I couldn't take my eyes off it. It was an old one, of the sort we'd had in school, with the western edge of Alaska in the top right corner, Kamchatka and the Kuriles below it, and the great mass of Asia running west to the Urals, and Europe beyond. The face of the world that must have once seemed as fixed and unalterable as the man in the moon himself. I could see the route we'd marched marked in blue ink. I'd guessed we weren't the first prisoners to make that journey. Elsewhere on the map, there were other inked corrections, place names in the Far North, and symbols which were too far away for me to read.

The walls on either side had red Circassian rugs hanging off them, and a bearskin. On his desk, Boathwaite had a kinzhal, a Cossack knife.

He offered me a smoke, and when I said no, he lit one himself. The smell of it was cedary, like pipe smoke. I noticed he had a brown stain on his finger from smoking so much of it.

"My wife is very happy with the way the garden turned out," he said. "She'll be sorry if you don't want to carry on your work."

"That's too bad," I said, "because I've lost the stomach for it."

•

So it was back to regular work with the others. I missed the garden. Sometimes, at night, while the place was settling down to its louse-ridden sleep, I'd picture it in my mind: the plants the way I'd last seen them, the hard yellow quinces that I'd mulched for compost, the damp cool of the lawn after rain. The other prisoners would have thought I was mad for giving it up. But I was happy never to be going back.

Facing that woman, I had felt like a beggar holding open the door of a restaurant for pennies and thank-yous. I hated the thought of them in the ease and calm of the garden I'd sweated to build, while I rotted in here, and Ping rotted, and they crunched ice cubes, willfully ignorant of us, living like beetles in this dung heap of a barracks.

Now I began to plan in earnest to escape.

4

I figured on breaking out come spring. Over December and January I traded most of my warm clothes with the other prisoners. I waited until the weather turned biting cold so I could fetch the best price for them. They paid me in the oddments that passed for currency in that place: smokes, drink, and bits of food. The random-seeming bits of trash we used to buy things from one another had a value that couldn't have been more fixed if they'd had price tags on them. So a foot cloth was worth two smokes, and a pair of woolen mittens would buy you a bottle of moonshine, and so on.

When I had amassed enough, I bribed the boss of the prison smithy, a fellow named Pankratov, to let me back in there for a week. They never let me forget I was the most junior and

I had to shovel charcoal and work the bellows, but it kept me out of the cold, and when it was quiet, I pulled little birds and flowers out of hot wire, which I sold cheaply to the guards for them to give their sweethearts.

That one week turned into two, and then three, and it looked like I might be there awhile, but a couple of the smiths got jealous over the trinkets I was making for the guards; and so, to keep the peace, Pankratov told me my time was up.

I missed the warmth, but my work was done. In between the fancy wirework, I had made pieces for a tiny grapple that I hid in my shoes while the guards were cooing over the little owls and forget-me-nots. I buried the pieces just inside the wall of the latrine.

The little that I earned from the guards, I traded for a pair of leather boots off one of the new arrivals. They were a little broken down from the marching, but I paid another prisoner to fix them.

A few of the old-timers said I was a fool to pay so dear for them this time of year. No amount of foot cloths could make them feel warm, they said.

These are the kind of things we talked about all the time. Every prisoner in that place was an expert on the tiny details that made our lives more bearable. In winter, every man who could get hold of them wore felt boots.

But I didn't have them in mind for winter wear. I needed shoes that would hold up for a thousand miles of wet spring walking.

•

I took half my bread away with me, morning and evening, as many of the prisoners did. But where they ate it or used it for swaps and card games, I dried mine in my bunk, and when it was hard, I took it out to the grain store and hid it in places I'd found under the eaves, hanging on nails or from wires so the mice couldn't reach it. I'd never done it myself before, but I'd heard you could make rusks this way. I stored it here and there, since if some were found, I'd still be left with the rest, and I thought I just needed enough to get me on my way.

Selling my warmest clothes left me underdressed for winter, and from eating less I grew weaker and my health suffered. Having once been one of the strongest there, I now began to fall sick with every fever that passed through the barracks.

The really ill were excused work and sent to the sick ward, but the place was so awful, and so full of consumptives, that most of us felt we were better off laboring through our fever.

One of the few signs of tenderness between us was that prisoners in the work gangs would notice a sick fellow among them and carry him through the day's labor. I'd done it often enough myself. We'd give the sick man the lightest bundles or, if we were working inside, let him rest on his feet leaning against the wall for as long as he could stay out of sight.

I say "tenderness," but it was no more than reason. Each of us knew that there'd come a time when we needed to redeem the favor.

The worst one swept through the barracks toward the end of January. I was wobbly at the early-morning milking. The men I was with put me down on a stool, and I began to shake with the almost pleasurable first shivers of a strong fever.

I was beside myself with the sickness. I seemed to be watching not Billy Erasmus, not Chingiz, not Gosha, carrying pails, but my mother and Charlo and Anna cooking Christmas dinner in the kitchen of our home. The light of the byre, which was so weak and watery, leaped up like a yellow flame, and there was a roaring heat all around me.

Gosha smiled at me. Makepeace is flying! She's been drinking. Look at her eyes!

I couldn't say anything, because the roar was deafening, and I recognized the sound: it was another plane coming. I stood up to tell them that we were all saved, and as I did, that yellow light turned blinding, and everything in front of my eyes melted into stars.

Gosha told me later that I went ghost-pale and fell to the floor with a crash that shook the walls. All I remember is things going dark and me worrying what would happen to all the bread that I'd hid.

•

I came to in the sick ward, soaked in sweat and raving to be let go. The place was dark and smelled like a butcher's. There were no guards posted. Because of the horror of the place, no one worked there and the sick were left to tend each other. As I soon as I was able to stand, I got up and left.

This time they took away my shoes to keep me put, but in the morning I stumbled out in the snow to reveille barefoot.

Boathwaite saw me this time. He had a word with one of the guards to keep me behind and give me my shoes back. I was too feverish to tie up my laces. One of my toes was white with frostbite. And when I walked, it felt like my limbs wouldn't move properly. They seemed to jerk forward in fits and starts like there was clockwork inside me.

I followed the guards, protesting to them all the way that I was well enough to work. But instead of leading me back to the sick ward, they took me to Boathwaite's office.

•

For winter, he had brought in a potbellied stove with a chimney that poked out of a broken window. It filled the room with a choking heat, but I was shivering so hard that my voice shook like a lamb's and my teeth seemed to rattle in my head.

One of the guards had come in with us and stood beside him at the desk.

"Seems you're determined to work," said Boathwaite.

"Yes, sir," I told him, trying to keep him level as the room danced around his head.

"You're sick," he said.

"Nothing too serious," I whispered between chattering teeth.

"Your winter clothes. What happened to them?"

"Gambling debts."

Boathwaite winked at the guard. "I heard you're none too good at cards." His voice echoed down to me, as though I was listening to him from the bottom of a well. "I heard you told the prisoners in the sick ward you got a plane coming for you. You planning to fly out of here?"

I shook my head.

"You ever even seen a plane, Makepeace?"

"No, sir. I must have been raving."

I thought then that perhaps my stash of bread had been found, or I'd blabbed about my plan to escape. In that case, they would certainly kill me.

"You're from the Far North, aren't you?"

"American, originally."

"Settler family?"

I told him yes.

"They tell me the settlers in the Far North are tougher than frozen mammoth shit," Boathwaite said, and the guard cackled.

I could barely hold my head straight. "I don't know about that," I said.

"Seems about right to me. Go get some rest," he said, and nodded to the guard.

I was too tired to fight. I barely understood what was happening. They hauled me down to the workshop and broke me out of my chains.

THREE

1

It was a couple of days before the change in my life began to make sense to me.

For the first time in almost three years I had a room to myself. My new quarters had a cot with a stained mattress, a tiny desk with an oil lamp, and a window that overlooked the parade ground. There were half a dozen streaks of brown on the ceiling above my head, each of them ending in a squashed mosquito carcass from the summer. There was no heat, but I had a pile of army blankets that stank of naphthalene.

Someone brought me food three times a day, and I sweated out my fever.

Part of me wanted to walk out the door right then, back

onto the highway, which was all silvered in the moonlight and would take me back the way I'd came. Likely as not, my house sat empty, with the pianola sagging to bits inside, and the dusty books and the bed frames. The garden would have seeded itself from old crops and grown straggly and wild. I had a hankering to be back there, in a place I knew well, among the memories of my loved ones.

But something more than the practical concern about the time of year and the provisioning for the journey kept me from leaving.

Out in the yard, the prisoners were crossing to their bunk-house.

In the twilight, you might almost think that I was looking out at the old world right here. There was a farm, and these were workers, idling in the cold night air in twos and threes on the other side of my filthy window.

One of them was Shamsudin. I knew him by his gait. None of the prisoners moved with urgency, but Shamsudin went especially slowly nowadays. Lately he'd begun to stoop a little too. He was one of the oldest at the base by now. This was our fourth winter in that place, heading into our fifth summer. We'd hadn't exchanged a word with one another for over a year.

The hard life at the base had aged him. I had noticed him working in the fields over the past months, resting on his shovel more often and breathing hard. There was a kind of defiant slowness in the way some of the younger guys worked, as though they were daring you to chivy them. But the older ones like Shamsudin worked slower because they were weakening, and they needed to conceal it. There was a casualness about the way they moved, but its root was deep fatigue. Sometimes you'd surprise one of the older ones where he wasn't expecting to be seen, flat on his ass behind a wall, legs splayed in front of him, his face slack with exhaustion and hollowed out like a corpse's.

There was no one in the base much past fifty. Disease and the foul weather tended to do for them after that. Even on the guards' side there wasn't much gray hair.

The oldest prisoners only had two hopes. One was that they would be made a guard, but it got less likely the older they became, and never happened at all if they were a muslim. The other was to find easier work in the Zone.

It was pitiful to see the effort they went to when they heard that a roundup of men was about to happen. They'd shave and comb their hair the night before. Once on old fellow they called Tuvik put on a fresh shirt he'd been saving somehow and pinned a bar of medals to it. He jutted his skinny jaw as the guards' eyes fell on him. They moved past without choosing him and his Adam's apple bobbed once or twice.

One of the half-Tungus prisoners teased him for it as we walked back to the hut. "Where did you steal those medals, Tuvik, you old thief?"

That was too much for Tuvik's wounded pride. "I fought two years in the Pacific war. I lived in a submarine and killed Japs and chinks like you with my bare hands!"

The Tungus boy laughed at him and fended off Tuvik's reedy forearms as he came to strike him. Tuvik's hands looked like bird claws in the boy's meaty brown fists.

The Tungus boy stole the medals that night and lost them the next day at cards. A week later, Tuvik died in his sleep.

It was the guards as much as anyone that fed our dreams of the Zone. When I was a prisoner, they'd drop casual remarks about what we'd find there. The refrigerators in the guards' village, the generators, our weapons—all of them were made there, they said. Someone even said they had a picture house.

I was curious to see it myself, but most of all I thought it would be good for Shamsudin to get there.

There was a growing sense of defeat about him. That day on the roof I had a glimpse of the man he might have been. Some of those others slipped into life at the base like they'd known no other—perhaps they hadn't, or known worse—but Shamsudin still carried about him some dignity, like a fading scent of the world he'd come out of.

It struck me that a man like Shamsudin would be welcomed in the Zone. He might have to do menial work at first, but any place with a little ambition would soon see the value of him, a man who had traveled and knew languages, who knew the name of every muscle in the human body. People like me were ten a penny in that place: practical, tough-minded ones who knew ways to grub in the tundra to stay alive. But Shamsudin had knowledge that could only be got from books. I couldn't say the use of all of it. Sometimes I know it seemed foolish and a little strange, like a silk tie round the necks of one of those prisoners. But what he knew had been thought precious by people who knew more than we did. What he had in his head had been hoarded up over centuries. It was precious enough for blood to be spilled over it. It took a thousand years of study for him to know the things he did—a thousand years of science and testing and people prepared to die to say the earth went round the sun and not the other way around. And once it was lost, it would take another thousand years to learn it again.

It made me sad to see him weakening. He seemed to go into himself and spend less time with the other muslims. I wished I could take him out of that place somehow. He reminded me of one those books that I used to hide in the armory. Only a person is always better than a book.

So at the back of my mind was the thought of the good I

might be able to do for him. And the good that could be done if I could find a way to link him up with the people in the plane.

The way things looked, he had at most two years to live. Perhaps less. Sooner or later he'd wind up in the clearing where they'd put Tuvik.

Each autumn before the ground froze, the guards marched half a dozen prisoners out to the woods to dig a deep hole. Come the thaw, they marched them out again to put the earth back over the fifteen or twenty bodies that had been dumped there over the winter. There was no ceremony to the burials. A couple of guards would slip the body into a sack and haul it out on a cart, toss it in the hole, and throw powdered lime on it. It waited there uncovered until the next one.

Weighing it up in my heart, it felt like I had a duty to do right by Shamsudin. There are reasons behind reasons, of course, and if you go into them too deeply, you end up tripping over yourself. Looking back at it now, I see I had some kind of feelings for him, since he was the first person to show me an ounce of kindness since Ping. And he had a way about him that reminded me of my father, I think, and I wonder if maybe I was trying to go back and save *him*. But if I search behind that, I come up against a plainer reason: since Ping died, it felt like I had lost the knack for being alone.

When I was a child, there was an old man in the woods who lived alone, miles from anyone, who we were warned from visiting. He was a Russian called Pankov who did big wooden carvings that he stood in his yard. We would sneak over to spy on him, and he would yell and chase us away if he caught us there. Being children, that was sport to us. "Madder than an outhouse rat," my father called him, and he slippered us when Charlo blurted out that we'd been over there.

Pankov died when I was about twelve, and a party of elders

from our town buried him in his yard. The hut he'd lived in fell a little more apart each year after that until it was all flattened, as though something big had sat on it.

I went there once or twice in the years that followed. Pankov had sculpted whole tree trunks into big, busy columns of snakes, and demons, and wriggling, bosomy women, that the elders politely ignored when they went to inter him.

Whatever had flattened the house—snow? woodworm?— had scattered its contents around the yard. And amid all the stuff you'd expect—torn bedsheets, candlesticks, moldy shoes, broken glass—was page upon page of musical scores, piles of them, with their pretty lines and black dots. What must they have meant to him that he went to the trouble of carrying all that paper out there with him, and keeping it, year after year, where there was no one to share it with—not an instrument, only the silence, and the little creaks and whirs of his own body failing bit by bit?

I didn't want to be like Pankov, sitting out years like a man in a waiting room, marking time until the fall that killed me, or the accident that left me unable to feed myself. But I could see how I might end up that way. Between the world of my youth, and the world I was in now, was a gap so big, I was finding it harder and harder to cross it even in my imagination.

Had I dreamed a world where people flew, and food was plentiful, and we, the settlers in the north, were seen as primitives?

Life in the base gave you all the evidence you needed of men's beastliness. And yet, looking back on long passages of my life, it felt like it was the solitary parts of it that made the least sense.

2

When I was strong enough, I took my meals in the guards' mess, where they served meat and some kind of almost-coffee alongside the things they gave the prisoners. The other guards seemed less surprised by Boathwaite's raising me up than I was.

It wasn't the paradise the prisoners imagined, but we had better food, and solitude. Strangely, there was a wariness among the guards themselves that I couldn't fathom. They had a few things: a steam bath, a little store where we could buy stuff with paper tickets. And there was indeed a whorehouse. I never had need of it, and even to look at the women on the stoop in daytime, chattering and brushing their hair out, put me too much in mind of Ping.

We all lived within the base, but there was a higher order of guard who lived in the village. Some of them had taken wives and settled down.

I hadn't changed my intention of slipping out of that place in the spring. In fact, now it would be easier. I had a greasy old sidearm they'd given me with a couple of bullets in it. And I knew where I could probably steal a horse. But there was something I wanted to attend to first.

.

In February, Boathwaite called a few of us together and told us he was sending a detachment of men to work in the Zone. There would be ten guards escorting them, and I would be one of them. The Russian called Tolya who acted as Boathwaite's deputy at the base was leading the party. He had been to the Zone many times. Of the nine others in the party, four including myself had never been there before, but even among the guards it wasn't the style to seem too curious or ask too many questions. We acted like it was the most normal thing in the world and we just did what the others did.

At the morning lineup, each of us picked two men from the prisoners in the yard.

The experienced guards went to some trouble to choose the strongest men, feeling through their clothes for muscles and checking their eyes for clearness.

When it was my turn, I went slowly along the line, trying not to dwell on the desperation in the faces of the men in front of me, acting like I was sizing them up. It was strange how different they looked at me, now I had some power over them. I dithered for a while to make it seem that I was weighing up my choices, then I nodded at Shamsudin and Zulfugar to step out of the line.

•

The prisoners who had been chosen were allowed to fall out and given two minutes to collect their things from the huts. They regrouped on the parade ground and four of us marched them out, all twenty of them, through the central gate of the base, across the clearing around it, and into a low two-story building that stood on the fringe of the guard's village. There were two big rooms on the lower floor. One was a refectory where they were served the same food as the guards got, only a little colder because it had to be carried over there. Next to it was a sleeping room with bunks that were sprung and more generous than the ones at the base.

For the next two hours they ate and were allowed to exercise out in the clearing. It was unaccustomed freedom to all of them. Next to being made a guard, it was the best that any of them could have hoped for. Most didn't try to hide their delight at being chosen.

It was unseasonally warm and bright. Just for a moment, the idea that some of us were prisoners and some guards seemed to fade. I was filled with a rare hope. From here to the Zone seemed like an easy step. I had no fixed notion of the future, but I could feel its shape, and for once it seemed like it wasn't a thing to be dreaded.

Shamsudin stood alone, eyes shut, face into the sun, his shoulders rising and falling with his breathing. At the edge of the clearing, the sunshine had melted the thin snow cover under the trees. Zulfugar squatted down in a mess of fallen oak leaves and dug at something with a stick.

He looked up and saw me watching and waved me over with his free hand. Just as I got to him, he yanked something out of the ground.

In his hand was a warty black ball about the size of a walnut. He held it out to me.

I took it from him. It was hard and somewhat like a nutmeg to touch. Zulfugar motioned me to smell it. *"Al-kamat,"* he said. "The prophet said it is good for the eyes." There was a glint of his gold teeth as he smiled.

Suddenly there was a shout behind me and something banged my arm. One of the other guards had charged past and shouldered Zulfugar to the ground. Zulfugar lay on his back in the leaves, looking puzzled. Two other guards had pinned him down with the muzzles of their guns and were shouting, "What's he got?"

"It's a mushroom," I said, "and by the smell of it, a damn good one."

"Yes," said Zulfugar. "Mushroom."

The guards let him up slowly. He dusted the damp leaves off his pants.

"For you, Makepeace." He walked back shakily to the other prisoners.

•

Around mid-morning, we took them back to their quarters and led them into the upper room. Boathwaite was waiting for us. The prisoners sat on the floor cross-legged like schoolchildren.

"All first-timers?" he said to Tolya. Tolya nodded.

"Now listen up. It's a privilege to be chosen for the Zone, as you know. I gather that some of you are already getting the idea. You share what you bring out. Those who picked you are entitled to half of your labor."

A couple of the guards chuckled, understanding him to be making a dig about the mushroom that had almost got Zulfugar killed.

It was beginning to dawn on me how some of them were able to live so well, with houses off the base, and wives. If you had enough workers in the Zone, it could make you a rich man. It was like what Boathwaite was doing, but on a smaller scale.

"Joking aside, this isn't easy work," Boathwaite went on. "I'm not going to bullshit you. Working in the Zone isn't heavy or backbreaking, and it brings plenty of rewards, but it's dangerous in other ways. The men who picked you chose you because they figured you'd have the smarts to use common sense, do what we say, and not get sick.

"You work a ten-day stretch and then you will be allowed a number of rest days back here. The harder you work, the more rest days you get. And for the best workers, there are privileges.

"I'm going to let Mr. Apofagato explain in detail what those duties involve."

Mr. Apofagato had jet-black hair and wore thick eyeglasses that fastened right round his head like welder's goggles. I couldn't place his accent, but I can tell you that he didn't grow up speaking English.

"Zone big," said Mr. Apofagato, slapping his hand on a wall map. "Almost four hundred square kilometers. Right here not Zone. Zone start far side of river. But not all contaminated. Your duties: mine objects. What objects? These."

He unrolled a handwritten chart and tacked it over the map. It showed about a dozen different objects, all carefully drawn in colored ink, and rough measurements around them. Some of them were familiar to me—electrical batteries, something like a wireless—but the others looked like nothing I had ever seen.

The guards around the room handed out sheets of square paper and pencils.

"Copy pictures," said Mr. Apofagato.

They did as they were told. Most of them weren't much for

artwork, and when Mr. Apofagato came round to check them, he tutted at their drawings and told them, "Write serial numbers; serial numbers important."

Shamsudin's surgeon's fingers made fine copies that were crosshatched to show shading and got Mr. Apofagato clucking with approval.

When the copies had been made, we took away their pencils, and Mr. Apofagato unrolled a smaller city map.

"Many sectors in Zone. This your sector. Mining these locations. Okay? Now copy map. Copy locations."

When they were done, he scrutinized their work again, then reached into the pocket of his trousers and pulled out a fistful of plastic discs. "Now very important. These dosimeters. Very important know your dose. When return Zone, give dosimeters, we calculate dose, can give medicine if high dose. Your health very important to us. You are valuable people." This last sentence he said with a weird high laugh as he handed round the plastic discs and supervised pinning them to their dirty lapels. "Any questions?"

"What kind of privileges do we get?" asked one of the prisoners.

Boathwaite stood up. "You get credits that you can exchange for extra food and alcohol."

Shamsudin raised his hand. "How do these dosimeters work?"

"Reactive film," said Mr. Apofagato.

Shamsudin raised his hand again. "If you know what we're looking for, and you know where it is, why don't you get it yourself?"

Mr. Apofagato's face wore a big smile as he answered, "Not my duties."

"Mr. Apofagato is doing valuable work here," said Boath-waite. "Now, take your notes and your dosimeters and go to the canteen. You have the rest of the day free. You'll be leaving for the Zone at first light."

Shamsudin and Zulfugar seemed uneasy to me, but the others swabbed their plates with hunks of bread and asked for seconds of meat stew, pointing at their blue dosimeter badges and saying, "I am valuable person."

3

We mustered at dawn by the gates. There were a dozen horses, and several sleds for bringing back what we found. They gave me an old rifle, some shells for it, a decent fur hat, and another set of clothes. It was army-issue gear, never worn, stiff and stale with the smell of potatoes. The gun wasn't much to speak of either, but in a pinch I could probably club somebody with it. We weren't given any advice on how to guard those who'd once been our fellows.

One of the prisoners was called Felix and he had a fine singing voice. His voice rang like a bell on the high notes as we rode through the thin light of daybreak.

My horse was the slowest of the bunch, so I ended up at the back with Zulfugar and Shamsudin.

They seemed glum to me, in spite of the good food and the mood of hopefulness among the other prisoners.

At one of the water stops I took the two of them aside and asked what was bothering them. Zulfugar wouldn't say.

"He opened his badge," said Shamsudin. "There was nothing inside it. Just plastic. All that talk of privileges and rest days were just lies to make us drink poison."

I asked Zulfugar if it was true. In answer, he yanked off his badge, smashed it under his heel, and showed me the innards, empty as a bad nut.

We were talking in low voices. I guess we all thought that if he had rumbled some deception, he would most likely be shot for it.

"Let me get you another of those," I said, and I called to Tolya that one of the prisoners had lost his magic badge.

His reaction confirmed their fears. He rode over to us and, instead of slapping Zulfugar's head or punishing him for losing it, reached into his pack, pulled out another, and made a great play of pinning it on him. It was like watching a magic trick you've figured out. Try as he might to misdirect you, the magician can't shake your eyes off the card that he's palmed or the rabbit twitching in the false bottom of his hat.

Zulfugar thanked him, but as we moved off once more, his eyes reproached me and he spat into the snow.

·

I had misgivings about the lies. It made me wonder where on earth we were headed. I was worried for Shamsudin and Zulfugar. And yet, the movement itself felt good to me.

The road to the Zone was the old highway to Yakutsk, bearing due north until it met the Lena River and petered out in a splash of rutted gravel. From then on it was a winter road. In the old days, the winter roads were prepared and smoothed as the cold set in, but nowadays we had to take them as we found them. They could be treacherous going and in places sometimes they didn't freeze properly because of hot springs near them, or the general warming, or in sections where the river narrowed and the water surged too fast to be held by the cold.

For days at a time, we had to turn off the Lena and make our way through the taiga. Then it was slow traveling, working our way through snow, until the ice on the river was strong enough to carry us again.

As we drew closer to the arctic circle, the ice on the river thinned once more and we had to turn back into the taiga for the last push north.

We shared rations with the prisoners and kept an easy pace. It was the closest thing to fraternal I'd seen in my days at the base. All the same, there was something that grew heavy and joyless in the mood of the prisoners as we made our progress north.

Usually you couldn't stop those fellows chatting. Now there seemed to be hours of silence, broken only by the clink of chains and bridles and the crunch of snow.

Every time we stopped to make camp, Tolya pulled a cerberus from his saddlebag and pointed it around the place. He had brought two of them. Once or twice he gave me one to use on the firewood before we lit it to make sure it was clean.

I'd never held one before. It was about the size of a sidearm but dense and top-heavy, with a dial in the top of it and a couple of wires sticking out the back. I got a thrill from using it, but it spooked the prisoners, especially when it gave out a noise.

Most of the trees were clean and safe to use, but there were copses of them that made the cerberus chirrup. It was the same as at Buktygachak: Poison had got into the fiber of things. Radiation had blown this way across the land. The trees had leached it up from the soil. It was locked into them, for now, but breathing their smoke would burn your throat and bray the inside of your lungs to mush. Whatever grew out of the soil there would harm you if you ate it. And any creatures that fed there would be poisoned too. One day, that place will be clean again, but it will be long after my lifetime.

·

Two nights after we left the Lena, we were woken by the smell of smoke and the crackle of woods blazing. We'd camped in the lee of a stand of trees.

That night there had been long discussions between Tolya and one of the other guards, a man named Victor. It seemed that one of them wasn't too keen on the place. We camped there anyway, but we gathered the firewood from further away.

When he saw the flames in the darkness, Tolya straight out panicked. His cerberus was going crazy from the smoke, howling and wailing like a beast in a trap.

The prisoners were up and panicking, too, shouting about being poisoned.

We struck camp then and there in the darkness, moving out of the path of the smoke, and traveling north, until at daybreak the burning forest was behind us and its coils of black smoke formed a huge cloud in back of us with a flat top like an anvil.

The faces of the prisoners looked bloodless and drained in the half-light from bad sleep and fatigue, so we stopped and rested for the remaining daylight hours.

The mood in the camp that night was sour as wormwood.

Tolya split the guards at daybreak and rode back with half of them to find out who had set the fire. They rode the long way round, staying away from the gray banner of the poisoned smoke.

I stayed back with the prisoners. Tolya had left me the spare cerberus for finding firewood. I went with Shamsudin and Zulfugar to get it.

I took them further from the camp than we needed so as to be more private.

Watching the two of them sweat over the saw, and sweat again as they loaded up the sled, I felt a little bad inside myself. Because of me they'd been dragged out of the warm on a lie to face who knew what?

I swung down off the horse. She nuzzled a tuft of grass at the foot of the tree. I looped the reins round a branch so she wouldn't go off and eat the dirty stuff.

Zulfugar had walked a little apart and was breaking branches for kindling off a dead birch. I went over to speak to Shamsudin.

He was working with a hand axe, stripping logs so they'd sit more easy in the sled. I hauled a couple of pieces alongside him, and I told him that I was sorry he'd been deceived, that I knew as little as he did, and that I gave him word that I would let nothing bad happen to him.

"That's not in your power," he said.

I didn't disagree, but I was thinking to myself that with a couple more horses we could all three of us get clean out of there before Tolya returned with the other guards.

Life at the base depended on separating the guards from the prisoners by the fact of their privilege. I wanted to tell Shamsudin that Boathwaite hadn't been able to buy my loyalty with the promise of a whorehouse and coffee made out of dandelion roots.

He dumped a load of wood with a crash onto the sled. "Zulfugar says there is a plague city north of here. He says we are being sent as grave robbers to steal from the dead."

"How does he know a thing like that?" I said. It sounded like it might be true, but it also sounded like the kind of wild rumor that the men liked to scare each other with. There was a kind of prestige attached to being the man with the darkest view of Boathwaite's motives.

I bent to pick up a stray branch and I found myself sliding backwards. The treads of my leather boots had filled with snow that spread out in a pancake of ice around my feet and wouldn't bite. I fell forward onto my front into the snow, almost laughing at myself because the fall was comical.

Shamsudin drew nearer and I thought he was going to offer to help me lift myself up out of the deep snow, but then I saw the hand axe glint by his side, and instead of laughter in his eyes there was something deadly serious.

I could never hate him for it. He had the look of a hungry dog measuring the length of his chain against the distance of a juicy bone, wondering if he was about to feed or choke himself.

He took one step forward. I had fallen awkwardly and my gun sat under me, so that I would need to wriggle to get it free—and even then, there was a chance it would fail to fire and he could brain me. I wonder what restrained him for those seconds. I'd like to think it was his affection for me, his decency, maybe his religion, or his training as a doctor: "First, do no harm," they say. Maybe running it through his mind gave him second thoughts and his intelligence got the better of him: the two of them, one horse, no easy way to break their shackles. Maybe he just lacked courage.

Shamsudin was the kind of man the old world must have turned out in millions: smart and charming, but with such a

slim connection between him and the earth. He had more stuff
in him than a book does, and if you cared to listen, he had a better sense than most how we'd ended up in this world; but still, a
beast like Hansom was better able to live in it. Those soft hands
delayed a moment too long. And then Zulfugar was back, panting and tugging his load of branches, and Shamsudin looked
aside like a guilty thing. And in that second I rolled over and
freed my sidearm.

Shamsudin raised his arms over his head. I wagged the gun
at the two of them. "Get this thing loaded up," I said. A glance
passed between them. There was an after-smell of danger in
the air.

We went back in silence.

.

Tolya rode back into the camp late that afternoon with a Tungus boy stumbling along behind him, his wrists tied and roped
to Tolya's saddle. One of the boy's eyes was puffy and closed, and
he had dried blood in his nostrils. He looked to be no more than
fourteen.

"This is who set the fire," Tolya said.

The guards circled the boy. He trembled as they looked at
him, his eyes cast down at his ragged fur boots, which were held
together with strands of rawhide. Everything he wore seemed
on the brink of falling apart. He reeked of wood smoke and his
face was blotchy with smuts. He called to mind a tiny mouse
that might die of fear in your hand if you picked him up.

Tolya cuffed the boy round his head and the others set on
him with kicks and blows.

He let himself be hit, standing listless and soft—whether
from real hopelessness or because he was smart enough not to
stiffen at the punches, I couldn't say. After a few heavy shots, he

flopped into the snow. His greasy shapka plopped down a little farther off.

The men beat him for a while. What is it about a prone body that makes men so murderous? Lucky for him, the snow where he fell was deep, and their felt boots muffled their blows. Also, unlike the prisoners, the guards were fat and idle, and they got tired after a minute or two of wading and kicking in the deep snow.

They left him and stood cursing and catching their breath. Tolya explained that the boy had been smoking meat in the forest at a little camp of his own that had been all burned out, and by the looks of things he'd been there months at least.

I picked up his hat with the barrel of my gun and dropped it closer to him. It didn't do to look too tenderhearted in front of those men, but I felt pity for the poor creature. I crouched down and spoke to him the few words of Tungus that I knew. He lay curled up in a ball and didn't even raise his head to meet my glance. He was dazed and it seemed like his nose was broken. There was a spray of blood and dribble around his mouth. I couldn't help thinking of Ping. It seemed like every encounter with a stranger spelled death or injury to someone.

Tolya and one of the guards called Stepan came up close behind me and asked what I was saying to him.

I told them they were fools for knocking him silly, because now we'd never get sense out of him. Stepan said he'd make him understand and shook him and yelled questions at him: Where are you from? Where are your friends hiding at? Who are you spying for?

This Stepan wasn't a bad sort, but like the others he was scared. Outside of the base, they knew nothing of the land they lived in, and their imagination peopled the place with monsters.

Here, only a few hundred miles north of where they lived, they felt as far from home and as uneasy about it as if we were on the moon.

One of the guards said to be careful because he might be a Wild Boy. Some of these Wild Boys lacked speech, he said, and ate meat raw, and some of them walked on all fours and could take out your throat with their bare teeth if they had a mind to.

I almost laughed in his face. I've been all over the Far North, and if there are such things as Wild Boys, I ought to have seen at least one of them.

It seemed clear to me the boy was simpleminded. So I said to them that that he was an idiot and that it would be bad luck to harm him. There wasn't much that they held sacred, but anything in the way of a superstition had a lot of power over them. They were apt to believe all sorts of nonsense about charms, and omens, and black magic.

They kept him tied, but they let him be after that.

When evening came we ate dried meat and bread we had brought with us, on account of the radiation in the game. The guards threw scraps to the boy, which he ate as he sat and rocked on his haunches.

At nightfall he crawled under a caribou skin beside the fire and fell asleep.

•

That night the stars were bright as anything. There were wisps of silver fog above the trees, and still the smoke rose from the burned forest.

I watched my breath rise up into the clear sky. The stars once had names, every one, and once shone down like the lights of a familiar city, but each day they grew a little stranger. I knew the polestar and the Dipper to travel by, and I'd had the others explained to me over the years, but was that the Great Bear or Arcturus? Andromeda or Orion's belt? Could you see Venus this far north in January?

The sky was becoming a page of lost language. Things as a race we'd witnessed and named forever were being blotted out of existence.

Once these rivers all had names—the hills, too, maybe even the smaller dinks and folds in the pattern of the landscape.

This was a place once, I thought.

We had been so prodigal with our race's hard-won knowledge. All those tiny facts inched up from the dirt. The names of plants and metals, stones, animals, and birds; the motion of the planets and the waves. All of it fading to nothing, like the words of a vital message some fool had laundered with his pants and brought out all garbled.

Here we were, within a day of the Zone, getting ready to filch from dirty land the things we no longer had the wit or means to make. And when the Zone was exhausted, we would be lucky to be this boy, stalking poisoned animals in a forest we could no longer name. He was our best possible future.

I lay down to sleep thinking that as much as I missed what was gone, maybe this was the best thing: for the world to lie fallow for a couple hundred years or more, for the rain to wash her clean. We'd become another layer of her history, a little higher in the soil than the Romans and the people that built the pyramids. Yes, Makepeace, I thought, maybe one day your mandible will show up under glass in a museum. Female of European origin. Note the worn incisors and the evidence of mineral deficiency from a poor and unvaried diet. Warlike and savage. And beside it some potsherds.

In the long run, the waters recede, the sun rises, and plants grow. I've never doubted that something will survive of us. Of course, I won't make it. And all those books I saved will end up mulch and birds' nests, I suppose.

But something will go on. It just gives me no comfort when I imagine the day when the deluge has finally passed, and the dark, slippery, once-human things that will be waiting to hatch out of the ark.

4

We were off and moving at daybreak, the clouds above us a mass of black and red. I don't know if it was the mood among us that morning, or the dead silence of that poisoned land, but I felt a deep misgiving about where we were headed.

I was afraid Tolya would kill the boy to save the trouble of keeping him, so I took charge of him and let him amble in back of me. He was docile like a herd animal and seemed to want nothing more than to trot behind my horse and share my water.

For two hours until mid-morning we made a long, slow pull up to the shoulder of a low hill. The boy and me were the last to get there. We found the others had stopped and were gazing out at the vista in the next valley.

It was the ruins of a city, and not a city like mine, with its middling houses dwarfed by the water tower, but a city of glass and concrete, with buildings that soared into the sky, and a bridge that spanned a wide, fast-moving section of the river. The city was still and gray, and birds wheeled over its silent streets.

The prisoners were staring, too, though some had taken the chance to gulp water or chew on the bread they'd been given. Tolya had a spyglass, and he passed it among us.

Through Tolya's glass, the city looked like a mouthful of rotten teeth, its buildings and windows hollowed out and lifeless, but its size was awesome. Way in back, on a rise in the rear of the city, was a tower that must have been a hundred yards high. It looked too spindly to stand without blowing over, and yet on top of it was a big disc with windows all around it that seemed to perch there in defiance of the laws of nature.

Over on the most eastern bend of the river, three chimneys, each of them painted in red and white stripes, rose from a vast square box. The building crouched at the water's edge, and from it sprang a net of wires that were carried on steel legs to the farther side of the river and fanned out beyond it into the distance.

After we'd rested, we descended to the edge of river and made our way along its bank to the bridge.

It took us maybe forty-five minutes to get there. Our pace slowed as we got closer. Not that we were fearful, but there was so much to take in. Every man's head was craning this way and that, drinking in the details. The prisoners who were going to go right to the heart of it seemed almost excited.

The riverbanks were lined with concrete slabs which had narrowed its original course. That was why, even in February, it hadn't frozen hard.

Beyond it, on the far side, those towers rose up. You had to wonder how many thousands of people might have lived here when the place was alive. And you had to wonder, too, how many thousands of places like this might have been built the world over. In the old days, at night, men in planes must have been able to see a city like this from the air, sketched out by the lines of its streetlights and the glow of its lit windows.

It struck me that my plane had gone out from a city much like this one—God knows, even bigger than this one—a place that had kept its knowledge and customs, a place where each person woke up each day to add their piece to the whole sum of endeavor that had been going on since who knew when, instead of waking up each day like Adam and having to feed and clothe yourself from the garden and think up names for the trees.

.

We only went midway across the bridge to where an empty block post divided the highway. There were rolls of rusting barbed wire scattered around it across the snow. That's where we were to separate. The prisoners were to go on without us. They were chattering like children. One of them peed off the side of the bridge, just for the novelty of it, his piss arcing and then breaking into fine spray before it reached the concrete supports below.

As we stood and watched, they went on, passing the central span of the bridge and moving leisurely forward, like a congregation taking their seats at a funeral. At that moment I envied them for what they'd find.

I feel awe and wonder at the lights, for instance, but I know it's nature's work. Standing on the bridge, looking across at that empty city, everything in the compass of my gaze had been set there by a human hand. Somehow those pylons had been strung with wire, and those towers raised, and roofs tiled. There had been food and drink for millions of mouths. I don't cry easy, but my vision blurred as I stared on the ruins of what we had been, and I watched the small band of men in rags move toward it to pick at it like birds on the carcass of some giant.

They'd entered a patch of waste ground at the other end of the bridge where the road split three ways—one each way along the riverbank, and a third that went on into the heart of the city, bearing right down a boulevard that was lined with tall, blighted chestnut trees.

A couple of them hunkered down on their haunches while they considered what to do next. That unfamiliar feeling they had—no one breathing down their neck, all that space around them—must have given them an inkling of freedom.

The guards whistled at them and Tolya shook his gun and shouted at them to get along. He told them we'd be waiting for them at the same place in twenty-four hours.

Gradually they moved off down the road in the middle, until pretty soon they were out of sight and only a few clouds of frozen breath hung in the air to tell you that anyone had passed that way.

Tolya stood watching them, almost motionless, just a couple of little bumps flexing on each side of his jaw as he clenched and unclenched his teeth.

Once the prisoners were out of sight, he was extra friendly to us. He pulled out cans of meat from one of his bags, some bottles of spirit from the still at the base, and a loaf of bread. There were ten cans and only eight of us, so he gave one of the tins to the Tungus boy. A couple of the guards weren't keen on eating something so old, but when they saw the rest of us tucking in, and smelled that it was still good, they ate theirs up. The Tungus boy could only manage a little of his.

It was some kind of meat in jelly and it wasn't to my taste, either, but this didn't seem the time to get finicky.

Tolya let a little spirit spill onto the snow and then poured the rest into the tin cups each man had brought with him. To the Zone, he said, and they all drank to the bottom and sniffed their chunks of bread to take the taste away.

I put my cup down without tasting it, which a couple of them didn't like. That was held to be bad luck, too—as was toasting with an empty cup, or leaving an empty bottle upright, or eating where you can see into a mirror, and too many others to list.

Stepan chided me and called for my cup to be filled. His cheeks were greasy from the canned fat and his eyes had lit up from the drinking.

I covered the cup with my hand so they couldn't add more, but I drank what I had so as to be comradely. It was the first time I'd touched alcohol for years.

They didn't offer the boy any drink, though. It was too precious to be wasted on him.

When Tolya pulled out the second bottle, I decided I didn't want to stick around there, either, drinking myself or watching them get drunk. I got to my feet and dusted the snow off my pants.

"Where are you off to?" Tolya asked.

I explained that I wanted to cross the bridge and take a look round.

Tolya came apart from the others with me a little way and said not to go deeper than fifty yards on the other side. Something in his voice made me go suddenly alert. I wished I hadn't had that drink.

There was the first notion of evening in the sky: the gray was heavier above us, and the shadows longer. We were standing out of earshot of the rest of them.

Tolya put his arm over my shoulders and turned me toward the far side of the bridge—not roughly, but forcefully enough that I knew he was serious. He pointed at a pair of lampposts on either side of the road to the downtown. "If you go any further than those, I can't take you back with you us. Do you understand?"

There was a peal of laughter from the huddle of men drinking.

He lowered his voice and his fingers gripped tight on the meat of my arm. "The city's poisoned," he said. "No one leaves the Zone."

I said that that was pretty harsh on the boys we'd sent in there.

He said nothing. It seemed like he had enough left in him of the old life to feel guilty about it. You could see he didn't like what he'd been sent to do, but still, he was one of those lucky enough to make his own destiny, unlike the prisoners.

Stepan yelled at us to come back and join them.

I jerked my head toward the little drinking party behind us on the apron of the bridge. "Do they know what you've got planned?"

"The ones who have been in before do. The others, not yet."

I guess something in my face betrayed what I was I feeling.

"Some are damned and some are saved," he said. "Be glad you're one of the saved."

Then he let my arm go and turned back to the others. He

sang a dirty ballad in Russian and made a show of being light-hearted so as not jar the mood in the gathering. Their jokes and oaths followed me across the bridge.

I stepped over the concrete divider. The wind had swept the top of the camber clean of snow, and where it had drifted, it had been chased into curling shapes. Here and there, the prisoners' feet had burst through the crust on top leaving tracks that were more like passing hooves than feet.

Be glad you're one of the saved.

I'd been saved to see this, I thought: a city stripped of life but kept intact by the power of the poison that had been spread on it; a dead place, but one that by its size and wealth might as well have been built by gods as men; a place that made a mock-ery of our patched clothes and our scavenged food. What kind of salvation was this?

·

I walked as far as the end of the bridge. Where I'd thought the prisoners had been resting, they'd been squatting. I suppose they were afraid to seek a more sheltered place, given the radiation they'd been warned about, but there was also something about the vastness of the city that made itself felt in your bowels. The few times I had to investigate a robbery—when robbery was thing to be concerned about—the robbers had shat right in the open of the house they were stealing from. It looks like a ges-ture of contempt, but it was the fear and excitement of doing the crime that made them need to void themselves. And so with the robbers we'd sent. They'd fouled the streets of this once-dainty, once-plumbed city.

Their tracks led up the central avenue to wherever Apofa-gato's map told them they should be heading. The trees and the big brick mansions crowded out the light, but fifty yards further on there was a break in the buildings, and the street lit up again. I could just make out furniture—chairs, tables, a dresser with its drawers gone—lying on its side in the snow, where it had spilled out of one of the buildings like the innards of a slaughtered animal. Much nearer than that, practically on the street corner, was a circular kiosk with some kind of posters glued to it that were too faint and far for me to read. I wished I'd had Tolya's spyglass with me. Just as much as the paved road and the tall buildings, the tiny details of the posters and the work they'd demanded—paper, ink, a press, gummed brushes—told a story about abundance and persistent antlike industry.

.

By the time I got back to the others, the drinking had made them mellow.

They wanted to know what I'd seen, so I told them about the size of the city. From their curiosity and easy laughter, it seemed that Tolya hadn't broken it to them yet that he intended us to kill the prisoners.

Hearing about the boulevards, and the furniture on the sidewalk, and the posters, they became reflective and one or two of them expressed a wish to see it, too, but Tolya told them it was already too dark and pulled out another bottle.

This one made them talkative, and they started to do a thing men rarely did in the camp unless you knew them very well: they talked about where they were from, their families, and their past lives.

Between them, they'd seen a lot of war and trouble. Exactly half of them had been soldiers of one kind or another. That was often the way of things. It seemed like the routine of soldiering fitted a man pretty well for life in the base.

One called Osip said his father had been an engineer and that he'd been him with once to Paris. That seized all our imaginations. It sounded like the most exotic place there was, and the other guards had a million questions about the food and the weather and the women. But when they pressed him on it, he didn't seem to know anything more about the place than the rest of us, or than someone could have got out of a book. He spoke in a tongue he claimed was French, but it could have been anything, for all we knew.

Stepan said he'd been in a plane as a child and visited the Black Sea. He said the water was warm as a bath. He said there were fields of vines as far as the eye could see. About flying, he couldn't remember anything except that it had made his ears hurt.

Tolya had been trained for the priesthood. He had been to an Orthodox seminary in the West and then sent to his own church in the Buryat region. He said his parishioners had been without a priest for so long, they did all his cooking and cleaning for him. He lived like a lord and spent most of his spare time painting icons.

He reached into his jacket and pulled out a leather pouch with a tiny portrait in it which he said was his own work. It went round the group, just like the bottle had, from hand to hand.

It was a Mary and Child, painted tiny as can be. Osip held it for a long while it and he actually kissed its tin frame before he passed it to me to have a look.

The icon itself was no more than two inches square. The frame was warm from Tolya's body. I'm no judge of that kind of workmanship, but it must have taken a steady hand to be able to paint that small with brushes.

Tolya said that when the hungry times came, his village was still living well. The villagers were well off for food: the hot

weather that brought drought to the south just made their growing season longer.

This village was about a hundred kilometers from Ulan Ude,
and traders began to come from the city and offer them high
prices for food. Pretty soon the villagers stopped selling. Prices
were rising so quick, that they figured better to hang on until
they topped out. Tolya claimed he warned the villagers, but
it did no good. The people who turned up next were full of
righteous anger that the villagers were chiseling them and starving their children. Then they came in a mob and took the food
and butchered the ones who resisted.

Felix asked how many of us had grown up in a proper city
like this one. None of us had. And none apart from me even had
parents who were city dwellers. That was no accident. Without
power or clean water, dysentery and thirst finished them off
quicker than any poison.

"What about you, Makepeace?" said Osip, not in an unfriendly way. I was the only one who had said nothing about my
past life. "How did you come by that?"

"Someone splashed lye on me," I said. There was a pause, as
though they expected me to go on, but I wasn't minded to tell
them about Eben Callard and the bad thing that had happened
to me.

Tolya put a candle in a battered lantern. We had to make do
without a fire because all the wood we'd gathered was tainted.
He stood the lantern beside him in such a way that the light
bronzed him and his fur clothes.

Suddenly it seemed to me like he'd planned everything this
way: the drinking, the stories, and now the lantern like a lamp
on an altar, just as he must have planned the services he read to
his parishioners in the old days. He said he knew how much we
must all miss the old life, and there was no chance of bringing it

back in our lifetimes. That was in the way of things: civilizations had risen and fallen and there was nothing to be done about it. Then he said we were lucky enough to be part of a plan to put things back on the road to how they were.

The icon had made its way round the group back to him. He held it in his hand and talked of his life in the seminary. He said that writings that were copied from monk to monk kept alive knowledge that would otherwise have been lost.

I'll give him this: he had a beautiful, deep voice and a kind of priestly calm about him. And the men had drunk enough to be suggestible. Once he started unfolding his story, he had us hooked, because the words we were hearing were what we all wanted to hear.

•

Once upon a time, he said, the Zone had been just what it looked like from the bridge: a big industrial city called Polyn, of more than a hundred thousand souls.

The part that lay on the far side of the river was at least three hundred years old. It had been founded as a port for river traffic. Fur and timber and gold coming out of the Far North used to be shipped from here to roads and railheads in the south. The loads moved on barges part of the year, and in the winter months, before the river was embanked and it still froze hard, they moved on the ice.

But beyond what was visible from the bridge in daylight lay a whole newer city. This place, almost a second separate city, had been built no more than half a century before our own time. It had been the most advanced city anywhere on earth. And it was put up here because the work that went on in it was meant to be secret.

A place with too many links to other cities wouldn't do, and a place that was smack-dab in the wilderness would equally attract the wrong kind of interest, so its founders planned it to look like nothing more than an offshoot of Polyn. The new city never had a name of its own, and for ten or twenty years after it was built, the government wouldn't admit it was any such thing. This secret city was known as Polyn 66, after the line of latitude it lay on.

The government drew to Polyn 66 the brightest people of the time—doctors, professors, scientists—and put them to work in factories and institutes of higher learning. You needed special passes to be allowed to enter the precincts of Polyn 66. The ordinary citizens of Polyn, for instance, were forbidden to travel there, and there were severe penalties if they were found there without the correct permission.

Aside from its being much colder than most of the scientists were used to, the life the city offered was a very comfortable one, with big apartments, high salaries, and good food, some of it brought in by air out of season.

There was no train to the city, and no road out of it. The only practical way to reach it in those days was by air. The taiga surrounded it on three sides like a moat of trees, and on the fourth side, Polyn stood between it and the Lena.

The story is that in its heyday, Polyn 66 was a real Sodom. Unless you have a real love of hunting and ice fishing, the Far North doesn't offer much for your leisure hours. They had theaters and an opera house and suchlike, but a great many people chose to spend their free time drinking and going to bed with others' spouses.

But it's what they got up to in their working hours that made them special. They were like the brain of the human race, puzzling out solutions to problems that had taxed us since we learned to make sparks from flint. No one alive can begin to guess at the sum of what they achieved, Tolya said, but it's fair to say there's not a branch of human knowledge that they didn't add something to. They made better kinds of fuels, more deadly weapons, more fruitful crops. They looked through telescopes at the stars and made plans for carrying us into space. The scope of their work gave them an outlook different to what an ordinary man has. Every day they wrestled with the births and deaths of stars and civilizations. They thought in terms of Genesis and Apocalypse, how to scorch the life out the planet and how to bring it back in the aftermath.

Perhaps they tackled things that we don't have the right to understand: how to breathe life back into a corpse, how to double the lifespan of a person, how to engender a child without the act of procreation.

But what they were most eager to find, Tolya said, was something called Daniel's Fire. He couldn't tell us any more about it than the name.

Because of the city's great importance, Tolya said, the government had never abandoned it. Its food supply had been more or less constant. And when war and shortages were threatening it with chaos, its inhabitants were moved to safety. They were put in planes and flown out west, and the city was left to crumble.

Left in the city was the fruit of all those years' work.

You remember in Genesis, said Tolya, that God puts an angel with a flaming sword to guard Eden after Adam and Eve have been expelled?

There are two forbidden trees in the garden: the Tree of Life, and the Tree of Knowledge of Good and Evil. God doesn't want Adam and Eve to eat from both, otherwise they'll become gods, so he bars their way and sends them into exile.

The government decided the same thing. Knowledge and power can make you a god. There are things in Polyn that used rightly will make you almost a god. So over the city they put a flaming sword.

When he said its name, some of the prisoners crossed themselves. You would never have known there was such a deep seam of belief in these men from the way they carried themselves in the camp. They'd squirreled god away inside them, like men who bury food in a famine, and hold up empty hands to their starving neighbors.

The word stuck in my mind for being so strange and pretty: "anthrax." I had never heard it before, and it sounded to me like an ancient god, one the Tungus might worship, or maybe a famous old asiatic city with minarets and a mosaic arch.

But there was nothing pretty about what it did to you. Tolya told us how the spores of it slept in the rubble, stubborn and long-lived. It killed people and it killed what they lived on. It opened sores across your body and ate into your lungs. It was a living thing, too, just a lot simpler than we are, and with its own implacable appetite for life. You wonder on what day a loving god created that.

Tolya said it was thanks to Apofagato that we knew these things. Apofagato was a scientist himself and he came from a family who had lived in Polyn. He understood the layout of the city, and that's why Boathwaite had brought him to the base from a place in the Kuriles.

I wondered if Apofagato had fled there like Shamsudin. He was another of those book-smart men, but he had been lucky enough to find someone who valued his know-how. With the instructions they'd been given, the prisoners were right now unearthing what we needed to restore more comfort and safety to our lives.

The men wanted to drink to that, but this is when Tolya grew grave and came to the point of his sermon. Though we needed what he hoped the prisoners had found, we couldn't afford to let them out of the Zone alive. He didn't like it anymore than they did, but that's how it was. The place was poisoned and the poison had to stay locked up.

The guards had listened intently as he talked, and when he stopped, they broke out with questions. They wanted to know about the poison in the Zone, and the objects we were taking out, and how you could be sure that what came out of the Zone could be made clean.

Tolya answered their questions and he puffed up those men with the notion they were doing good, embroidering their task with a lot of words like "dedication" and "sacrifice" that reminded me of those odd telegrams from the Almighty that would burst in our silent worship at home. Maybe I'm simple, but they ring in my ears with the same dull thud you get when a stone bangs against an empty coffee can.

The world has shrunk to simple facts, and the simpler the people, the better they cope. My father spoke six languages but he couldn't hammer a nail straight. He could speak with presidents and governments, when there were such things, on matters of law. He was one of those who negotiated the grant of land that became our home. He had yards and yards of words to dress up his vision of what our life should be, but he couldn't so much as make a fist when the time came to defend it. He spoke constantly of bringing good to the world, but I don't think the good he brought would cover a penny piece. It takes no words to do good.

What Tolya said reminded me a lot of how my father talked. Where my father saw the handiwork of god, all I ever saw was sunlight on ice or two blue eggs in a nest. And where Tolya said he saw holy men preserving the lost jewels of human knowledge, all I saw was a team of burglars getting ready to shoot their accomplices.

·

The drink I'd had gave me a thirst that shook me out of my sleep sometime after midnight. The moon was as big and pale as a duck egg, and it dazzled me as I stumbled after my water bottle. The water was frozen hard in it, so I had to slake my thirst with a handful of snow. I looked at the sleeping forms in the darkness and decided that this was where we would part company. You can build your new world without me, I thought. I would try to get back to my lake cabin before August. I would get myself a hunting dog. I would pick cloudberries and plant broad beans. There's so many things worse than a solitary life.

I shook the Tungus boy awake. He woke silently, like a good backwoodsman does, and I gave him the jagged lid of one of the meat cans to saw through his bonds with.

Osip's carbine was next to him. I took it and changed it for mine. My gun was a rusty old thing that I didn't want to trust my life to. He murmured a little at the noise, but he was pretty far gone in drink.

By the time I made the swap, the boy had sliced the lariat into pieces. I handed him the reins of my horse and pointed him the way we'd came. If he was smart, he'd keep to the trodden path and his trail would be invisible.

He swung up into the saddle and left without giving me a backward glance.

I slipped the spyglass into my jacket, then gathered my things quickly and untethered Tolya's horse, which was the fastest.

A ringing sound came up the concrete banks of the river. I'd hoped the boy would have the sense to stay in the deeper snow to muffle the clang of the hooves, but eagerness had got the better of him.

The noise didn't wake anyone yet, but it made the horse skittish and she wouldn't let me mount her. I tried to wrangle her around the right way in the darkness, beseeching her inwardly to be silent. She startled this time and let out a whinny, and there were a couple of groans as sore heads came to.

By the time I was in the saddle, I no longer had the jump on them. I could hear Tolya fumbling for his weapon. I didn't think through what I did next. It was like the split second before the draw when all your hours of practice take over, and the gun's out and smoking before your mind's caught up to it. If reasoning played a part in it, I suppose it must have told me that I could take my chances and try to outrun them on a trail they knew better than I did, or I could make for somewhere they wouldn't want to follow.

I urged the horse up toward the block post, past the rolls of rusty wire, and I kicked her flanks, and she pinned her ears back and we made straight for the Zone.

The moon was bright enough for them to have a clear shot at me, so I lay as flat as I could to her neck.

I didn't bring her up at the kiosk. I clamped my knees tight and we galloped on down that wide empty street, flat out for a couple of hundred yards. The space between her footfalls seemed to stretch out until we were airborne, hurtling through the arctic darkness like a thing in flight, over the rubble under the snow, the discarded furniture, tramlines, anthrax, god knows what else. The city expanded in front of us: the streets multiplied, the houses fanned out like trees in a forest, enfolding, embracing, hiding us—this dirty, dead, poisoned old city. And for the first time in so many years, I knew what it was to be free.

5

At daybreak I found myself in the main square of Polyn, where I came upon a huge bronze head glaring out over a vast field of snow.

The man was a bald, bearded fellow with an asiatic squint and the snow was banked up to his jowls like a starched collar. He'd only been cast from the chin up, but he still stood more than fifteen feet high. I rode round him twice, leaving a wheel of prints.

If that was his tomb, I owe him an apology, because the next thing I did was to shinny up his nose and sit my ass right on his big bare dome to watch the sun come up over the city.

There was no warmth in those first rays, but there was something icy and beautiful in the way they sparkled on the bronze head, and lit the red marble of its base, and gleamed on the windows of the big, square buildings that surrounded us on each side.

The head sat on a raised plinth at one side of the square and faced directly east, into the sunrise and out over the old city. As the sun rose higher, the square grew more dazzling bright: three or four acres of blinding, virgin snow. No wonder that bronze head was squinting.

I could see by the tracks in the snow that the prisoners had used the square to orient themselves. It must have been the clearest landmark on the maps they carried. There were tracks entering it at different points on two of its four sides, but all of them exited the same way: westwards, past the two block posts that marked the separation between the new city and the old.

The tallest building in the old city was probably no more than ten stories or so, but through the spyglass I could make out some on the other side of the block posts that were twice or even three times as high. There was something so heartless and sharp about their shape: plain, straight sides, gray as granite, unadorned with any detail—nothing to tell you they'd been built by a race of men. And even the biggest of those was dwarfed by a blue metal crane which stood beside it like a huge headless bird.

You'd think somehow a city would miss its people, that at least it would look incomplete without a line of washing or two, someone idling on a street corner, some children hurrying to school. But Polyn 66 looked no more short of people than a cemetery does. It was perfect just how it stood, all concrete and right angles, and governed by that giant's head.

To tell the truth, I think the city would have been a little spoiled if it had had people in it. Humans limp and loaf. They slouch, don't walk in straight lines, spit on the sidewalks. The city I could see through the glass looked like it would stand to attention for eternity.

•

The snow cover was pretty general, but here and there were tufts of brown grass that were tempting to the horse. I couldn't let her eat anything like that in case it had leached up poison from the soil, so I muzzled her with a feed bag to keep her from grazing.

I had half a sack of kibble for her, which would also take the edge off my hunger, but when that ran out I didn't like to think how I would keep us both fed. I could eat the horse if it came to it—it wouldn't be the first time—but it would be a long walk home.

As I scoured the old city for something to melt snow in, I was struck by how orderly it had all been left. Windows were mostly intact. Front doors were shut and padlocked.

On the road back to the bridge was a big yellow mansion. Its front door lay off its hinges, all warped and swollen by the weather. Rags and broken furniture were piled up in the opened passageway. I'd seen similar sights enough times over the years in Evangeline to recognize where someone had broken in looking for firewood.

It was a grand old building with two pairs of columns holding up its portico and the number 1897 laid in tiles beneath it. I found a shower curtain, a pair of rusty ski poles, and the remnant of a fire at the foot of the stairwell.

My first thought was that one of the prisoners had decided to disobey his instructions and shift for himself, and I went on up the stairs half expecting to run into him. But when I found him in the apartment on the first floor I could see he wasn't one of ours.

He lay on his front on a big Turkish rug, wearing the same fetters on his feet as ours had. I was afraid to touch him, so I turned him over by hooking his arm with an umbrella I found in the hall cupboard.

I'll never forget how light he felt. It was like a shell with no snail in it. I could only turn him so far, because something on his other arm had suppurated and glued itself to that heavy carpet, but there was no meat left on his face and by the look of it he was a year or two dead.

In the bathroom, I found the remains of a killed pig. That pig might have been what did it for him. Mushrooms are the worst food to eat in a poisoned place, because their roots are so high and widespread, but pig is scarcely better, since mushrooms are what they feed on.

The staircase led up five stories where there was a second, narrower set of stairs that gave out onto the roof. The light off the snow was dazzling after the gloom inside.

I fell to my knees and licked snow melt right off the slates.

The rooftop commanded a view out toward the river. From it, I could clearly see the block post on the bridge and figures moving beyond it. Through the spyglass I was able to tell the men apart, and I could watch them idling around their camp. They had a small fire going, so they must have found some clean wood somewhere. I knew their heads were hurting from the slow way they dragged themselves about.

Toward eleven, the first prisoners began appearing on the approach to the bridge. I didn't see them arrive, because I was too busy melting snow from the roof in a pail. The lack of food in the Zone didn't worry me so much, but without water, the horse and I would die in a couple of days.

The second or third time I went up on the roof, I saw the guards had changed into white one-pieces with hoods and masks to cover their faces.

It was hard to keep track of numbers. The guards all looked identical, and the prisoners had been made to sit in rows on the side of the bridge nearest to me.

One by one, they were called forward to hand over whatever they'd found. They stood up, laid down the things they had, and then crossed over to the other side.

When they were done, one of the guards came forward and hosed down the pile of dropped objects with a fumigator he wore strapped to his back. It was a weird-looking thing, something like a cross between a weed sprayer and the smoke machine we used to use to put a hive of bees to sleep.

I was all caught up with watching it when the first shots rang out. The next thing, a couple of the prisoners had broken free and were trying to get back across the bridge, but they could only manage a slow, loping run because of their chains.

There was a volley of shots and one of the prisoners fell down. The other kept going for ten or fifteen yards more. He didn't fall flat. He slipped down and died upright but on his knees, like a man at prayer. I'd never seen anyone die like that before. You wouldn't think gravity would allow it.

·

The temperature began to drop again as night drew on. The eaves stopped dripping and the slush in the roads hardened into ice.

I'd stabled the horse inside the stairwell, but I was planning to spend the night outside where the air was cleaner and I could keep an eye on the guards.

From the roof, their fire was a tiny yellow spark in the

blackness. The city was so still that an indistinct grunt or laugh occasionally carried all the way across the river.

In the last hour before sunset I broke into an apartment on one of the upper stories to try to find a blanket.

The place had been left in perfect order: there was a vase of dried flowers on the kitchen table, a pair of sofas with anti-macassars, a glass-fronted case of books in Russian, a dusty television, a standard lamp with an old frayed wire.

The bed in the main bedroom had been stripped, and on it sat two zipped bags of sheets and blankets. A photograph, a clock, and a copy of the Bible lay on the bedside table.

The second bedroom was half the size of the first and held a single bed.

On the corkboard next to the dressing table were photographs of a dark-haired teenager. In some she was ice fishing, in others eating cotton candy and standing in the glass bubble of a huge Ferris wheel in a city I didn't recognize.

Even after years of standing empty, there was something sweet in the air of that room: some faint smell of dried roses behind the mustiness and the rat and roach poison that had been so conscientiously laid around the skirting boards.

I found the girl's diary in the second drawer of the dressing table. It was all in Russian, but I knew what it said without having to read it. I could tell that it warned off snoopers with threats and spells. It rated the boys in her class for their promise as lovers and husbands. It charted the monthly cycles that were the first proofs of her womanhood, and it looked forward impatiently to a future that was already dust. I knew because I'd had one just like it.

In the story of Goldilocks, the little girl sneaks into a bear den, eats the animals' food, and finds a place to sleep. That night

I felt I was that story in reverse: a stinking, scarred bear, reeking of blood and gun smoke, turning up in a world of clean sheets and flowers.

Sitting on that bed, I felt some part of me emerge the way a snail does, soft and flinching, reaching up to the sunlight with its tender horns.

So little of my life was human—at least, not human in the way the girl who had once lived here would understand it.

I thought about Ping, and if her baby had lived: maybe I could have made her a room like this one, and lost myself in the turning years, knowing I'd dug my patch, and fixed my house, and loved the people I was supposed to. The bronze head in the square spoke of a race with grand notions, but my bet is that all most people ever wanted was this.

In the drawer where the diary had been stood a jar of cold cream, the cream inside all stiff and waxy with age. I smeared a fingerful on my wind-burned lips. The taste of it numbed my tongue the way soap does.

I put the jar and the diary back and slid the drawer shut. It stuck, and as I jerked it free, I heard something rattle at the back. I drew it out: a perfect oval, flat and heavy, that sat in my hand like a turkey egg. It was so cool on my palm, I took it for a paper-weight at first, until the fading sunlight showed the etched shapes on its upper side that told me it was a memory stone.

•

Around three that morning it started to snow again. It can't have been the sound that woke me up, because there was none. Maybe it was the change of light in the room. It poured out of the sky like feathers from a split pillow: big warm-weather flakes.

It seemed to double the starlight as it whirred down past the glass of the bedroom window. I came to consciousness on that girl's bed, watching it fall, and I felt a kind of peace in me. It made me glad that this scaly old world still has so many pretty things in it.

I must have drifted off again. Next thing I knew, the horse was hollering, and I was halfway down the stairs, shouting at whoever it was to get gone, with my gun cocked and my eyes still barely open.

There was a mess of snow in the hallway and someone had tried to unfasten the horse's bridle. They had fled at the sound of me yelling.

I swung myself into the saddle and chased out after them.

It turned out there was only one. I followed the tracks he had left as he labored through the snow with his chain on. I've hunted down some men in my time, but this one didn't take much catching. He was all broken with the weather and the short rations. The best he seemed able to do was to huddle in a shadowy alleyway and pray I mistook him for something else in the darkness.

He waited and waited, hoping I'd pass along. Thinking of the plague and the withered man in the apartment, I didn't want to get too close to him, but I had no intention of leaving him be, either, so that he could make more trouble.

After what seemed like a foolishly long time, I shouted out to him that if he didn't show his face, I'd kill him as a stranger and sleep no worse for it, and then I broke and closed the breech of my gun with a snap so there was no mistaking my intention.

He shuffled forward out of the darkness on his knees and begged me not to shoot. When he looked up at me, the first flush of dawn in the sky behind me lit up his face. It was Shamsudin.

He squinted up at me and said my name as though it was a question. His voice was croaky and thick with thirst.

Telling him to wait where he was, I went and fetched one of my pails of water for him. He clutched it in his arms and put his face in the bucket to drink. Between gulps he raised his head and sat with his eyes closed, panting with relief and fatigue. The water dripped off his beard and back into the pail. When he offered the bucket back to me, I told him he could keep it.

I guess I was pleased to see him alive, though I had no desire to let him near to me. It could have been Charlo or my own pa in that place and I still would have kept upwind of him and ten yards between us. I didn't believe that the guards would have killed those men for nothing, or go to all that trouble with their masks and suits because they felt like it. Tolya knew more about the Zone than I did, and he didn't trust to luck to stay healthy.

Shamsudin asked me about the others.

I said the guards were waiting on the other side of the river and as far as I knew all the prisoners but him were dead.

That seemed to surprise him less than I expected, then I saw that he had fallen asleep. His face looked old and hollow and the skin of it hung in baggy folds.

I whistled him out of his slumber. It was cold enough that he would never come round if he slept there.

He stumbled after me groggily. I led him to the stairwell and covered him with a heap of bedclothes from the apartment.

•

At dawn I went up to the roof to watch the sun come up over the city. It lit the glass in the distant windows of the second city: gold and bronze, and some the greenish-blue of cut ice.

I took the memory stone up with me and laid it down so it could drink in the sunshine for a few hours and come to life. It looked even prettier in the daylight, bright and shiny as a knife blade. It had an ebony screen. There was some tiny writing on the front in Russian and a row of buttons marked with symbols that I couldn't recognize. They moved with a faint click at the lightest touch. On the back was written the only words I could understand: *Made in China*.

·

The guards struck their camp and headed off an hour or so after sunrise. They moved slowly along the eastern bank of the river. I lay on my belly and followed them with the glass. They had just enough animals for the journey back. The sleds were loaded up with the things that had been brought out of the Zone.

All the bodies had been left where they had fallen. The one that had died on his knees had keeled over in the night. The others lay piled under the fresh snow too far away for me to count them, even with the glass.

I put some kibble in a pillowcase for Shamsudin to eat when he woke up.

It was a nuisance keeping him in this half-assed quarantine, but I didn't know what else to do. I wasn't certain that he was a danger to me, but I couldn't risk it. I thought it was best not to touch him, or anything he handled or ate, and not breathe the same air.

He came around toward mid-morning. I watched from higher up the stairwell as he munched the food I'd left him.

The sleep and water seemed to do him some good. He looked less deathly and he had some of his old poise back.

I said to him that the guards had gone and we were free to go.

Free to go where? he asked.

I shrugged and told him he could go where he liked. As for me, I was headed home.

He gave me a mistrusting look. I sensed that business in the woods still hung over him. I said I wasn't minded to pay him back for thinking of killing me. I found it easy enough to forgive; I might have done the same. As far as I was concerned, we'd let bygones be bygones.

At that he came closer and offered to shake my hand on it.

I told him not to mistake me, and that I was shaking his hand in spirit, but that there were diseases and strong poisons in the Zone and either one of us might have picked them up. I said until it was clear that we were both well, we should give each other a wide berth.

Shamsudin surprised me then by bursting into tears. He was tortured, he said, by the thought of what he'd sunk to.

I told him not to mind it and that supposedly better men had sunk to a lot worse.

·

Before I left I collected the memory stone I'd put on the roof. It was warm to the touch but there was no life in it. I squeezed every button and even tried shaking it. The thing was just no good anymore.

As I drew back my arm to pitch it into the river, its screen picked up the sunshine and cast it into my eyes. It was bright enough to make me wince. I held it in my palm and turned it this way and that in the light. The glass of it was so true that it worked like a mirror.

I hadn't seen my face up close for so many years, and to tell the truth, it looked a little better than I remembered.

Twenty years seemed to have taken the anger out of the scarring. I was a sight older, but my face looked more comfortable with itself. Not pretty by a long chalk, but no longer hideous. Or maybe I'd just imagined it was worse than it was.

I decided to reprieve the mirror. I would hang it from a string above my seeds to keep the crows off. I liked the idea that it would have a second life as a bird scarer. I put it in my coat pocket with my tinder and flints.

After a hunt, I found a hammer for Shamsudin to break open his chains with. He went at it for a while and managed to get the chain off but couldn't crack the fetters.

•

We left the Zone around noontime. There were about four hundred yards of slush between us and the bridge. I walked the horse but I kept ten yards ahead of Shamsudin. Whenever the squish of his footsteps got too close, I pressed on a little faster.

Just stepping onto the bridge, I immediately felt different. I realized that I'd been breathing shallow the whole time I'd been in the city.

The first body we came to lay a yard or two beyond the block post. It belonged to the man who had died on his knees: Zulfugar. I didn't linger there. The shell they used must have had a soft tip, because it had sprayed a peacock's tail of his insides across the snow.

I pushed on to the campsite at the far side of the bridge. I was hoping that, being a horse down for trip home, Tolya would have had to shed some rations, but all I could find at the spot was empty tins and bottles and their cold cooking fire. I raked the embers with my toe just in case they had dropped some food.

Shamsudin was dawdling on the bridge. I looked up and saw him stood on his knees by the body, head bowed, saying a prayer over the dead man, and I shouted to him not to get too close to him.

He yelled back an oath at me in a thick, choked voice.

I drew my gun and ran back after him, struggling to keep my footing in the slush and telling to him not to touch the corpse or I'd shoot him. I was breathing hard by the time I caught up to him, but my gun sight was steady enough on his forehead.

His eyes were all flared up. He jutted his chin at me as though to say he'd get as close as he wanted. Then he turned away from me, grabbed Zulfugar's sleeve to pull him up sitting, and hoisted the body from its armpits.

It was an awkward lift and he tottered as he got to his feet.

I don't know if he thought I'd shoot. I don't think he cared by then.

He buried the body in a bank of shale at the river's edge. I watched him from the track as he dug out a trench with his hands and pieces of flat stone. It was not much more than a foot deep and it took him a while to get the body covered.

•

We made our way slowly south as the light lengthened and the sky turned all blue and gold. Shamsudin and I never said a word to each other until sunset.

When we stopped, I cut us both branches to lie on. He offered to help but I said he should keep his distance. His coat was still spotted with gore from the corpse. He'd buried his friend and as good as buried himself, but he wasn't going to bury me.

I made his bed a noisy one so I could keep an ear on him.

The weather was warm for early March, but it was cold and comfortless without a fire and I was too hungry to sleep.

I was watching us both for signs of sickness. I didn't want to die now—not here, within an ace of being properly free.

The twigs Shamsudin was resting on rustled as he shifted his place.

I told him that in a day or two, we'd be able to hunt the wildlife and burn wood. There were fish in the rivers just south of here. We were too late for salmon, but there was pike perch and grayling. We'd leave them on the ice and carve them into frozen slices: stroganina. There were leaves and mosses we could eat. If it came to it, I could make famine bread from pine bark. I asked Shamsudin if he'd ever eaten horse flesh.

He said, Not knowingly.

I told him he was in for a treat. Horse makes a fine sausage, and the steaks are sweet and tender. The Yakuts eat the liver frozen raw, like meat ice cream.

Shamsudin said that in Harbin once he'd eaten a meal that went on for forty courses, and more than ten of them were goat.

I asked him where else he'd been. He reeled off a list of cities and then asked me where I'd traveled.

Of course, I had to tell him that Polyn was my first city proper, but I'd covered a lot of territory in the Far North.

"Makepeace," he said, "you are a savage."

He didn't mean it unfriendly, but the truth is it stung a little. I'm sensitive on that score. My ways are rough. I've done brutal things. There's a shame in me at my ignorance, and the gulf between me and my parents.

"Civilization and cities are the same thing," Shamsudin said. "And that place is not a city. It is a tomb."

I asked him how much he'd seen of it.

More than enough, he said.

•

Shamsudin told me that the prisoners had split into pairs almost as soon as they got across the bridge.

There had been excitement at first. They had a little food each. They felt free. The ones like me who had never been to a city were in awe of it. For the men like Shamsudin, there was some sadness, a sense of impossible return, the feeling of seeing a dead friend's face in a dream.

He stopped his story for a moment and I knew he was thinking of Zulfugar.

Some of the prisoners ignored the maps and went to scavenge food or tools. The rest made their way through the city, following the route I'd taken.

The maps they had copied led them to the square with the big bronze head in it and then beyond, to the industrial part of the city, the place that Tolya had called Polyn 66.

There was an immediate change in the look of the place. There were no more churches with onion domes, or timber houses. The buildings were all taller, newer. Tanks and army vehicles lay abandoned in the street. Zulfugar got nervous, thinking the road was mined.

Shamsudin shared my view that our crew were only the latest to visit the Zone. In an alleyway where he'd gone to piss, he stumbled on a heap of sticky rags, thighbones, and a chain.

Little by little, the other pairs of prisoners dropped away.

Human nature being what it is, some were content to pick up any old flotsam and head back with it. Shamsudin laughed as he remembered what they had taken: old car batteries, the ball cock of a cistern, the cogs from a sewing machine.

But others headed into the ruins of the city with a grim resolve. They used crowbars to break into old storerooms and stacked makeshift sleds with what they found there, hoping rather than trusting that Tolya would deal fairly with them.

Shamsudin and Zulfugar pressed on into the city, looking for one of the places marked on their map.

When they found it, it turned out to be a playground. There were shoes and cans scattered around the place, a rusty carousel, a steel rocking horse, and swings that had rotted.

Night was falling and Shamsudin was ready to turn back, but Zulfugar had it fixed in his head that the map was wrong. As a soldier, he'd served sometimes with maps that had been tweaked to fool the unwary by hiding the location of important things, and he figured the true destination was about two hundred yards further off.

It took some scrambling to get over its outer wall, and Zulfugar cut his hand open. He tied it with a rag and boosted Shamsudin in through a window.

The drop on the inside was much further than he expected. He stiffened up as he fell and hit his head upon landing. He lay unconscious for a while, but he couldn't say for how long. When he came to, he looked up and saw the window was too high for him to climb back out again. He felt something drip warm on his hand: he had broken his nose in the fall.

He said a panic seized him at the thought of dying alone in there. He shouted himself hoarse calling out to Zulfugar. The foundations were deep and it was pitch-black inside. Then, after a while, his eyes began to adjust to the darkness, and the pain of the fall abated.

He stood up and began feeling his way around the walls of the building. It seemed to him that the floor sloped upwards slightly in one direction, so he headed that way, hoping it would lead him aboveground.

The bunker was vast. Shamsudin said that at times he thought he was going out of his mind, and at other times he feared he had died and was fumbling along in the corridors of the afterlife.

After what seemed like hours of wandering, he felt broken glass under his feet and, looking up at the window he'd fallen through, realized he'd come full circle.

That's when he gave up hope of escaping the labyrinth. He cursed god and threw himself against the wall, hoping to dash out his brains, but the darkness gave way in front of him. He found he'd stumbled through a kind of doorway into an inner chamber, and in this place he noticed a pale blue light coming from under a metal door.

To his astonishment, the door swung open when he pushed it. It led into a huge storeroom lined with metal shelves twenty feet high.

Stranger still, the blue light was not coming from a window but from a shelf of blue flasks that were crackling and glowing.

Shamsudin was a man of science, but he said he had never seen anything that was like them, or the power that was in them. He reached for the drawings he had made at the base, but found he had lost them and his map in the fall.

As he told me this, I heard the branches under him rustle. He was fumbling inside his jacket. I put one hand on my gun stock. I must have drawn breath as I did it, because he looked up at me. He was yards away from me, but I could see his face clearly—the deep shadows in his eye sockets and the glint of gold in his teeth—as though lit by candlelight.

What he had taken from his coat was one of the flasks he had described. I had imagined it like a lightbulb, but the light it contained was neither solid nor steady. It moved and shimmered. It looked for all the world as though someone had caught a part of the Lights in a mason jar.

He stood it in the snow between us.

The closer you got to it, the stranger it was. It had the

power fire has of drawing your eye into it so you'd notice the tiniest things. The light had texture and depth, like flame does, like the towers of Polyn 66 seen from far off, but it had a quality of water too: moving, folding, closing, sending off little shoots of blue flame, rolling back on itself as though it was gathering its strength again. And all the time I could hear a faint hiss coming off the flask, like a live thing breathing. I wondered if this was what they meant by Daniel's Fire.

Shamsudin had taken two of them from the rack and used their light to guide himself through the cellar.

The light was too faint and scattered for him to see far with, but he was able to figure out that the space he was in was circular, and after about another hour of fumbling he found a ladder bolted on one of the internal walls. It took him up to a trapdoor in the roof.

It was a big, heavy steel trap with bolts across the inside, but even when he'd undone them, he couldn't lift it. Leaf mold had settled in the hinges and was holding it closed. There was a crack of daylight visible where the door sat in the hatch and he could smell fresh air. In his desperation to be free, he battered at the door with his fists and it opened a little, and one of the flasks dropped.

Shamsudin said he'd flinched and covered his eyes, expecting a crash of glass, or sparks, or flame, or worse; but the flask fell ten, twenty feet and bounced as though it was made of iron. He left it there, laying in its own pool of blue light like a lantern at the bottom of a well.

He had been underground so long that he thought Zulfugar would have given him up for dead, but not only was he waiting where he'd left him, nursing the wound on his hand, he'd also saved Shamsudin's share of their rations which he'd had for safekeeping.

Shamsudin ate his food and told him where he'd been while Zulfugar took off his ragged mittens to touch and marvel at the flask.

By this time, it was getting close to the hour of the rendezvous. Zulfugar said they would have to leave or risk getting there late. He stood up first and offered Shamsudin his hand to hoist him to his feet.

Shamsudin looked at him in surprise and asked him for his other hand. Zulfugar showed him its back and front. The wound had knitted up without a mark.

Zulfugar grabbed him fiercely by the coat and told him, God is great.

I asked Shamsudin if he was sure it was the flask that did it. He swore five ways that it was and said that it healed some smaller scrapes of his own.

Then Zulfugar asked Shamsudin if he thought he would be able to find his way back to the room where they were stored.

Shamsudin said he thought that with a rope and a lantern the return could be made pretty smoothly, though the truth was that he dreaded going back there.

A change had come over Zulfugar. He puzzled over his drawings and found a number that matched one on the flask. His joy had given way to a kind of nervousness. It's the same when a green cardplayer gets dealt a winning hand and he finds himself all sweaty and anxious at the thought of scooping the pot. Zulfugar was hatching a plan to barter the flask for their freedom.

He said that if they went back to the bridge together, the guards wouldn't hesitate to strong-arm the flask off whoever had it. Instead, he told Shamsudin that one of them should return while the other remained in the Zone, guarding it.

His proposal was that Shamsudin should go back empty-handed and tell Tolya exactly what he'd stumbled upon. In return for leading the guards to it, he was to ask for a week of rations and a horse.

Time was ticking by. Shamsudin had misgivings about the plan. He had a timid spirit, and his natural inclination was just to hand over the flask and trust to the good faith of the guards.

Zulfugar would have none of that. He was pacing in the snow, ramping up his demands like the fisherman's wife in the fairy tale: two weeks of rations, a month of rations, a horse each, a gun.

Right at the last minute, Zulfugar decided Shamsudin should be the one to stay behind. Maybe he didn't trust his friend. More likely, he felt he was the shrewder bargainer.

The trouble with Zulfugar's plan was that it credited the guards with too much intelligence. I don't think anyone but Apofagato knew exactly what we had been sent to the Zone to find. You could copy pictures until your hand got cramped, and write down all the numbers you liked, but until you saw that flask, with the light pulsing in it, you would never believe such a thing existed.

I could see it right in front of me and I had a hard time crediting it.

Also, Tolya's speech about the Zone had all the guards panicking. Even watching them through the class, I could see they wanted to get their job done as quick as possible.

As Zulfugar waited on the bridge with the other prisoners, he must have sensed that he'd miscalculated. Instead of being let loose on the other side, they were being corralled together like pigs waiting for the bolt.

He'd turned to flee. Maybe he risked a bullet, thinking that if he could just get back to the flask, he thought it would make him better. I'd seen what had unfolded next from my perch on the roof.

That flask might be able to heal a graze or close up a cut hand, but it couldn't fix the hole they put in Zulfugar.

.

We made good time over the next two days in spite of the dearth of food. Shamsudin walked quicker without the chain, and we moved so fast that we had to watch that we didn't over-take the party of guards.

I didn't dare risk hunting or a fire those first two days—not because of disease or radiation, but because I feared revealing our position. But on the third night I snared a pair of rabbits and started to build a tiny fire to broil them on.

That evening Shamsudin got a fever. It was by no means warm yet, but he complained about the heat, and even by the moonlight I could see his face was basted in sweat.

He had taken it into his head that his flask, as well as mend-ing cuts, would be proof against disease, and he had started lay-ing it on himself when we stopped to melt snow or let the horse feed.

I teased him for it. I told him that it was no medicine, but pure juju. But he was ready with a theory about how it worked and even suggested I try it.

"I'll take my chances with the germs I have," I said, "rather than sharing yours."

Anyway, he was at it with his magic jar, rolling it over his sweaty forehead and up and down his arms, which he said ached.

That gave me a bad feeling, and the truth was I didn't feel so great myself. Also, the horse was skittish and off her food.

I thought it would be a twisted kind of justice for us to get sick now.

Digging in my pocket for the flints, my hand closed on the memory stone. I drew it out without thinking. When I had put it away three days before, the thing was dead. Now its face was all etched with green fire and the lights on it were winking and alive.

The thought crossed my mind that it had drawn its power from the bottled lightning, or that whatever had been broken in it had been knit up by its closeness to the flask. But I pushed the idea out of my head for a piece of foolishness.

Shamsudin had noticed me pause and asked what I had.

I showed it to him and he told me how to make it play.

It lit into life at my touch. Its screen took color and moved with pictures that showed the city as it had been, its streets all come to life, filled with people and transport.

You couldn't see her at first, but there was a girl's voice in it, telling you what the pictures were. She was speaking in Russian, which I couldn't make sense of, but Shamsudin translated.

She said this is my school, this is where I live, this is my friend Darya—who was a girl giggling and covering her face with her hand—this is my father who is packing to leave.

It became clear that all the bustle in the city was people getting ready to go.

I understood why she'd made this thing. I've often wished I had a keepsake like it. It was a sampler with patches of the past worked into it. It should have been with her in the city she had gone to. It seemed a pity that she had forgotten it in a drawer.

Then it showed her on her bed. The picture went wobbly and you could hear a girl laughing in the background.

Lyudi budushchevo, she said, or something that sounded like it.

Shamsudin sat up and said she hadn't forgotten it all: she'd intended it to be left.

People of the future, she was saying. Whoever sees this message. I was born in the city of Polyn, Russia. I am eighteen years old. This is how I lived. This is who I was.

This is how I lived. This is who I was.

When Shamsudin said those words I felt a chill run through me. I saw that skull of a city with the life gone from it.

I thought of the mounds of coins and ribbons beside the highway. And the scratches on the cell-walls at Buktygachak. And the bronze head guarding the empty square.

You never expect to be at the end of anything, Boathwaite had said. But then, he had his brother's arrogance. The end is where you end up. You always end up at the end of *something*. So what is it that keeps you shambling out to the stable when it's sixty below, doing up the saddle with your fingers stiff with cold, or riding out in summer when you can't breathe for dust?

There are many words I've seen written down that I've never heard spoken. This is one I wouldn't know how to say exactly, but I know it's at the back of every other fear.

It doesn't make sense to fear it, because you're never around when it happens. Fear hunger, or cold, or the pain of sickness— but this? And yet, this is the one that preys on me. I bumped up against it in the darkness hearing her say those words.

I fear *annihilation*.

Boathwaite can say what he likes. A sane person knows they're headed for the end of something. But the thought that things will continue, that there'll be kind words at their funeral, or even just a pulse of blood in someone, somewhere, that dumbly recalls that they were here that gives the rest of it some point. A sane person expects that.

That girl had cast her message adrift on a sea of time so that she could live again briefly in the mind of whoever saw it. Maybe she didn't know that, but that's how it was.

Everyone expects to be at the end of something. What no one expects is to be at the end of *everything*.

·

When I woke up in the morning, there were six inches of snow on me. I was a little feverish, but Shamsudin was badly ill. His skin was gray and he was breathing hard. He kept saying he'd be fine, and he insisted we move off as normal, but he barely got ten yards before he stumbled.

He said not to get close, but I was all done with that. I figured I was gone, or as good as gone, if he was.

I helped him up from the place where he'd fallen and I laid him back down on his bed and covered him with all the blankets we had. Then I boiled some soup from the rabbits and gave it to him, spoon by spoon, as he lay shivering.

Between bouts of sweating he was able to sleep, and I held his head in my lap. He felt like a baby. I thought about Ping and as I pictured her face I told him I loved him.

He murmured in his sleep.

The flush of fever in his face made him look almost youthful again.

After an hour or two, he woke up and asked me if I held out hopes for the afterlife.

I said no, but if anyone deserved it, he surely did.

"I have been in Andalus," he said. "I think paradise will smell like the flowers of bitter oranges."

I said I had always thought something similar.

By then he had exhausted himself with speaking and just

held on to me until the two of us were moved to a feverish intimacy, clinging together in loneliness and fear of death.

•

When the sickness got bad again, he raved and told me to shoot him. In his lucid moments he wanted to talk about his childhood. He said his mother had always been proud of him. I said I didn't doubt it. Just like the girl from Polyn, he wanted a witness.

When the sun came out, I opened his jacket to get some fresh air on him. His skinny chest burned like fire.

Later that afternoon, sores broke out on his face and the infection spread to his lungs so he had to sleep upright. The horse had sickened, too, but I didn't have time to tend it.

I boiled up some herbs in a bucket for him to breathe them in. That seemed to help him and he slept easier that night.

At first light I was up to gather more plants. I found a bunch of them. And while I was doing it, I caught sight of a deer. I had my gun with me, and I thought, To hell with it: either the sickness will get us, or Tolya's men will get us, but at least this way we won't die hungry.

I was pretty dizzy with fever myself, and it took me three shots to put her down and half an hour to drag her back to our camp.

She was a young female who must have got separated from her herd.

Shamsudin was sitting up but groggy, and I shouted out that we had fresh meat. It struck me that it would do him good to eat the liver, so I butchered that out first.

By the time I was ready to cook it, I could hear that his breathing was rattling again.

I went over to him and his eyes were glazed and he gripped my arm as he breathed hard, struggling like a man in a race. His tongue seemed dry and spongy however much water I tried to put down him.

Maybe if I'd used a bullet he would have died more comfortable, but I couldn't do it.

About noon Shamsudin died, then the horse died. But I lived. Well, that's the kind of luck I've had.

FOUR

1

After the horse died, I had to go on foot. I delayed setting out in order to bury Shamsudin and then I moved on southeast, feeling my way through the taiga for the start of the highway that would take me home.

It was the worst season to travel. Meltwater made even the smaller rivers impassable. And if you got wet, and then the temperature dropped, you ended up with your pants all armored with ice.

I'd always been a wiry and uncomplaining sort. Four hours of sleep would get me back to myself after a day's work. Now I was aching and short of breath. I'd stop every hour, then every half hour, then every fifteen minutes. Finally I was walking for a hundred yards and resting for five minutes. I carried my belongings on a birch frame which dug into my arms.

Soon I was too weak to hunt. The ground was soaked through, so with the last of my strength I lopped the branches off a larch and spread them out for a bed. Then I crawled onto it and waited to die.

I must have lain there for days as the sickness worked its way through me. Day and night wheeled about the sky. On the third or fourth morning, I sat up and drank a pint of water from the stream in my cupped hands.

Why I should have been spared, I couldn't think. I heard a tale later that the plague in Polyn was an artificial one, engineered to be deadly to men but to spare women. It wasn't out of any sense of chivalry: just practical to kill male soldiers and leave females behind to wait on the victorious army and bear children. It sounds unlikely, but not unlikelier than many other things I know to be true.

As soon as I was strong enough to stand, I hoisted up my pack and stumbled on. I picked fiddleheads and ate them as I walked. A couple of them had caterpillars on them and I munched them too because I was so hungry. I was thinking about counting my shells and seeing if I could spare some to hunt with when I smelled a terrible sweetness on the wind.

About two hundred yards further on, I came upon a heap of bodies stacked like logwood. Some were half dressed but most had been stripped, and their limbs were naked and waxy in the sunlight. The remains of the caterpillar went bitter in my mouth.

They had been killed with blades and some were only trunks. Tolya's head sat on top, mouth downcast, winking out from under drooping eyelids.

The bodies were soft with decay, and ants were busy on

their mouths and eyes. I guessed they had been dead two or three days.

The tracks of their attackers had melted away with the snow, but here and there were dropped objects—a boot, a saddle-bag, saucepans—that made me think the struggle had been in the dark. The guards were well armed. I doubted that anywhere else in the region were there such guns and weapons as they carried. It would have taken a large number to subdue them by force. But the relief of surviving the Zone and the power of their guns might have made them unwary. If someone had come stealthily, sneaked up on them at night, they might have been too drunk or bleary-eyed to defend themselves.

I blacked my face with dirt, loaded my carbine with all the shells I had, and skirted the track until darkness fell.

It was the mildest night we'd had since autumn. The land was shedding winter like a wet dog shaking itself dry. Now and again a chunk of damp snow flopped out of the branches and made a sound like a footfall. Each time I heard one drop, I flinched.

I sat and snoozed under a tree for a couple of hours before dawn. When I opened my eyes, it was still dark. There was silence, then I felt a blade at my throat and a hand close over my mouth. It smelled of soil and caribou meat.

The prick of the knife in my neck forced me up on my feet. I wasn't aware that I was scared, but I peed myself, like I had that time in the lake. A little light was coming in to the sky, but it wasn't any comfort to be able to squint down at my chin and see that whoever had got me was wearing Tolya's watch.

He marched me out to the track and gave a low whistle. Horses and men appeared from the woods.

The heap of bodies wasn't more than two miles behind us.

They talked quietly in a throaty language that I guessed was Yakut. I'd never had much dealings with the Yakut, but I knew them to be a tough, horse-herding people. They had flat, dark faces like Kazakhs and were dressed in a ragbag of clothes. I spotted a few hats and coats that I remembered as belonging to the guards. What surprised me most was that, bundled up as they were, I still recognized women among them.

I knelt in the slush, listening to their chatter. It sounded like a conversation you might overhear at a market, except they were haggling over me. The higher voice of a woman was as forceful as any of them. I could guess what they were saying: Mercy or no mercy? Kill her here or over there? Who gets to keep her stuff?

My hand felt raw and wet. I'd lost a glove stumbling out of the woods, but that didn't seem to matter anymore.

Whoever held the knife in my throat joined the conversation from time to time. I dreaded hearing his harsh raised voice in my ear, because whenever he spoke, he pressed the knife harder and I had to tip my head back to keep him from cutting me.

A faint blue haze was beginning to light the sky from the east. Flawless arctic blue. I knew for certain there was nothing waiting beyond it. No other worlds. No Mother, or Pa, or Charlo, or Shamsudin. No Ping. And yet, I found myself muttering the words of the Our Father over and over again, as though it was something to bite down on so I wouldn't cry out in pain.

Someone else came up beside me. A hand wiped the dirt roughly off my face. A new voice spoke and talked on a while. The knife stopped cutting into my windpipe and I fell forward onto my belly.

The ground had the earthy damp smell of mushrooms. I lay there nose down for a while as they argued back and forth above me.

No one stopped me as I got to my feet. Standing beside me was the boy from the Zone, the Tungus boy. The man who was arguing with him turned away in disgust.

A woman with a chapped red face was breastfeeding a baby. On a little pony beside her was a pale-skinned girl of about ten. Her eyes were so light that she couldn't have been native and she had fair hair curling out of her bushy fox-fur hat. I almost cried out in surprise, but she looked straight through me with the stony gaze you'd use to aim a gun. Tolya's icon was fixed to the lapel of her coat.

One by one the Yakuts went back to their horses until only the boy stood beside me. He never met my eye or gave the least indication that he knew me.

I watched them drift away into the forest. The woman with her baby rode behind the man wearing Tolya's jacket, and the white girl didn't give a backward glance.

Soon there were only two of them left in the clearing with their horses, the boy and the man with the knife. The boy patted the flank of his horse, but instead of swinging up into its saddle, he handed me the reins and got up on the other horse behind his friend.

He looked back at me for an instant with the blank face of a stranger. There was no kindness or understanding in his expression. I can't say what he might have been thinking.

It would be nice to suppose he did me a good turn for the one I did him. But there's no telling how grace works. I don't even know if there's a word for "mercy" in Yakut.

The imprint of his empty eyes stayed with me when he turned away. He dipped his head as the two of them rode under a branch which scattered snow down his back. In ten more yards they had vanished, and the drip of the thaw swallowed the sounds of their hooves.

I thought of the curt way I turned him loose that time by the riverbank, and of times out hunting when I just held my shot on a whim or threw back fish because they were too small. They never lingered to speculate about my motives.

It would be consoling to think there's a pattern of justice in things, but I've seen enough to be sure that there isn't. My father would point to what the boy did and say it was the redeemable part of his humanity. Maybe—rarer than a tadpole in a hailstone—that's what it was. But if I killed ten caribou, butchered them for their meat and skins, and then freed a snared rabbit just for the pleasure of watching its fluffy behind vanishing in the bracken, would that make me Saint Francis? I'd be deceived to think so.

The horse licked my bare hand. My pack and glove lay under the tree where I'd been woken. I found them, swung my stiff body onto the horse, and aimed her nose at the sunrise.

2

I kept away from the track we'd come out on in case Boathwaite had sent a party to find where we'd got to. It meant slower going, but I had the whole summer to get home in.

At night I'd see my route in the sky, mapped out in a pattern of stars. The Lena takes a great swerve to the west, but it ends up almost due south of Polyn, right near the base. I was planning to cut out that bend altogether and ride southeast until I struck the commissars' highway. As long as I kept on roughly in the right direction, I couldn't miss it. It was a straight line east to west. And once I was on it, there was less than a thousand miles between me and Evangeline. I could be home in six weeks.

Some evenings I'd pull out Shamsudin's blue tube. It had bumped around in my pack, but nothing could put a scratch on it. Once I fell asleep holding it. I had bad dreams and my fore-head and cheeks were sore the next day, as though I'd spent too long in the sun.

·

I stopped to fish one evening, hooked a pike perch, and then found four duck eggs in a nest. I made a fire and cooked one of them with the fish.

Overhead, there were cranes coming back from their winters in the south. Their long white bodies looked pink in the dying sunlight. They are holy birds to the Tungus. They use their bones as calendars and mark the phases of the moon in notches on them. The shamans say they ride them up to the ninth heaven, where the spirits live and make mischief with human souls.

It's all fairy tales to me, but I did see a shaman heal a sick woman once. She was a Tungus woman who'd had a stillborn child. It had left something awry in her womb.

The shaman had on a heavy coat of skins with jingling metal beads on it. The beads made a map of the stars. Before there were ever books, those coats were an atlas of the skies. He danced around her body for almost an hour, until a weird web of what looked like blood appeared on the skin of his drum.

I couldn't speak to the shaman myself, but I asked him questions afterward by way of a half-Tungus guide.

The shaman said he felt himself rise up through the air as he drummed. The air around him became thick and watery. He claimed it was like being lost in fog, and every now and again the fog thinned, and he was aware of the breathing in the hall. Then he rose up through a final bank of cloud and landed in a clearing.

He followed a path along a mountainside, past a skeleton he said was his father's, toward a lighted tent.

The sick woman's body was inside it, in the shape of a pile of stones with a vine growing out of it. The shaman ripped out the tendrils of the vine. The nearer he got to the center of the plant, the thicker they got; in the middle, they were a couple of inches round, and furry and hot like the shaft of spring antlers, full of new blood. And at the heart of the plant was a shriveled-up thing: the miscarried child whose soul had got lost on its way back from earth.

I don't know if he made this up to fool me or if he believed himself. It doesn't make a whole lot of sense to my mind. But after that dance, I heard the woman was able to conceive.

It seems like wherever it goes, my mind always comes back to dead children. That Tungus girl's. And Ping's. And mine.

Mine was born dead after a three-day labor. It was the worst pain I've ever known. In the chaos that had been brought to the city, there was not a doctor to be had.

They took him away and buried him somewhere. We never mentioned it again. I was sixteen. I was never close to a man after that, although I think I could have been. It just wasn't how things were.

•

My looping route toward the highway took me through a village with an old church in it. The houses around were all rotted and overgrown, but the church was solid enough, with a big wooden cupola and a bell still hanging in it.

The door opened and the air inside had a hint of incense and new whitewash.

Someone called up from the cellarage in Russian. I was too

amazed to recall any words of it beyond *bog*, which, crazy as it seems, is what they call god. Then a man clumped up the stairs with an armful of books. He looked taken aback to see me.

I couldn't have been more surprised to find a chuchunaa, and, come to think of it, he resembled one a little, being tall and having a long white beard.

We didn't have enough words in common to say much to each other, but we were able to talk in dumb show.

He was the priest of the village, and he had a helper, a kind of junior priest called Yuri. Yuri had a beard, too, but his was jet-black, and he smelled strongly of onions. I'd put his age at fifty and the priest's at seventy-five.

•

How they'd managed to survive—just the two of them, with Boathwaite on one side and the Tungus on the other—and keep the church in good repair, I don't know. I guess they'd just clung on there like a pair of limpets.

They lived in a little house in a yard alongside the church. I put my horse in an empty stall in their barn and they fed me.

We had a kind of soup of salted cabbage and some sausage, and I marked out my route to them on the tabletop.

They rolled their eyes when I showed them where I was going.

It was too bad that we couldn't say more. I had so many questions.

After dinner, they took me down into the cellarage and showed me all the books they had squirreled away down there. The old priest kept giving me things to hold, talking about them, and then looking at me closely as if to check I'd understood. Of course, I had no idea, but whatever it was he was talking about, he was proud of it.

Yuri could see I was foxed, and he kept trying to distract him, but the old priest wouldn't be told. "Here it is," he seemed to saying, "I've got it all squared away. Here are my jams, here are my jellies," as he dusted off another book or roll of papers.

After about an hour they locked up the church and we went back to the house. Yuri boiled up some kind of herb tea.

We couldn't say anything to each other, but sitting among them felt like the first happiness I'd known for so long. I wished I had something to give them in return. Then it struck me that I did have some words in their language.

I took the memory stone out of my pack, set it on the table between us, and showed them the girl from Polyn. They weren't happy until they'd seen it half a dozen times.

They loved it, the old priest most of all, slapping the other on the back each time they watched it. *Lyudi budushchevo!* he laughed, as though it was the best joke in the world.

I was pleased to see him so lively, then a terrible feeling came over me. I understood that he'd taken it as a picture of the present. They thought that was an image of the place as it was today. If I hadn't seen where it came from, I would have formed the same idea.

Here they were in their outpost, guarding their trove of holy books, waiting for news of the outside world, and it seemed that I'd brought them good tidings.

The misunderstanding made me heavyhearted. I said to them, "You've got the wrong idea. This is a picture of the past. This girl is dead. The city looks nothing like this."

But the words I was saying were just so much noise to them. They believed what they wanted to. I was the harbinger of something good. Any day now, people would begin to drift back. There would be damp beds airing out in the street. Shovels would turn over the soil in long-neglected gardens. The silent bell in the cupola would call a congregation to service, and someone would pin a medal on the old priest's chest for taking such care of his archive.

They made me a bed on a ledge above their tiled stove. I told them I'd be happier on the floor, but they insisted. It was too warm and soft for me to sleep well up there, and I was troubled that I'd deceived them. Seeing what false hope had done to them lowered my spirits.

The next morning they were just as cheery. They gave me buckwheat groats for breakfast and asked to watch the memory stone again.

I gave the stone to the priest and told him he could keep it. He tried to press an old book on me in return, but I refused.

The two of them walked me to the edge of their empty village and kissed me three times good-bye.

I looked back half a dozen times and they were still there, watching me go.

•

Spring was on the land. There was no snow to be seen anywhere. One hot noontime, I decided to bathe. I tethered the horse and stripped at the edge of a stream. My feet were so pale, they looked bluish.

Although the river was shallow, it was swollen and faster than it looked. I almost took a tumble as I stepped in. I braced my legs against a rock as the current eddied around my knees, then squatted down to let the water wash all over me. The cold made my head ring.

After I'd got myself clean, I laundered my clothes on a rock and then left them to dry in the sun.

I lay on the bank, soaking up the heat like a lizard, fighting the urge to drift off, but the sound of the river lulled me to sleep. I must have slept for an hour or more, because I woke up groggy, with my vision all bleached out from the sunshine.

It took me a moment or two to come to my senses: there's the horse, munching green shoots off a tree; there's my damp clothes; here's me, naked, with dried mud up to my ankles that looks like a pair of socks.

And suddenly, over the sound of the river running, I heard a buzz, very, very faint but growing stronger. Up in the eastern part of the sky, maybe a quarter of a mile up, was the sliver glint of a plane.

I stood there naked, shouting myself hoarse and waving my clothes as she passed overhead.

Judging from the angle of her flight, it seemed like she'd come out of the Far North, maybe from Alaska.

By the time I thought to fire my gun, the plane was in the southwest part of the sky.

I loosed off four or five signal shots, but she gave no sign of hearing me. The bullets would have been barely more than faint pops above the sound of the engine. The plane slipped away into the deep blue of the sky like a tiny silver fish. But as she vanished over the trees behind me, I was certain I knew where she was headed.

3

It took me two days to reach the base. I rode like a madwoman.
I don't recall that I ate at all. Sometimes I'd dismount and walk
alongside the horse to let her rest. All that time, I could hear my
heart banging in my chest with hope.

Seeing that plane the first time at the lake, I'd never known
hope like it. I was a castaway. The plane was a sail, luffing and
snapping to a new course as it came to find me. I would walk
on its warm deck with my pretty feet. There was silk and cloves
in its hold, coconuts, oranges. Well, I guess it brought on the
hooey in me. There's a little in there. I am a woman.

The second plane gave me a different kind of joy. This time
it was the cavalry, it was the law in armor. I pictured it touching

down on the base like a twister, ripping the huts out of the ground, scything down the guards. Imagine those captives free and bent on revenge: they'd kill Boathwaite like a dog and scorch his slave camp to the roots.

．

I neared the base around noon and dismounted where the forest began to thin. The land around the walls was bare. It had been clear-cut in the early days for timber and to strip the cover from the approach. I hung back out of sight behind a stand of trees.

My first glimpse of the base was through the spyglass. I could see the mismatched tiles on the roofs beyond the palisade and smoke rising from the smithy and the cookhouse.

The wind brought the hum of the latrines across the open ground. Everything looked more small and grubby than I remembered. My eye was jaded after the marvels of Polyn, but it's also because the snow was gone. Snow flatters poor workmanship. It covers up dirt and makes the crooked look quaint. And it keeps things from stinking.

I started to make a circuit of the base, keeping close behind the fringe of trees. There were no men to be seen, but just beside the front gate, no more than twenty yards outside the walls, stood the plane.

What a beautiful thing it was, like a muscle or a blade: all-purpose.

There was a ripple of heat haze above its top wing that made it look like it was still in motion.

As nearly as I could remember, it was the same kind as the one that had gone down by the lake. The colors of its hull were red and white and it had a door in its tail like the one I had smashed open that time on the hillside.

It had a weathered look. The dents and patches on the wings hinted at the labor it took to keep it flying. And yet, I could scarcely believe that the creatures who made that thing were human.

Everything at the base had a handprint on it. Everything took its scale from the shape of a man and the work he could do in one day. I could judge with my eye how long it would take to raise a stretch of wall or level the simple road that ran around it. I could probably name every tool they used to build it.

But to make that plane—was it six months or a century? What mysteries were at work in its engine?

It looked as out of place standing on that bleached grass as the wristwatch had on the herder's arm.

I am in awe of this broken pianola and the nameless crafts-man who fitted her with brass wires and felted hammers and a spiked drum to read the piano rolls. I've saved these piles of books for the knowledge that's in them. I've seen Polyn. I marvel daily on my morning rides at the beautiful skeleton of my dead city. But to turn words and numbers into metal and make them fly—what bigger miracle can there be?

It's a kind of heresy to say so, but I think our race has made forms more beautiful than what was here before us. Sometimes god's handiwork is crude. There is no more ugly thing than a lobster. There's not much pretty about a caribou. It has an ungainly walk and its touchhole voids droppings when it strains in harness. Was there a straight line on earth before we drew one?

But that plane in flight didn't pump and lurch like a big bird does. It moved steady and level, and faster than any bird I've ever seen.

The truth is, I half expected its crew to be gods.

And what would they know of us? What had they seen

from the sky? What would men like that make of the brutal facts of our life at the base?

I thought they would feel about me the way I felt about the simple understanding of the Tungus, with their shamans, and spirits, and chuchunaa.

.

I rode back into the bush to wait that night and ponder. I am rash by nature. I act best in the heat of the moment. Given too long to think, I can fall to brooding.

More for company than anything practical, I set a small fire and fed it with long, slim, twigs, holding on to the ends of them until they were almost consumed by the flame.

A dry wind blew and fanned the embers to orange.

Over the years since I'd seen the first plane, it had become my North Star. Just knowing about it was a comfort to me. I'd touched its hull with my own hands. I'd buried what was left of its crew. I had poured all my wishes into it. It was a vessel that held everything my world was not.

But now that it came to dealing with the living, breathing people that were on this new one, my nerve had failed.

All sorts of bewildered feelings were stirred up inside me.

Part of me was dying to know more. But another noisy part was saying it was better to leave now, knowing the first one wasn't a fluke, and not go further, which was bound to lead to ugliness and disappointment.

Big as the plane looked to me, hope was too heavy a cargo for it to carry.

I still wonder if there could have been anything on the plane that would have made what I'd gone through seem worthwhile.

It's so hard to think now what might have been on it, instead of what was.

What happens lays down a steel track over all the flimsy forms of *what might have been*.

I've been around this many times. I see myself in the wood, feeding the twigs into my solitary fire. And I see the empty plane sleeping by the gates of the base. I move myself, like a picture on a memory stone, until I'm riding backward to Polyn, giving Shamsudin the kiss of life on the way, trudging backward to the base with Tolya and the prisoners, the years of confinement, the months of work returning Boathwaite's garden to a wilderness.

Back and back I go, to before Ping's death, to when this city had life in it, to before the bad years, until I'm standing at the Bering Sea with my father, watching the Chukchi pack the innards back into a walrus and set him adrift on the water. And at each moment, I think, Here? Or here? Is this the choice that set the points for what followed?

Whatever way I come at it, it always plays out the same. The bad thing happens. The city burns. Those I love die. The plane crashes. I search for another. And when I finally find one, it has Eben Callard on it.

4

He was older, of course, yet somehow that surprised me. And even after spending some time with him, I found that his face was still overlaid by the younger one that I had spent so many hours remembering.

"I knew a Makepeace once," he said. He snapped his fingers for someone to pour him a drink. The blind can have a bossy way about them. I lied and told him I was from a different city.

He sat in the chair behind Boathwaite's tin desk wearing a dark broadcloth suit, staring straight past me with those cloudy eyes. His shirt was white and newly pressed.

"Your voice is familiar," he said. "It must be that settler accent." He never gave any hint that he might have known me. "Boathwaite spoke highly of you."

I still had the dust on me from my long ride. Six of his men were posted around the room. They were armed. Two wore bandoliers. They'd patted me down for weapons when I'd come in.

At dawn, I had ridden up to the gates. The itch to know had overcome any thought I had for my own safety. If I'd had any inkling who'd been on it, of course I would have made for home. But I never connected that plane with anything in my own past. In my mind, it came out of the orderly world of my parents with a promise as straight and green as the twig in that dove's beak: dry land this way, turn your ship around.

The sentry knew me by sight, but another man—one of Eben Callard's, it turned out—was standing guard beside him.

They called someone out of the guardhouse to take the horse. I didn't know the boy. There was straw in his hair and his face was crinkled from sleep.

I was sorry to see the horse go. There was no easy way out of there without her, but my desire to know about the plane had overmastered my every other thought.

All the omens were poor. The sentry gave me a sly and uneasy look as he hauled the door open. And on the far side of the parade ground, a rough wooden cross had been dug into the dirt, and off it was dangling a body.

The wind had sprung up, and when it blew, it caught him like a sail and made the joints of the crosspiece creak.

Though the face was black and swollen, I could see from his build that it was Boathwaite. There were wounds to his body and head, and his arms had been nailed through the wrists. His belly was all bloated with gas.

From the manner of his death, I guessed the prisoners had chosen it themselves.

He looked like he'd been dead at least two days. They must

have turned on him in a fit of revenge soon after the plane landed.

I'll confess I was taken aback. I'm no lover of mob justice. People making their own law is an ugly sight.

Shamsudin had said that civilization meant city life. I wasn't sure about that. To me it meant streetlights, plumbing, schools, and things worked out by reason. I can't see the reason in deliberate cruelty. It makes a fetish of what's most base in us.

But I had to trust that the men in the plane were wise enough to know what they were about. No one else had died. The walls were intact. The place had not been razed. Maybe the body on the cross was the price of that order.

·

Whatever upsets there had been, I still held my old rank as a guard. My room was just as shabby as I'd left it. The dust on the window looked like milled gold in the sunlight.

Out of the window, I watched the place coming to life. First the reveille and the weary prisoners dragging their chains out of the bunkhouse. How ragged they looked.

After fifteen minutes, one of the new guards came in and said Mr. Callard would see me. By the time I reached the office, I had a pretty good idea what I'd find.

On the walk over, his man said to me that he'd lost his eyes defending a woman's honor. That made me smile.

The first meeting was short. He wanted to know where I'd been. How come I'd survived. I told him as little as possible. They excused me to go back to my room and clean up.

Someone brought food and water and a change of clothes. They gave me a rough towel with a tablet of green soap on it. I scrubbed myself and cleaned my hair with it in the washroom. I could only think that it had come on the plane. It had been so long since I'd seen any. We used to make our own in Evangeline. Fat and lye is what you use to do it. *Jezebel.*

There was a little scent in this one. It seemed to make my hair go stringy. As I washed, I thought of how I would escape. First light. I'd take another horse. I'd take two.

Tears made my eyes go blurry. It was the disappointment of it. After all this. I was the one holding a garbled message. I thought I was a caretaker, shoring up the few things I could against annihilation, trying to be worthy of the traditions of my ancestors. I'd always been so proud that I lived in this world. But I was just like Pa. I needed another world to redeem the present.

I've looked back at my pages and found I've written: *I don't need things to be otherwise.*

•

You know how it is when the most cussed and determined bachelor falls in love, he colors what's left of his hair and gets his heart broken? Or the teetotal lady who does the flowers in the church, has her first sherry at sixty, and dies a drunk?

I'd walked through life like a cat on ice, testing each step before I took it. Now it turned out I'd tiptoed into a bear trap.

It's something when disaster walks in through an open window. But what could you do? Every life has some of that. But when you barred yourself into a strongbox, rubbed your hands, and spent years telling everyone how safe you are . . . That's the trouble I'm talking about. Everyone sees it coming but you. That's in the nature of a blind spot.

The years stretched off in front of me like a frozen winter road. The hope that I'd fed on, that I'd held in secret like a stash of hidden money, was gone.

How had I lived before Ping or the plane, without the sense that any other life was mortised to mine, or the thought that somewhere children were walking to school, and the dead getting buried, and a pianola playing in tune? Sitting in the dark all winter, waiting for the candles to run out. Trying to catch an echo of the life that had been here. Waking in the dark. Cleaning my guns at night. Crunching out to the stable with the saddle over my shoulder.

My life didn't even count as suffering. It was one long cruel joke that the wind had written on the snow.

5

There was an odd smell in the air which I remarked on to the guards who came to get me toward midday. They said the stills were going full tilt to brew fuel for the plane. It meant the kitchens were shorthanded and most of the inmates on half rations.

I questioned the wisdom of that, privately. For all his short-comings and cruelties, Boathwaite never let the prisoners go hungry. The food was often dull, but it was plentiful. He'd known as well as I did that well-fed people were more biddable.

They escorted me across the parade ground. I knew the way as well as they did, but I guessed they'd been told to keep a close eye on me.

Up in the fields, the men were laboring as slowly as ever, weeding and mending fences, grumbling and moving livestock.

Things looked much like they always had. And yet, some odd changes had taken place in my absence. With Boathwaite and Tolya dead, the running of the base had fallen to a man named Purefoy. He was settler stock himself, but a shy man who I'd always felt Boathwaite trusted because he didn't have the dash and swagger of a natural leader, or carry much weight with the other guards.

Empty bellies, the old boss gone—there was more than the fumes from the stills in the air. I was almost too cast down to smell it, but sure enough, alongside the stink of brewing, and the dirt, and the latrine, there was a sharp whiff of mutiny.

They had laid out Boathwaite's room for a banquet. I didn't feel like eating anymore. Purefoy and a half dozen of the senior guards were there. They had shaved and put on their best coats and three or four of them had brought their wives. You could see by the way the men bowed and scraped to Eben Callard and his men that they felt themselves to be country cousins.

The women sat by themselves at a separate table, wearing old-fashioned formal clothes. I couldn't help wondering about Boathwaite's widow and that little girl of his.

·

There was a place laid for me at the main table. Eben Callard sat at the head of it and there were fourteen or so places set round it. Much of the food had come from the base, but there was plenty there that must have traveled with them on the plane, since we had no way of growing or making it there. There was sweet wine for the women, little heaps of orange salmon eggs, bowls of lump sugar, candy, and canned crabmeat, and bottles of cognac with labels on them.

At a signal from one of the guards, we took our seats.

It was a strained and nervy gathering. No one was sure if we were meant to start eating.

Eben Callard rolled a shotglass of cognac between his fingers. "We don't visit often," he said. "We don't want to leave a bad impression. Things have had to be done. Some harsh decisions had to be made. But I don't want to dwell on that now."

He was speaking of Boathwaite. Even now his body was tanning in the sunshine out in the yard. I wondered what they considered to be his crime. He must have run the base as they asked him: turning the raw prisoners into farmhands and sending gangs of them out to the Zone to scavenge from Polyn. Maybe he'd been a little softer in command than they wanted? Had he failed to bring enough back from the Zone? Or was it some lingering politics that I had no sight of, like what had seen me imprisoned by Boathwaite's brother?

I guessed that whatever happened here was a sideshow to the world Eben had flown out of. Maybe his standing there hinged on his adventures here in the north. I knew now that on the other side of the straits something limped on. It hadn't abandoned us; in fact, it seemed to look to us for its salvation.

My mind was snapped back to the room by his mentioning the Zone. His white, sightless eyes had fixed on me at the end of the table. "The last trip threw up some promising things. We're looking forward to learning more before we leave."

He proposed a toast and put his glass to his lips. The level in it barely altered, while all around the table the guards emptied theirs. Purefoy proposed a toast in return. People began eating; the drinking became general and loosened the mood in the room.

The guard next to me served me with roasted meat from a tray. I remembered him as a bully. Flushed with drink, he boasted of his young wife and whispered indiscreetly about what I'd missed.

"They gave him a last chance one year ago. That's when they sent the Jap out from Alaska." He nodded his head at Apofagato, who sat up at the far end of the table.

He'd been to the Zone himself, he said. Trouble was, Boathwaite was too damn soft. A dozen or so prisoners a year would never make a dent in that place. They needed to turn the whole base out, march them into the Zone en masse.

When he said "soft," I thought of the pile of the bodies in the snowmelt on the bridge.

"You can't make an omelette without breaking eggs," he said.

•

The afternoon dragged on. The bottles kept coming. I didn't drink and neither did Eben Callard. By mid-afternoon, the noise in the room was a roar. Men took turns making outlandish toasts. The guards' wives were flushed and giggly.

Suddenly Eben Callard's voice cut through the buzz of drunken laughter. "We haven't heard from Makepeace," he said.

I said I didn't mean to give offense, but I'd drunk as much as I wanted.

The room quietened. He said he hadn't had a toast in mind. He'd wanted to hear me speak about the Zone and what we'd found there.

So I told them what I'd seen, more or less, leaving out my own visit to the city. I told them about the Tungus boy, and the poison, and how we shot the prisoners on the bridge.

That phrase "too soft" that the man next to me had used kept coming into my head. I told them about Zulfugar and the soft-nosed bullet that had cored him like an apple.

I wanted them all to know—the women, too, since it was done in their name. And I told them that we had come back empty-handed.

They heard me out politely and without interest, as if these were things that we didn't speak of but were plain to all of us.

When I was done speaking, Eben Callard thanked me for my account of the trip. "Sure you've been straight with us?" he said.

I told him I had.

"Because some of my men followed your trail into the bush and went digging."

He signaled and someone brought a sack into the room. I knew what was in it. I'd buried it near the ashes of the fire the night before.

Eben Callard reached in and pulled out the mason jar with its waves of light. He held it up with both hands, as though he was going to bless it. The room went quiet enough that you could hear the faint hum of all that light moving.

"I wish I had eyes to see it," he said, "because I hear it's a pretty thing."

6

Why Eben Callard needed to make theater out of proving me a liar, I don't know, but after he had, he had his men take me down to a room in the courtyard where they left me for a while, bound fast, before they hauled me out to question me.

They took to me another room with shades over the windows, where, in spite of the heat of the day, they had a stove lit which they'd rake from time to time with pokers, with the plain intention of letting me think they were going to burn me. They said they wanted to know why I'd lied and where the thing had come from and why I had hid it, but the truth was, I think they were just itching to knock me around the place.

One of them stepped forward with a roll of papers which he spread out in front of me.

"I want you to look carefully at these drawings and tell me if any of the things the prisoners found are shown on it."

There were six sheets of thin waxy paper with drawings on them in a kind of faint blue ink. The pictures were drawn with a very exact hand and measurements and figures were inked in alongside them. There was writing in Russian, too, but I couldn't read it. Some of the images I could recognize—there were suits and masks like the guards had been wearing, something that resembled a rifle—but others were simply too strange for me to make head or tail of.

I shook my head in a weary way and told them that all we'd found was the flask, and they had that.

·

They let me alone to sleep, and around noon the next day there was a knock on the door and someone slid in a plate of food. It was sausage, stale bread, and beetroot soup. I recognized the sausage as leftovers from our feast. It had grown more leathery and little drops of oil had gathered on its cut ends.

The door opened again and two guards showed Eben Callard to the spare seat in the room.

"Make sure her hands are tied," he said.

The guards roped my arms to the chair and yanked the cord tight. They left the room at a signal. The shutting of the door seemed loud over the silence that followed.

Being alone with him after all that time wasn't as strange as you'd think.

"How do you look, Makepeace? They tell me you're marked."

"I look about the same," I said. "What happened to your eyes?"

"You want the long answer or the short one?"

I told him I didn't mind either.

He passed his hand over the tabletop in a steady, thorough way until it lighted on the handle of the spoon. With his other he found the soup bowl, then he stirred it up until the broth went cloudy like his sightless eyes.

"Before Evangeline, you know, we had a big property outside of Esso. That was the place we left America for. It was really something. The earth's volcanic and rich and there are hot springs right under the city. You just sink a pipe and you've got hot water. We had heated greenhouses, tomatoes all year. We were on the side of a mountain you could ski down and only a couple of hundred miles from Peter-Paul." He sighed with the recollection of it. "And I bet you thought life was good in Evangeline.

"Then all the changes came. We got overrun. There were Russians and Evenki and some Koreans who had been there from the beginning. They formed a militia and kicked everyone else out. They didn't care if we had a title to the land. For the next five years it was snakes and ladders with no ladders. First run out of Esso. Then run out of Evangeline by James Hatfield's people.

"You know that we lit out of there with nothing? A bunch of men came to our house with torches. They said someone had raped James Hatfield's girl and I was supposed to have done it.

"I offered to go out and talk to them, but my father said not to. It was the middle of the night. There was no reasoning with them. They'd have strung me up there and then. While we were arguing about what to do, they set the roof on fire. We grabbed what we could and escaped out the back.

"It was my nineteenth birthday. I should be bitter about it, but I'm not, because that was the start of all the good things that happened to me."

He kept stirring, sifting through the contents of the bowl in silence, then he let the spoon drop.

"We had to set out for Magadan on foot. It was summertime. I don't know how we stayed alive on that highway. The things I saw made life in Evangeline seem like Sunday school. A couple of times we skipped off the road and traveled in the taiga, getting eaten alive by the insects.

"We got a ride part of the way with a trader, a Jew from Odessa called Eli Rozenbaum who was on his way back from Polyn. We were lucky to find him. He drove us through the worst of it. You know what a *vezdekhod* is? He had one of those with its cab piled up to here with weapons: guns and things I'd never seen before. There were roadblocks in those days, but they were built to stop foot traffic. Eli drove at night, and whenever he came across one, he'd floor the thing and crash right through it.

"He helped us on a boat to Providence—what the Russians called Provideniya. That little pinch point between the old world and the new. Only a handful of miles, but every time you come this way over it, it costs you a day. He warned us about going there. We told him were planning on paying some Chukchi to take us across to Nome. My mother had family in Barrow, if we could get there. Before he left us he gave my father a pistol to protect himself.

"The voyage took two weeks. You ever been to Providence? It's a hellhole. There used to be a fleet there, but they'd all been discharged. The town was crawling with hungry sailors looking for money, looking for a way back west. Ugly, stained buildings. The Chukchi were terrified of the Russians and wouldn't come near the place. There was one warehouse full of freeze-dried potatoes that had been rations for the fleet. A gang of sailors were selling it off. We paid them a pair of gold earrings for enough to feed four of us.

"It was stupid of us, but we were desperate. They marked us out as worth robbing. We hunkered down that night in an abandoned apartment. We were asleep when some sailors broke in and started to beat up my father.

"In the struggle, the pistol rolled out of his pocket and I let off three shots at them. They were homemade shells. The first two killed one of the sailors. The third blew up in the breech and the metal splinters took one of my eyes out.

"The noise of it scared them out of there. We left town as soon as we could and went on foot to a Chukchi village on the Bering Sea.

"My father clung on for a few days. My mother gave the Chukchi all we had to take us across to Diomede. You know there are Chukchi on Diomede, like us, neither Russian nor Yankee?

"We buried my father at sea. Just slipped his body into the water. We felt it was better that way. We didn't want him to lie in foreign soil. What I would have given to bury him in America. We were near enough Alaska to be able to smell it, but with no way to get there.

"The Chukchi on Diomede gave us a shack and my mother taught in their school for a while. But it was tough on us. Losing our dad. Losing our home. Stranded among savages—no disrespect to them, they couldn't have been kinder to us, but we didn't come to that place to live like that, all the dirt and drunkenness. You know how native people are.

"The straits were still icing up some winters. I remember

my first sight of sea ice on the foreshore, looking out toward Alaska. It looked unreal through my one good eye, flat as a painting, all the mist and sand and gray water. I swore to God that if he could find us a way to get there, I would be his servant in everything. That was the day everything changed.

"I went back to the shack and who's there but Eli Rozenbaum. He'd run into some Chukchi fishermen who'd told him about us and he'd come to help. He paid gold for us to get to Nome and found a boat there to take us on to Barrow.

"Waking up that first morning in Barrow was like coming round from a bad dream. I mean, it wasn't like it *was*, but compared to everything we'd seen . . . Waffles and fruit for breakfast. I never tasted anything so good in my whole life. My aunt said her sourdough starter was a hundred years old. I looked at my mother with my mouth open when she said that. As bad as they thought things were, to have that *continuity* . . .

"Through the winter, Eli came back every couple of months to check on us. He was back and forth to Chukhotka and brought us news. Soon it became pretty obvious to even me that he wasn't just visiting out of neighborliness. He'd taken a shine to my mother and was courting.

"Our relatives weren't keen about it, with him being a Jew and everything, but my mother was a widow and she didn't have any better offers.

"She wouldn't hear anything against it, and she like to tell them it wasn't the first time He'd sent a Jew to save us.

"They were married in the spring and I went to work with Eli.

"Eli had a business going up here. He'd take moonshine and bullets and whatnot and pay Tungus to go into the Zone for him and fetch weapons and tools. He'd bring them back to Alaska to sell. Dealers came up in private planes from all over to see him. They had a notion where he was getting it from, and bitched about his prices, but none of them could have done what he did.

"I started traveling out with him. I know the Far North like you do. I understand the mind of the Tungus. Eli came to depend on me. We were able to clean out whole sections of Polyn and get the stuff back to the States, but every time, it got harder and harder to get labor. The Tungus were getting sick and dying and they'd refuse to go. Each time we'd have to tap up another village. The Tungus there still hate us for what happened in the early days.

"We started to think, There must be an easier way to do this. There were all these masses of people dying for food, and there's us hurting for workmen. That's when we stumbled on this place. It was an old garrison. We stocked it with men, and twice a year we send them in to earn their living.

"I took them myself at first. I never went into the Zone itself, but I liked being near it. Radiation didn't bother me at all, but that other stuff—that's fierce. We couldn't risk *that* getting out of there. The first couple of times we brought them back to the base. So many people got sick, we had to kill everyone and start again.

"We didn't like doing it. We didn't do it lightly. But we can't get by without what we get from the Zone. It's as plain as that. It's not pretty what we do. But I'm not ready to ask my wife and family to live like the Tungus.

"And to be honest about it, most of these prisoners will never see the Zone. There's old men here who would have been dead years ago without the base. We give them food, we give them work. If you take away the years they've gained from the years that have been lost, I'd guess it comes out all square."

He was silent for a while.

"And how did you lose the other one?" I asked him.

He shifted in his chair. "That one's a cataract. Too much staring at the sun. But I can see enough in it to know who you were.

"The thing about the Zone is, over the years, the easy pickings have gone. It's getting harder and harder to find what we want, yet the best stuff is supposed to still be in there. Things that make the flask you found look like a slingshot. And medicines. Cases of cells. Daniels's Fire. That's why I sent Apofogato out. But Boathwaite picked this moment to go soft on me."

I wondered if, because I was someone from his own past, he felt the need to acquit himself in front of me. I stayed quiet and let him open himself out to the silence in the room.

"He wanted to wind it up. Marriage and having kids made me more of a fighter. I need to be out here, laying my skinny ass on the line so they can live like they ought to. But it made Boathwaite soft. Marriage for him meant sitting in his garden with his wife and daughter, eating ice cream."

For a second, Eben seemed to hear a voice in his head accusing him of cruelty—some echo of his conscience stirring— and he flashed angrily at it. "I don't say I like it, but I do it, and I go home, and my wife don't know, nor will my kids. I do it so they won't have to. It's not a choice between good and bad. It's a choice between what is and what might be."

The slick words I remembered from before: always a plan, always a way to talk something into its opposite. But as I watched him, I was struck for the first time by a doubt about him, against all the evidence of my memory: what I *knew* of him, or seemed to know.

"It's easy to look smart, less easy to do good. You can only live in the world you find yourself in. These prisoners are fed because of me. There's cities with a future across the water because of what I've done."

That seemed to satisfy his conscience. I remembered his changeable moods. Suddenly he was reflective.

"You wonder: Where does the time go? It seems like suddenly you're old and the years are driving on. Merciless.

"I can't pretend the world we have is a match for what was. We live very simple. Don't get the wrong idea from the planes.

"There's things we don't know anymore. Things we don't have. Things we can't make. Our settler parents—what they did was easy. But out of the chaos they left us, I'm trying to make something. It's an awful duty, you know, taking care of the future. Who on earth would have thought it would fall to *me*?"

"Don't be so bashful," I told him. "I can't think of anybody better. This world has your handprints all over it."

So far I had heard him out in silence. All that ancient history between us meant nothing to me. I knew thousands of people had stories worse than his. But he wasn't dumb. He could hear the hatred in my voice.

"I never laid a finger on you, Makepeace," he said. "I've done some ugly things—I'm the first to own it. But I'm innocent of that." He fixed me with the blown bulbs of his eyes. "It wasn't me. But I don't blame you for believing it was, because the truth is uglier than you can imagine."

Suddenly my old tired body ached from all its rough usage and I wished I had something stronger than soup to drink.

"Remember Rudi Velazquez?" Eben went on. "About five years ago, he showed up in Alaska and looked me up at my office. I hadn't heard from him for years, but I recognized his name and I had him shown in. There were a few niceties, this and that, how's so-and-so—you know how it is—but I'm a busy fellow so I asked him what was his reason for wanting to see me. He told me he was sick. I'd known that as soon as I'd heard his voice. It was old and papery and shaking his hand was like holding a fistful of sticks. Now, as it happens, I know a good doctor in Barrow, and I was pleased it was this, because, generally speaking, what people want is to borrow money from me, or for me to find me work for them. I'd told him I'd be happy to help and was ready to have him seen out, when he said it wasn't that he was after and he'd like to have word with me in private.

"Now, that's something I rarely do. I'm still pretty quick and I'd back myself against any man in a grapple, but without my sight I'm at disadvantage. I have to be careful how I do business. So I had him patted down again and sent my bodyguards out of the room.

"There was a long silence. I told him I was pressed for time. Still nothing. Finally he blurted it out. He said he wanted me to forgive him. He said I'd taken the blame for something he'd done. I told him not to mind it, the past never weighed on me that heavy in any case; and besides, I couldn't imagine Rudi doing anything so bad it could stir his conscience."

I knew otherwise but I said nothing.

"Rudi said this thing had been preying on his mind. He was keen for me to know in detail and whether I forgave him or not, that was up to me. Confession's a powerful thing.

"He said it was him that had broken in to the Hatfield residence that night with a gang of men he'd hired down by the old firehouse. He'd had to pay them half up front to get a deal and they were drunk when he went to meet them. He had a bad feeling about it, but he went ahead anyway. The men were out of control. He lost a grip on things as soon as they got to the house. You know the rest.

"I told him it was *your* forgiveness that he needed, but for my part, I could see his remorse was genuine and it wasn't up to me to judge him.

"He seemed pretty happy with that answer and left soon afterward. It didn't rest so easy there with me, though. It didn't feel quite right. I knew Rudi once, and it didn't sound like the kind of thing he would do. We have all had to adapt, but for Rudi to break in and steal? It got to bothering me so much that I had some of my men follow him.

"They said he was living with some distant relative of his in a street full of crippled houses that were sliding into their own foundations. He spent most of each day in bed in this screwed-up room, not a straight angle left in it, coughing up into a bucket.

"So finally I went to see him. I said, 'Rudi, something's bothering me about the story you told. And don't for a second think that I don't forgive you, because I do—and in a way I ought to thank you, for if they'd never run me out of town, perhaps I would never have made it here like I have.' And I thought to myself, Maybe it would have been me in this crooked room, preparing to die. 'But what's bothering me is this: I just don't believe that you, on your own, would have decided to rob James Hatfield.'

"And he said, in his rattling voice, 'I didn't.'

"'If that's the case, why did you do it?'

"'Someone sent me,' he said.

"'And who was that?' I asked.

"'James Hatfield.'

"For a moment, I thought I'd misheard or the consumption had reached his brain. But then, just after, it was like a big light going on in my head.

"What do lawyers say?" Eben went on. "'Cui bono'? We got set up. Your father was running out of friends. Turning the other cheek sounded grand, but it wasn't practical. He knew that, but how could he climb down from his mountaintop and say he'd changed his mind? A man as rigid as him.

"A wiser man would have known how to move with the times. He *could* have thrown his hands up and said: 'I was wrong. This thing's out of control. Mike Callard has the right idea. We need to arm ourselves and protect what we have here.' But the thing about your old man is he had no humility. He had to be right, even when he was wrong.

"And what made it galling for him was my father, a new-comer to the town who'd depended on your father's charity, winning over all those wavering souls. Your father must have wrestled with himself, seeing the corner he was in. Yes, he had an uncomfortable choice to make.

"Rudi said your father came to him and laid things out. He told him he needed a provocation. Rudi was supposed to break into your house with a gang of men, rough the place up a bit. No one was to be harmed, just smash up this and that. Enough for him to blame us for it, run us out of town, and use it to ex-cuse a change of heart on carrying arms. I can almost hear your father's voice saying it: 'Why, even Simon Peter raised his sword to defend our Lord!'

"Rudi didn't want paying himself. He was doing out of re-spect for your old man. Your father had given him a little money as wages for the men, but he didn't take any. He was very par-ticular that I know that. It was never meant to go as far as it did. Things got out of hand. That's the tragedy. Rudi said your fa-ther couldn't live with it and the remorse killed him.

"Rudi said he never felt anything but admiration for you.

And he was sorry how it had changed you. He said you kind of went into yourself after it happened. You were always so outgoing, couldn't keep still, always moving, like a ball in a bagatelle. You had big dreams, I remember. Move out east, back to the States. You never had the spirit of a small-town girl. He said there was a time when there was just a handful of you all living in the rubble of Evangeline like refugees. He said he'd see you every day, circling the place on horseback, like a—what's the word he used?—a wraith. Depressed the hell out of him to see what had become of you. I remember how you were, too, Makepeace, bright as a button. You were a pretty thing too. A lot of us were sweet on Makepeace Hatfield.

"I understand why you lied to me about the Zone. But we're not enemies. Look at me: time hasn't been kind to me. But two hops and you can be out of here. Take us to where the flasks are and we can ride that plane to Barrow. People live very well there. It's like it was here in the old days. Very neighborly. Very respectful. And bit by bit we're building something we can leave our children. Not all fathers are like yours, Makepeace."

He stood up and took something out of his pocket. "I brought you dessert," he said, putting it on the table in front of me.

"I'm sorry if what I said has hurt you, but I thought it was better for you to know."

He called to the guard to see him out of the room. There was a step down to manage on the way out, and he wobbled somewhat as he took it, but aside from that, you would never guess his eyes had gone.

·

The guard loosened my hands.

I thought at first he'd left me behind an apple, but I soon

knew what it was. The first I'd ever seen. An orange. I scraped the skin with my nail and it let out a smell that seemed to have flowers and mint and burned sugar in it. After a moment I could smell sea spray too. But I couldn't bring myself to eat the thing.

·

There was an electrical storm that night, as big as any I can remember. It kicked off with a drum roll of thunder way out to the east of us, toward the coast, toward Evangeline. Then the sky darkened and flashed, throwing down chunks of ice so big that I thought we were under attack. It pounded the yard, and rustled the trees, and slammed the tin roofs of the prisoners barracks.

·

All my life I spent with people whose whole task on earth was bound up with acting rightly, and I guess I got the habit of it.

Now I had found myself standing in a world where right had perished. I had always believed that right was like north to my father: a thing as real as sunlight, a place on the map, the arrow on a compass. It was the unalterable facts of duty, love, and conscience. But our world had gone so far north that the compass could make no sense of it—could only spin hopelessly in its binnacle. North had melted right off the map. North was every which way. North was nowhere. For so long the plane had been my north. And in a strange way, so had Eben Callard. I was anchored by the bad thing just as by the hope that in a distant city some semblance of order, of right, was giving meaning to my world. But we were long past that place. I stood in the dark, trying to make sense of a room that was lit by flashes of light through a keyhole.

An hour or two past midnight the hailstorm ceased and the air grew quiet and fresh. I rattled on the door with my tin cup to get the guard, then I told him I had a message for Eben Callard.

7

It took them another day and a half to distill ethanol for the plane's spare tank. The plan was to take enough for two flights and miss out the base on the journey back.

They let me back to sleep in my old room and I was up at dawn, waiting by the plane in the caramel morning light as the horses were loaded up a ramp at the back. The animals balked at the stink of oil and spirit, but the guards shoved them in and fixed them in slings to hold them through the journey. I know in the old days that even the Tungus flew sometimes, and they moved their prize caribou by air. Then we took our places among them, some of us on boxes, others on the seats that swung down from worn latchings on each side of the plane. The inside was painted sky blue, with Russian words stenciled on it. I felt for all the world that I was in a shed. It didn't seem possible that it would ever be able leave the ground.

We were sat there for almost an hour before the props started turning so I had plenty of time to think about what I had chosen. I felt that Shamsudin would have approved of the deal I'd struck. "Civilization and cities are the same thing," he'd said. I wished he was coming with me. I wasn't too old for a change.

Eben was the last to get in. He was helped up to a seat beside the pilot in the front of the plane and put on some headgear to talk to him with.

At the takeoff, we rumbled across the grass outside the base so slowly, I couldn't see how we'd lift before we hit the trees. Then, just when it seemed the pilot had misjudged the takeoff, the note of the engine changed, and she rose up, and an invisible weight pressed me into my seat.

The horses seemed more calm about the notion of flying than I was. They swayed a little as we lifted but never stopped munching out of their feed bags.

I had to turn awkwardly to look through the windows. I could see the ground dropping away beneath us as we turned in a wide arc over the base. It was spread out beneath us like a toy fort.

The men who were marching out to work all turned as one to look up. The bare ground around them was brown and faded like a worn bearskin. Summer and winter are the two moods of the north, but so different that you'd take them for different places.

And then we were over the taiga—one green vastness all the way to the horizon, here and there slashed with little rills of white water. The size of it made my neck prickle. At its distant edges I could make out the faint curve of the globe.

There was a roar in the cabin that was too loud to speak over, and some of the men dozed. The ones beside me were jumpy during the flight. They watched me carefully, not quite believing I would be helping them willingly.

It wouldn't have been hard to grab hold of the steering and plunge all of us into the trees. But I was as good as my word.

•

It took us half a day to cover the same distance it had taken weeks to ride. Toward noon we got a signal from the cabin that we were passing over the Zone.

You had to see Polyn from the air to understand what a masterpiece it was.

It lay bleaching in the sun underneath us, like the bits of a broken machine: streets fanning out from the hub of the main square; the river alongside it like a sheet of hammered lead, reflecting the sun back up at us with a dull glow; and that big head, no more than a bronze pimple.

The pilot brought us down on a stretch of flat ground by the riverside. We seemed to speed up as we landed, until the trees were rushing past us, and it felt like we would certainly crash; but the plane bounced a couple of times like a skimmed stone and then pulled up to a stop.

The sunlight was fierce as I climbed out. The props died gradually into silence until all you could hear was the boisterous sound of the insects. The mosquitoes plagued us from the moment we touched down. We wore head nets to fend them off, but any bare skin they'd settle on in a moment, and gorge there until you killed them or until they flew off, fat and giddy with blood.

It took a while to unpack the plane. The horses had to come down the ramp again and they took some cajoling. The men smoked constantly and they bickered and shouted, nervous about the place we were in.

We made camp a good way from the bridge because the pile of bodies was stinking. It was a lot different from my last time there. They'd brought bedding, fresh food, and clean firewood from the base—not to keep warm, but for smoke to put off the insects.

The pilot slept in the plane that night, but the rest of them spent the night in the open, sleeping in shifts so there was always someone keeping one eye on the Tungus—and another on me. They still didn't trust my change of heart.

•

Apofagato had told me I should shave my hair off as a safe-guard—anything to stop dust leaving the Zone. So at first light I snipped it short with some clippers and finished it off with a razor.

The guards were asleep. Eben Callard had a private tent and two men to guard it. Like he'd said, he had to be careful how he did business.

I had some tools but no weapons to speak of, and I knew there was nothing I could do to stop the double cross. I just hoped if they'd decided to kill me, they'd do it quickly.

My hair lay all around me in mousy tufts. It was darker than I'd expected, but for the first time in my life I could see there was gray in it. I stroked my naked skull with my fingers; it felt queer and slick to the touch. It was a comfort to cradle it, somehow. It was warm and there was a pulse in it. It reminded me of Ping.

The last thing I did was to throw away the keepsake I had

made from the wing. I'd been wearing it so long, it left a smudge of gray on my skin. I took it off and pitched it into the river. It rose and dipped like a bird in flight, then vanished. I thought that whatever hopes and convictions she had cherished, Makepeace was just another mask that life wore as it fought to renew itself, unsentimental, unsparing, fighting ugly.

I didn't doubt that Eben had told me the truth. Bill Evans had a rule of thumb he used to size up suspects. It wasn't foolproof—what is?—but it helped to get a handle on people. He called it the law of opposites. He said the truth of a man is the opposite of what he wants you to know about him. If you want to understand someone, you have to find a way to catch hold of his shadow. By Bill's reckoning, the man to fear is the one always harping on about goodness.

My father felt exalted by the thought of the things he had given up to live his life. He believed that he was a better man than those people who had clung on to riches and city life, who had been slower to see the changes in the world. But the truth was he wasn't even as good a man as Eben Callard.

Eben was cruel and blunt and practical. He called himself a Christian, but his real beliefs put him closer to the Tungus. There was no right in the first religions, no goodness to confuse the shamans—just the way things were done, just what served life and what didn't. And no room for hypocrisy.

The prayers my father had offered were the prayers of the Pharisee. He spoke of god and sacrifice. But his god was his own vanity, and the sacrifice had turned out to be me.

•

I crossed back into the Zone a few hours after dawn. The town was quite different with spring on it. The chestnut trees were in flower on the main streets, and the sidewalks seemed coated with a kind of sticky sap that had been thrown down from some of the branches. But in general, there was something sicklier and deader about Polyn in the summer. In winter it had seemed frozen—or maybe asleep, like the princess in the fairy tale. But in summer, you could see she wasn't just dead: her corpse was flyblown.

It took me till early afternoon to find the place Shamsudin had told me about, and I spent another hour fixing holds to the wall with the tools I'd brought with me. I tied a rope to one of them. Then I squeezed myself though the broken window and dropped down into the basement.

It wasn't exactly how Shamsudin had described it. The way he had told it, the storeroom was near the place he'd come in, but there was nothing like that nearby. The chamber was much bigger than I'd expected: it was a walkway almost the size of a road that was lit with hidden skylights, and ways coming off it every ten yards or so. It was a labyrinth all right, but on the white tiles of the floor I could see traces of dirt and dried blood where Shamsudin had been before me, so I let him lead me down.

Following his prints was like tracking a wounded thing— the way they doubled back on themselves, went nowhere in particular, and seemed to rest, exhausted, in one place before continuing. They still told of his despair. The man who left these marks had only days to live, I thought. And as I followed him deeper into the labyrinth, I wondered how long I had, and I thought about the double cross. I figured it was fifty-fifty that they'd shoot me on the bridge.

The storeroom was much deeper than he'd explained, down several ramps and staircases that he'd never mentioned. I doubt anyone else could have found it. Only someone who'd lost all hope of getting out by another way would have floundered this deeply into the building. Out of all the combinations of turns and corridors, he happened on this one. There was almost a divinity in that—until you remembered how he ended.

Deep, deep inside the bowels of that thing, I found a bloody handprint head-high on a pair of double doors, and beyond those, the storeroom.

It was filled with rack upon rack of jars, filled with their flickering blue essence. They looked identical at first, but when you examined them more closely, you saw tiny variations in shape and design, until I wasn't sure if there were even two the same.

I've been in some strange places in my life, but there was something about that room that was so unforeseen. It felt stranger than a tomb, like something divine, but in a religion unknown to me. I thought of the shaman dropping in on the bones of his ancestors. At that moment, if you'd told me that each one of those jars contained a human soul, I might have believed you.

I wasn't minded to hang around in there. I put four in my bag and lit out.

·

The prisoners at the base used to joke about "overfulfilling the plan": they said it when some newcomer to their team worked too hard and seemed likely to make them look bad. The first few times they'd say it as a joke, but if the person kept on digging or threshing as though his life depended it—usually in the hope of impressing the guards—then there might be a beating, or worse. Once I saw a man have his toes taken off with a shovel. The long-term inmates knew it did you no favors to exceed expectations.

I was keen not to overfulfill the plan. There was easily a

dozen planeloads down in those stores, but it seemed to me that there would come a point when I'd brought out so much they wouldn't need me anymore. If that happened, I guessed they'd cancel my ticket to Barrow.

•

The evening light was melting back into caramel once again by the time I hit the avenue of chestnut trees and bent left onto the bridge. The sound of hooves and laughter echoed from a long way off along the concrete wall of the river, just as the gunshots did the time before.

I dismounted at the bridge approach and walked the last stretch to the block post. There were only two guards waiting. I slung my pack over the concrete division and let the guards spray it off.

I hitched the horse and dropped my tools on the city side of the block post, just how we agreed. I had an uneaten apple in my pants from my lunch and I offered it to the horse. She nosed it uncertainly, her nostrils quivering. After a moment she drew back her lips and bit. Then I started to undress, moving gingerly because of all the biting insects. Pretty soon I was standing there naked, slapping away the mosquitoes from my flesh, waiting for the guards to call me across.

Gradually, more men started appearing to watch.

There was no sign of the spare clothes. If they're going to kill me, they'll do it now, I thought.

I heard a shout. Eben and Mr. Apofagato were riding slowly back from the plane toward the bridge. The guards were waiting for a signal from him.

Eben rode loose and relaxed, letting the horse be his eyes and choose a path through the broken rubble. "How'd it go?" he yelled.

"I made a start," I said.

"Only four, but they look like good ones," said the guard with the sack. He held one up in the sunlight. His eyes raked over my bare skin as he waited.

Eben pulled a rifle from his saddle.

"There's a lot more back in there," I said. "Maybe hundreds of them. But it'll take time to tease them out." My voice sounded thin and fearful. Somehow, to die naked in front of them felt like the biggest indignity of all.

Eben gestured with the rifle in the direction of my voice. "You'd better kill the horse, like we agreed," he said.

That was the math of survival. Horses were plentiful. Letting one sicken and infect the rest was a risk not worth taking. They could breed another horse, but another Makepeace, who knew the lie of the city and where the flasks were hidden, would take a lot longer to come by. At least, that's what I banked on.

I stepped over the division. The guards sprayed me down with carbolic soap and handed me the change of clothes. The soap stung my eyes. I stepped into the pants and boots they'd given me. The boots were too big and my feet swam in them a little, but I was overtaken by a wave of relief so strong I felt like I might weep. The evening light seemed to hold the promise of so much life in it. I wanted to live forever and cherish the beautiful things I'd seen: Polyn from the belly of that plane. The girl in her memory stone. The stillness of Evangeline without a soul in it. Looking up at the night sky crowded with pinpricks of light, I'd sometimes fancied I could see a Makepeace on another star, a different me, living her last days surrounded by grandchildren. In Alaska I would grow old. There would be time for other things. The life I'd missed. The pit of my belly swarmed with a radiant peace.

"It seems a pity to shoot the horse," I said. "I was thinking I could use her tomorrow."

Eben shrugged. "What does Apofagato say?"

Apofagato shook his head. "It can develop symptoms within twelve hours. I strongly advise against."

"You heard the man." Eben flipped the gun in his hands and offered me its stock.

It was a beautiful old repeater with a lever on the underside of its barrel, at least a hundred years older than I was, with luminous gray metal and its wood almost the same shade of chestnut as the horse. I complimented him on it. Bill Evans had had one a lot like it. It took the same big shells he had used in his handgun.

"It's a Winchester," said Eben. "There's a story behind it that I'll tell you one day."

The horse had a white star on her forehead. I sighted the gun on that and then lowered it again. "You might want to dismount in case they startle," I said.

Apofagato swung down out of his saddle onto the dust of the bridge, but Eben stayed put, cocksure as ever. "Don't mind me, Makepeace," he said. "Just get it done. I want the other animals to stay clean."

I squeezed the trigger. The gun cracked and kicked my shoulder; then the horse swayed, drawing up her front foot before she fell to the ground.

At the crack of the gun, Eben's horse reared up and then slipped. For an instant he was fighting to stay on her. The two of them fell together in a blur of bodies, the horse twisting before she hit the ground. I thought at first Eben had broken his leg, but he was back on his feet in a flash. Apofagato gathered the reins and was gentling the horse with his hand when Eben snatched them from him and yanked his crop from the saddle. He lashed at the animal. "You bitch!" he cried, leathering her

sides until her eyes rolled. It seemed like a few strokes would satisfy his anger, but his rage seemed to feed on itself, growing
more savage, as though it had its roots elsewhere, in some ancient cruelty. The pain and the fear of pain made the guts of the
horse tremble. He thrashed furiously, with an action that was
suddenly so familiar, I could almost hear the bedstead jingling.
There was spit on his lips as they twisted into another curse.
"You Jezebel!"

He turned to where he knew I was standing.

"Give me the gun, Makepeace," he panted. "What you waiting for?"

Jezebel. The word crackled through my memory like a
splash of acid. A bird called back in the city I had just left, and
the eddying water behind him seemed to be still for a second.
My feet in the borrowed boots moved awful slow as I stepped to
my right to find a clean angle. I heard Bill Evans voice in my
head coaching me to move into a firing position: move to your
right, lead with your right leg—never cross over yourself.

Two of the guards were still laughing. One had turned away
to light a smoke. Eben frowned at me, impatient for the gun.

I put two shells in him before he had a chance to raise his
eyebrows, and the second of them pitched him clean over the
side of the bridge.

The current swept him under us in a moment. He seemed
to be lying facedown in the water. I picked off another guard
as he went for his sidearm. The others were slack jawed with
disbelief. Apofagato surrendered his horse to me without a
murmur.

8

I hoped to ride hard like I had the last time, but in the days that followed I got sick like never before.

I started to puke on the morning of the next day. I couldn't eat or keep food down.

I thought at first it was the sickness we'd all feared, but it wasn't anything I had picked up in the Zone. It was something I had caught off Shamsudin—the oldest disease of all.

It didn't seem possible that such a hasty intimacy could amount to anything. A month had passed and I had thought nothing of it. I was getting on in years and I had never been regular, with the food and hardship we had at the base, and every month I half expected my body to shut up shop. But it was more tenacious than that: like some crazy innkeeper laying out fresh linen each night for guests that never come.

I passed across the face of the land as summer came and went. By the time I swung north for the last stretch, there was frost at night and the first green showing of the Lights.

The last few years of weather had broken up the highway, and in places I had to pick my way slowly or dismount. It didn't matter to me. I was in no hurry. I had plenty to contemplate on my journey back.

I'd never known the north so beautiful as it was then. I'd find myself rapt by the tiniest things: a stripe in a stone, the blue crown on a honeysuckle berry—the ones the Russian prisoners called a zhimelost. I saw a tabby cat stalking through the long grass, the wild offspring of some long-dead pet. It fled when it saw me: no memory of a human face. There was a tumbledown house nearby. I crouched in its foundations to pee and found a four-leaf clover.

At other times in my life I'd seen animals or plants that had no business there, but now I seemed to come across them every other day: a parrot once—a flash of bright green the color of pondweed, and its unmistakable beak. Another time a plum tree. And once—I swear—a monkey, its pink face fringed with a tiny lion's mane, chattering its bared teeth at me from a silver birch.

I have no idea how they got there, but it took hold in my mind that they were salvage from a busted ark. I pictured it to myself, split or run aground somewhere, and the animals freed from the wreck, breaking out of crates—a whole menagerie crawling and hopping north, tracing the route of the rivers that flowed to the cold.

For the first time in as long as I can think, I knew a kind of contentment. And for once, the world wasn't a thing to fight against.

Rain was falling when I reached my city.

I was lucky to have the business end of a long summer ahead of me. I worked like a crazy thing to get some food in the ground and a spare room ready. By the time the first snow came, I was too big for the morning ride.

In fact, I was in the stable when it happened. I stayed on my feet throughout, clutching on to the tack pegs to keep up and terrifying the horses with my screams. It all went quicker than the first time. Just as I was finally doubling up in pain, out popped a fierce-looking little thing with a shock of black hair and the dark face of a Tungus, paddling with its limbs and squalling, and a cry more like a mew than a scream.

9

The other day I counted the books I've saved. There are 2,075 of them stacked up in the armory and 177 that I've laid by in the house. I also counted sixteen boxes of candles that I've stashed in Charlo's old bedroom. They're packed a gross to a box, and if you keep the wicks trimmed they burn for just above two hours. Each box is twelve days of constant light. There's something more than six months' worth of them altogether.

Of course, you barely need a light all the months of summer. You can read at midnight in June without one. If you read. It gives me a headache at any time of year.

The point about the candles is this: One day soon I'll have to scavenge more boxes again. I have a good guess where I can find some more for now. But one day there'll be no more to be had. One day the candles will all be gone, and the wicks, and all the jars of spirit I have left.

I'll have to make do with blubber lamps like the Chukchi have, or get used to living in the dark.

There isn't a life to be had in this city anymore.

We're not the last just yet. About a year ago, I saw smoke coming from the chimney of the Velazquez house. It gave me a fright at first, but it turned out to be strangers, a man and a woman with a child of about five months old.

How they got here, I can't guess and he wasn't able to tell me. He's Chinese or maybe Korean. She looks part Yakut, part Russian.

We don't have dealings with each other, but we nod when we pass. I left some cabbages and tiger balm on their stoop in the fall. And they left some kimchi for me.

Last winter was a fierce one, as bad as the ones in my childhood; but I know they lasted it, because at the end of March I saw him dragging a sled of ice blocks back from the lake. I haven't seen her or the child for a while.

If things go well for them, maybe they'll hunker down, make a life here, have another child or two. But I don't rate things better than fifty-fifty for them. That's the way things are.

Since I was fifteen years old, I've been watching the world I knew go to hell. The only part of it that behaves how it should is the half-acre of vegetables in back of my house, and even those have grown fickle as the seasons have altered.

Time is narrowing on me. I guess I could still leave here if I wanted: try heading south again, or maybe find a boat to take me to the States. But I don't expect I will now, knowing what I know. There are so many things that I wish could have turned out different. There's no way back for me in this lifetime.

That plane I rode in was the last I ever saw.

These years that I've written of were the fall of my life. I'm pushing on into my own winter now. This hasn't changed: old age is as cold as it ever was.

I'm growing old and thin. I've had to cinch my gunbelt tighter each year to hold what's left of my hips. I'm frailer too. But I still ride at dawn each day, round the fading circle of what was once this city. And I'm still greedy for whatever's left to me. I can't open my eyes soon enough each day to see you, my darling.

.

The road's been quiet for a long time. The only thing moving on it is dust devils in the summer months. Sometimes I look at it and wonder: What became of all that *life*?

I expect the base is gone by now. I wonder if the grapple I made still twinkles in a broken-down corner of the grainstore.

Those prisoners are bound to rise up sooner or later. You can't keep your foot on a man's throat so long without facing the consequence of it. And when they do? What then?

They'll kill the guards, fall out over the women, scatter in the bush, and their offspring—if they manage to have any—will end up like the tabby that I saw, meowing round a cold hearth, flinching at the sight of a stranger.

.

The cranes lurch south each fall. Each year the wilderness re-claims a little more. Each year the taiga riots on another tract of the city. Each month that goes brings closer the time of your departure.

And once you've left, I see it going like this: five or ten years after, or maybe sooner if I'm lucky, the horse will throw me on a cold morning, or the stove'll catch while I'm sleeping, or I'll just keel over among the cabbages—I won't have the puff I used to and it's heavy work chopping those stalks out. Down I'll go, nose in the dirt, and breathe my last.

There's not one iota of fear in me about it. I wouldn't have you stay for anything. But I can't think too hard about the world I've bequeathed to you, or the gulf between your childhood and mine, or I start to feel guilty for it.

Once I thought I would make this for you to read. I planned to give it to you, copied out in a fair hand, with all the spellings checked up against Pa's dictionary. But now I see that the best thing I can leave you is your own blank page. This can stay with the other books I've saved, in the way of a memory stone, or one of those Tungus ribbons on a branch at the start of the journey, or the end of one, chalking up a little prayer against annihilation.

When you're ready to light out of here, take the Winchester and the fastest pair of horses and go. Let it be on a bright day in winter for better traveling. And until the wind fills them, I'll be able to look down from the tower on the firehouse at the tracks you leave across the snowfields north, and say to myself: Ping's on her way home.